Advance praise for Meg Donohue and *How to Eat a Cupcake*

"*How to Eat a Cupcake* is a sparkling, witty story about an unlikely, yet redemptive, friendship. Donohue's voice is lovely, intelligent, and alluring. Grab one of these for your best friend and read it together—preferably with a plate of Meyer Lemon cupcakes nearby."　　　　—Katie Crouch, bestselling author of
Girls in Trucks and *Men and Dogs*

"Beautifully written and quietly wise, Meg Donohue's *How to Eat a Cupcake* is an achingly honest portrayal of the many layers of friendship—a story so vividly told, you can (almost) taste the buttercream."　　　　　　　　—Sarah Jio, author of
The Violets of March and *The Bungalow*

"A heartwarming and unpredictable tale of friendship, family, and frosting."　　　—Zoe Fishman, author of *Balancing Acts*

"An irresistible blend of sweet and tart, this book is truly a treat to be savored."　　　　　　　　　—Beth Kendrick, author of
The Bake-Off and *Second Time Around*

"Deliciously engaging. Donohue writes with charm and grace. What could be better than friendship and cupcakes?"
　　　　　—Rebecca Rasmussen, author of *The Bird Sisters*

"Donohue's sweet debut is a clever exploration of how a West Coast mean girl grows up and gives in to friendship, love, and dozens of delicious cupcakes. . . . Donohue's culinary romantic thriller will keep readers hungry for more."
　　　　　　　　　　　　　　　—*Publishers Weekly*

D1042788

About the Author

MEG DONOHUE has an MFA in creative writing from
Columbia University and a BA in comparative literature
from Dartmouth College. Born and raised in Philadelphia,
she lives in San Francisco with her husband, two young
daughters, and dog. This is her first novel.

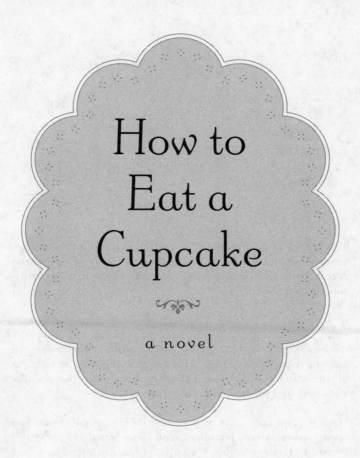

How to Eat a Cupcake

a novel

MEG DONOHUE

WILLIAM MORROW
An Imprint of HarperCollinsPublishers

This book is a work of fiction. The characters, incidents, and dialogue are drawn from the author's imagination and are not to be construed as real. Any resemblance to actual events or persons, living or dead, is entirely coincidental.

HOW TO EAT A CUPCAKE. Copyright © 2012 by Meg Donohue. All rights reserved. Printed in the United States of America. No part of this book may be used or reproduced in any manner whatsoever without written permission except in the case of brief quotations embodied in critical articles and reviews. For information address HarperCollins Publishers, 10 East 53rd Street, New York, NY 10022.

HarperCollins books may be purchased for educational, business, or sales promotional use. For information please write: Special Markets Department, HarperCollins Publishers, 10 East 53rd Street, New York, NY 10022.

FIRST EDITION

Designed by Cassandra J. Pappas

Library of Congress Cataloging-in-Publication Data is available upon request.

ISBN 978-0-06-206928-3

12 13 14 15 16   OV/RRD   10 9 8 7 6 5 4 3 2 1

For my parents, whose love and support embolden my dreams.
And for Phil and our girls, who are my everything.

June

I

Annie

PEOPLE FREQUENTLY MAKE the assumption that I'm unreliable. I chalk this up to the fact that I'm perhaps a bit too creative and flour-flecked in my dress and I'm not a hedge fund manager, dot-com entrepreneur, or lawyer. Oh, and my hair is curly, which I guess pegs me as unpredictable. Hair, apparently, is the new window to the soul.

Of course, no one actually uses the word "unreliable" when they describe me. Instead, they throw around coquettishly hyphenated words like "free-spirited" or "independent-minded," which mean they think I'm one of those flighty, dim, devil-may-care gals who arrive forty minutes late for everything, if they arrive at all. The accusation could not be further from the truth. When I tell you I'll do something, I do it, thank you very much. When I say I'll be there, I'm there on time.

Still, I'll admit that as I stood in the middle of the St. Clairs' stone courtyard for the first time in nearly a decade, I ever-so-briefly considered turning on my heel and getting the hell out of Dodge. Before me, an enormous hulking beast of a mansion—the closest thing I had to a childhood home, home to the best and worst friend I'd ever known—loomed silent, windows

4 · Meg Donohue

glinting in the early evening sun. While I stood there, hesitating, the bright, confident scent of Meyer lemon cupcakes wafted up from the box in my hands. It was hard to decide which was worse: envisioning the fallout of going back on my word to Lolly St. Clair, or being scoffed at by a dozen plucky cupcakes. I drew myself up as tall as my five-foot, three-inch frame would allow and marched across the remainder of the courtyard and up the front steps.

A long-faced maid with crisply parted black hair and swipes of blush as aggressive as war paint opened the door. I immediately pegged her as a temporary hire for the party. Visible make-up on staff members had always been near the top of Lolly St. Clair's lengthy list of pet peeves, and, foreseeing the torrent of scorn that would inevitably befall this unsuspecting woman, I felt a twinge of sympathy for her. Or was that solidarity?

"Hi," I said. "I'm Annie Quintana."

My presence seemed to baffle her. I didn't blame her for being confused; I wasn't wearing the black staff uniform, but I also wasn't dressed up enough to be a party guest. She stared at me, blinking her mascara-caked eyelashes rapidly, and finally looked down at the box in my hands.

"Oh," she said. "You're here with the cupcakes."

"That's right. I'm here with the cupcakes. They brought me as their plus one. I'm a lucky girl!" I gave a little laugh, but she didn't seem to be in the mood for camaraderie. I was beginning to suspect Lolly had already had a few choice words with her. She turned away, mumbling something over her shoulder that I interpreted as an invitation to enter.

I took a breath, lifted my chin, and then followed the maid into the St. Clairs' soaring foyer. The frenetic, multicolored Jackson Pollock painting I remembered well—and later studied at Cal—still hung above the rich brown tufted bench I'd sat on so many times as a kid. Twin curving mahogany staircases were bathed in the sunlight that poured through a round skylight two stories above. If the foyer was any indication, nothing had changed in the St. Clair house over the last decade. I wasn't surprised. Evelyn and Thaddeus St. Clair—Lolly and Tad to their inner circle—were fixtures in the most exclusive echelons of San Francisco society and steadfast in their good taste. It was like walking into a time warp. I half expected to look up the stairs and see Julia St. Clair smiling her Cheshire-cat grin down at me, her schoolgirl uniform tailored to near-couture perfection, Jewel's twangy yodels spilling out from her Disc-man headphones. Thankfully, this was impossible. Julia, like me, was now twenty-eight years old and long removed from her Devon Prep plaid. Last I'd heard she was living in New York City, vice president of a venture capital firm. *Just what Julia St. Clairs' bank account needs*, I'd thought when news of her impressive-sounding job had trickled through some funnel of e-mails and landed with a twinkly little plunk in my in-box: *a few more zeros.*

As the maid led me into the kitchen, Lolly St. Clair material-ized in front of me, her slender, Chanel-clad arms wrapping me in a surprisingly robust embrace. If I'd put on some weight over the previous ten years, Lolly seemed to have somehow shed the same amount from her already thin frame. She felt fragile in my arms, as bony as a bird. A tiny, squawking, bizarrely strong bird.

"Oh, thank goodness it's just you!" she rasped into my ear. "I nearly died when I heard the doorbell. I'm sure you haven't forgotten that early guests are as welcome as the plague in this home."

Before I had a chance to cough menacingly into her hair, Lolly pushed me to arm's length, her fingernails biting into my shoulders. Her pale blue eyes searched my face. I returned the steady gaze, but any changes in Lolly would have required a magnifying glass to identify. At sixty-one, she glowed with a Faye Dunaway–esque, bobble-head beauty, her hair dyed and coiffed in a perfectly appropriate white-blond, jawline-skimming do. Thanks, undoubtedly, to the efforts of a highly skilled surgeon, her skin was luminous and taut without succumbing to that trout-in-a-wind-tunnel look so many women her age seemed to be sporting.

Having completed her own inspection, Lolly pulled me close again. "Hello, my dear," she said quietly. "Lovely little Annie."

I was determined not to fall into the web of memories that her voice instantly spun through my head. Instead, I looked over her shoulder at the kitchen. But this was a mistake. Immediately, my body grew tense. I guess I'd assumed the St. Clairs would have changed something in the kitchen—if nowhere else—out of respect for my mom, or out of sadness, or regret, or even just to avoid any morbid associations. But everything looked exactly the same. There were the sand-colored granite counters webbed with intricate gold veins that my fingers had traced countless times; the stacked ovens Julia and I had baked pizzas in during slumber parties with a gaggle of middle-school girlfriends; the long rectangular window framing an absurdly postcard-perfect view of the sparkling bay and majestic Golden Gate Bridge that made my heart beat a little more strongly each and every time I saw it.

Home. The word pierced my thoughts like a poison dart. Is there any more complicated word in the English language? So much packed into one simple syllable. In Spanish, there's only one word for both home and house: *casa.* But we English speakers like to complicate matters. My eyes fell for only a moment on the white marble-topped kitchen island where my mother had spent so much time so long ago. I tried very, very hard not to look down at the floor where my mother had been found.

"Well," I said, extricating myself from Lolly's arms a second time. "I see you've really let this place go to hell."

Lolly barked out a laugh, wagging her finger at me. "And I see you're exactly the same. I'm finding it hard not to ask if you've studied for your history test, young lady."

"Go ahead," I said, warming to her. Even with those sharp little nails, Lolly really wasn't so bad. "The answer will be the same."

She sent the maid, who'd become remarkably less dour in Lolly's presence, to bring in the rest of the cupcake boxes from the car I'd borrowed from my friend Becca. It was Becca, in fact, who'd convinced me to accept Lolly's request to cater the desserts for her Save the Children benefit. *Are you insane?* Becca had sputtered when I told her I was planning on saying no. *Think of all of those rich people eating your cupcakes! You're going to pass up that opportunity for what? To make your eight millionth almond croissant for Valencia Street Bakery? To walk another mutt around Dolores Park, scooping up baggies of crap?* It was, all in all, a convincing argument. And so there I was, back at the St. Clairs' as hired help. Lolly's bonbon-sized diamond ring had nothing on the chip on my shoulder that day.

The truth, I knew, was that Lolly could have had her pick of any pastry chef in San Francisco. She threw lavish events at least once a month; her address book was thick with caterers and party planners and nonprofits worthy of St. Clair fund-raising soirees. But she had continually contacted me over the years, sending precisely worded e-mails and leaving the occasional brisk voice mail, undeterred by my infrequent response. It wasn't that I didn't like her, but just that I had spent much of my life attempting to untangle myself from the St. Clair world. I knew Lolly well enough to know that she was the classic give-her-an-inch-and-she'll-take-a-yard type. Still, when she somehow discovered that I was working as the head baker of a small café in the Mission—a historically Latino neighborhood I sincerely doubted Lolly had ever driven through, much less dined in—I had to respect the woman's tenacity.

"My favorite!" she cried, opening the box of cupcakes the maid had left on the counter. "I can't believe you remembered. Lemon. What a relief. I was a teensy bit nervous you'd bring some awful *modern* flavor. It's bad enough I'm serving cupcakes to grown-ups—no offense, Annie darling; they're all the rage, aren't they? But if you'd brought some ridiculous flavor like *mojito* or *wasabi*, I just don't know what I would have done. If I wanted to taste *lavender*, I'd spritz air freshener on my tongue." Lolly cringed as much as her taut face would allow. "Sometimes I fear the whole world has forgotten how delicious subtlety can be. Thank goodness for the classics." She hesitated. "Did you . . ." She paused again, studying me. "Is it your mother's recipe?"

"As best as I can remember. I never found her recipe book." I glanced again at the marble island at the center of the kitchen. "Actually, I thought while I'm here I might look around for it. That is, if you don't mind a broke baker snooping through your fine silver."

"I suppose we can make an exception this one time. We never did have anyone move into the carriage house after . . ." Lolly's voice dropped off. She studied her pearl-colored nails, collecting herself. When she looked up, the ripple of emotion that had momentarily crossed her face had stilled. She took a deep breath through her nose, her chest swelling beneath her pewter blouse. I imagined her looking in the mirror each morning and thinking, *Impeccably arched brows? Check. Sculptural cheekbones? Oh yes. Megawatt smile? Indeed. Now, let's go save some children.*

"Well, live-in help didn't seem necessary," Lolly continued, "once you girls were both off at college. It's just me and Tad now, rattling around in this big old house."

I tried to keep my smile in check. Lolly and Tad might not have their household employees living on the grounds anymore, but I was willing to bet my best cupcake recipe they were still surrounded by helping hands every waking moment. After all, for nearly twenty years, the helping hands had been those of my mother.

When she was sixteen years old, pregnant, and disowned by her devoutly Catholic family, my mom, Lucia Quintana, fled Ecuador for a cousin's couch in South San Francisco and remained there until the day she landed a nanny job with the St. Clair family. Even though I knew those details of her story as well as I knew the recipe for classic yellow cake, I still found them hard to understand. How had my tiny, teenage mom, her stomach just beginning to stretch her shirt uncomfortably taut, summoned the courage to leave her whole life behind and ride a network of buses thousands of miles to a foreign city where she knew only one person?

Through a program offered by the city, she eventually found herself perched on the edge of a plush, opal-colored couch in the grandest living room she'd ever seen. Using the faltering English she'd picked up cleaning homes for the previous two years, she'd explained to Lolly St. Clair that she had a daughter, Anita, the very same age as Lolly's Julia. The fact that she had a child turned out to be a bonus in Lolly's eyes; complications during delivery had ensured that Julia would be the St. Clairs' only child, and Lolly thought it would be nice for Julia to grow up with a playmate. Though I heard this version of the story many times over the years, I knew Lolly well enough to know that her motives hadn't been entirely self-centered. Beneath her well-tended exterior, Lolly hid a soft spot for those in need, and who was more in need than a single, unemployed immigrant with a toddler in tow? Not long after that interview, my mom and I moved into the carriage house of the St. Clairs' Pacific Heights compound. Right up until the day she died, neither of us ever lived anywhere else.

———

As I arranged six dozen cupcakes on the white Limoges plat-
ters Lolly had set out, I admired my handiwork. Lolly had
been right to worry about my flavor tendencies. In my mind,
there was nothing better than a cupcake with a funny little
twist. I liked bold pairings of fresh ingredients slathered high
with decadent, old-fashioned waves of icing—organic pear and
chai tea cake topped with vanilla-ginger buttercream was one of
my current favorites. But Lolly St. Clair had more classic taste,
and so I'd made an array of delicately flavored Meyer lemon,
vanilla, and mocha cupcakes for the benefit. The cupcakes were
smaller than my usual oversized creations, and I'd topped them
with smooth buttercream icing on which I'd placed fetching
little fondant birds and butterflies that I'd molded by hand. The
cupcakes looked, in a word, lovely. But how did they taste? Two
words: *freaking delicious*.

Lolly insisted I join the party, but not before she gave my
clothes a silent head-to-toe appraisal. An ancient anger bub-
bled inside of me as she dubiously added up the pieces of my
outfit: purple knee-length tunic, black leggings, chunky turquoise bracelet, gold hoop earrings, my dark, wavy, ever-
untamable hair falling loose down my back. At least I'd stepped
it up from my usual thrift store finds. *That's right*, I thought,
sticking my chin out and meeting her gaze straight on. *I don't
fit in.* Despite my defiant train of thought, all through Lolly's
evaluation I was anxiously spinning that bracelet around and
around my wrist.

Pride forced me to cross back through the foyer and join the
party. Already, the St. Clairs' large, formal living room was alive
with rustling silk dresses, clinking crystal glasses of Napa-grown
liquid gold, and darting, black-suited waitstaff. Everyone looked
perfect: toned and tan and dentally enhanced. Apparently, there
was a dentist in Palm Springs offering a special on poolside teeth
bleaching and no one had bothered to tell me. I felt a bit like I

had wandered into a camp for rich grown-ups and everyone had just transitioned from a mildly robust day of water activities to the mess hall, except instead of canoes there were yachts, and instead of a mess hall there was a chandelier-studded, velvet-draped great room with multimillion-dollar views.

Do any of these people actually eat? I wondered, lamenting the thought of trays of cupcakes with single bites removed being dumped into trash bags at the end of the night. When I was offered a glass of wine, I gratefully accepted it and made a beeline for one of the three sets of French doors that opened onto an enormous slate patio.

It was among the final days of June, just past the longest day of the year, and remarkably clear and warm for a San Francisco evening. The heat lamps on the patio hadn't even been ignited yet. Again, that view: shimmering bay, bridge the color of red velvet cake, sun just beginning to turn the sky a startling shade of peach above the Presidio's gray-green slope of eucalyptus trees. To the south, the island prison of Alcatraz rose somberly out of the water; I wondered if the sight of it made some white-collar criminal who might be living in Pacific Heights sweat a little as he swilled his five-o'clock martini. Stifling a grin, I leaned over the edge of the railing, drank in the view, and then drank down my wine.

"Annie! It *is* you, isn't it?"

That voice. I spun around. Before me stood Julia St. Clair. Tall and willowy, she had cut her shiny curtain of blond hair so that it fell razor-straight and ended bluntly at her shoulders, making her look sophisticated and vaguely Parisian. Her face, under the stylish hairdo, was as placidly beautiful as ever.

"Julia!" I said, feeling my calves tense. It was something that happened to me when I was anxious, as though my body, of which I only required running when I was late for a bus, nevertheless managed to tap into a biological instinct for flight. *Just being near this woman,* my legs seemed to be warning, *decreases your chance of survival!*

Julia hugged me, enveloping me in her rose-petal scent. "You look surprised. My mom didn't tell you I'd be here?"

"No," I said coolly. "She didn't."

Julia either didn't notice or chose to ignore my tone. "Funny. Well, I'm living at home now. *For* now, I should clarify." She smiled, glancing down at the sparkler on her left hand. "I'm engaged. Couldn't bear the thought of planning a California wedding all the way from New York City, so here I am. We're getting married up at the vineyard in the spring."

Actually, Lolly *had* mentioned that Julia was engaged. Her fiancé's name was Wesley something-or-other, a Silicon Valley whiz kid. What Lolly hadn't mentioned was that Julia was back in San Francisco. *Sneaky lady!* I thought. *Hell, downright Machiavellian.* I had to give credit where credit was due.

"Congratulations," I said, keeping my voice neutral even as my tongue went dry in my mouth. Seeing Julia brought me back to a time when rumors had buzzed around me as dark and thick as a cloud of flies. "That's great news."

"I know, thanks. God, Annie, how long has it been? Ten years? Not since, I guess . . ." Julia faltered and I didn't jump in to save her, enjoying the rare crack in her confidence. But then she shook her hair back and plowed forward. "Not since your mother's funeral."

"That's right."

We were both silent for a long moment, looking out at the bay.

"I miss her," Julia said.

I looked over sharply. There was something plaintive in her voice, a quiet desperation I couldn't help feeling was about more than my mother's death. Julia St. Clair had always had the type of serene, classic beauty that practically begged to be

studied, and I tried to view my onetime friend through the eyes
of a stranger. Her features were understated, less dramatic than
her mother's, more pretty than glamorous; she had the look of
someone who had never known less than eight hours of sleep per
night, who opened her eyes each morning to the smell of lilacs
and lattes, who wrapped herself in a cashmere blanket when she
flew first class to Rome, which was often. Her nose was patri-
cian, long and thin, but not *too* long or *too* thin, her skin a flawless shade of cream that had never been blemished by a pimple.
At twenty-eight, there were no traces of burgeoning laugh lines
around her rosy lips or true-blue eyes, but I knew that I myself
had made Julia laugh countless times when we were children—a
loud, infectious belly laugh that broke her composed face into an
unexpectedly cockeyed, cat-got-the-bird grin.

Of course, that was back when I still cared about making
Julia happy, before I realized that the person releasing that peal
of laughter was a manipulative, lying, cruel young woman who
was trying her damnedest to ruin my life.

"Anyway," Julia said, turning to face me. "It's really good
to see you again." The way Julia said these words—with equal
parts earnestness and surprise, as though she could hardly believe
them herself—set my teeth on edge. She hesitated, a shadow
passing over her face, and seemed on the verge of saying more.
But then, just as a heaping tablespoon of curiosity was being
mixed into the complicated and fairly toxic concoction of feelings I had for Julia, we were interrupted by the voice of the very
man who, once upon a time, had put one of the first nails in the
coffin of our friendship.

"Well, look at the two of you!" I heard from behind me. "If
someone had told me this shindig was going to be a reunion of
the prettiest girls from Devon Prep, I would have gotten here a
lot sooner."

Coming from anyone else, this line would have sounded

smarmy. But coming from Jake Logan—Jake Logan of the blue-green eyes, the puckish smile revealing that ever-so-slight gap between his front teeth, and the impossibly adorable dimples—the line produced in me a feeling I could only, and not without embarrassment, describe as puppylike in its unchecked delight. I know, I know: how cliché to fawn over a grown man with dimples. But! *He called me pretty!* I might as well have wagged my tail and rolled over.

How was it that ten years after graduating from high school, I still had a crush on Jake Logan? He'd been one of those kids who'd probably avoided an attention deficit disorder diagnosis by a year or two, always bouncing from one activity to the next, quick-witted and effortlessly talented at ostensibly everything and acutely, though somehow not obnoxiously, aware of his charm. Standing before me now, he didn't seem much changed from his teenage self—perhaps a bit broader through the chest and shoulders, a little more poise in his easy stance, a steadier hold to his gaze. But men nearly always age annoyingly well, don't they?

My stomach did a not-so-little flip. Why the hell had I decided to wear that *stupid* purple tunic? Julia, of course, had on a strapless navy miniskirted dress that might as well have been a field hockey uniform for all of the casual confidence she emitted. *Round two: Julia*, I thought. Jake Logan, after all, was Julia's ex-boyfriend. The whole surreal scenario called desperately for more wine. I grabbed another glass from a passing waiter and was surprised to see Julia do the same. Julia had never been much of a drinker in high school, though of course we were underage at the time. Not that that had ever stopped me.

"I can't believe my mother still has you on her invite list after that de Young Museum gala when you got so drunk you knocked over the champagne fountain!" Julia said to Jake, laughing as she touched his sleeve.

"Please," Jake stage-whispered. "You're blowing my cover in front of Annie! She hasn't seen me in ages. There's a sliver of hope that she might think I'm all grown up and responsible now."

"Not a chance, Jake Logan. I've got your number," I said. I looked down pointedly at his feet. "No one who wears flip-flops with a suit is grown-up and responsible. A peddler of surfboards to i-bankers? Perhaps. Responsible? 'Fraid not."

Jake laughed. Now I saw that the skin around his blue-green eyes crinkled in a new way. His dimples shone through a light brown scruff he could never have grown in high school. If anything, the changes made him more attractive.

"Touché. Note to self: Lose the suit." He clinked his wine-glass lightly against mine. "So, Ms. Quintana, other than cutting overconfident men down to size, what have you been up to these last ten years?"

Wait. Was it possible that Jake Logan was actually flirting with me? Before I had a chance to answer him, Julia jumped in.

"Annie's a pastry chef." She turned to me. "A *fabulous* one. I tried one of your cupcakes already. That lemon one—it's pure summertime. Remember when you were seven and the thing you truly wanted most in the world was a cupcake? You weren't thinking about world peace, or the economy, or, I don't know, *life* . . . you just wanted something delicious and special and homemade. Remember?"

And there goes Julia's third sheet, I thought as wind swept the patio.

"I'm pretty sure all *I* ever truly wanted was a snake, but maybe that's a boy thing," Jake said. His amused gaze lingered for a moment on Julia, making me wonder just how many of his old feelings for her remained. Then he looked at me, and for a brief moment I benefited from all the warmth that had built in his eyes as he'd gazed at Julia. "So these cupcakes," he asked, "are they . . . Ecuadorean?"

I couldn't believe he remembered where my mom was from. When I tried to recall the few interactions I'd had with Jake during high school, what immediately surfaced was the memory of being stung by his look of contempt during my humiliating walk to the principal's office near the end of that devastating final year at Devon Prep. Prior to that, I suppose he had occasionally taken a benign interest in me, but nothing strong enough to risk breaking rank with Devon's dominant crowd. I only made a couple of friends in high school: Jody, the poet who had terrible acne and a tendency to mutter, "This is *definitely* going in my collection" whenever classmates snickered at her dorky, overeager comments; and Penelope, the painfully shy pianist whose face turned a remarkable shade of ground chuck each and every time a teacher called on her. Yup, it was the artsy-fartsy girls and me getting by together as best we could all those years. After the rumors about me started, though, even Jody and Penelope couldn't risk association, and I didn't really blame them. That was the year loneliness gave my sense of humor a run for its money.

"Not exactly," I told Jake now. "There isn't a long Ecuadorean cupcake tradition for me to draw on. I guess it's in the genes though. My mom was a wonderful baker."

"So it runs in the family. And now you're a pastry chef."

"I actually work very hard to eschew labels," I said. "I am quite literally the most accomplished eschewer of labels you'll ever meet. But if you called me a baker, the pretension police *might* look the other way. I make desserts and breakfast treats for the Valencia Street Bakery in the Mission. It's a hole-in-the-wall. And I walk people's dogs. We must not forget the dogs."

"Never," Jake said solemnly.

"You're being too modest," Julia jumped in. "Those cupcakes . . . really, they're delicious. I'm so impressed."

I looked at her and allowed a beat of silence to pass before saying, reluctantly, "Thanks."

I was having trouble knowing what to make of Julia's apparent kindness. If she realized how bizarre it was for three of us to be chatting away like merrily reunited old friends, she certainly wasn't letting on. Did she really not remember what she'd done to me? How she'd turned on me in the years leading up to my mother's death? How her actions had changed the course of my life and caused irreparable damage to my relationship with my mother? What she'd said at the funeral? I shook my head, irritated to find myself rehashing the events of that year after I'd spent so much time working to put it all securely in the past, and excused myself as tactfully as a short woman with two large glasses of wine snaking through her veins was capable of doing. I had nearly reached the living room when I heard Julia's laughter, a loud, flirty, artificial sound that hung in the warm night air. I glanced back. Her hand was touching Jake's arm, their foreheads mere inches apart. *Awfully close for a happily engaged woman*, I thought as I turned and made my way out of that house, determined, yet again, that it would be the last time I allowed myself to be pulled into the duplicitous world of the St. Clair family.

The St. Clairs' squat, stucco carriage house sat flush against the city sidewalk at the front of their property and served as the final line of defense between the public and the mansion. A garage and gated porte cochere formed the lower half of the carriage house; the top floor contained the two-bedroom apartment my mother and I had lived in for so many years. Leaving the mansion and its still-crowded party behind me, feeling the courtyard's uneven cobblestones below my feet, and walking up those familiar steps to the carriage house apartment prompted a dizzying wave of déjà vu to wash over me. I found the key in its usual spot underneath a stone duck beside the door and slid it into the lock. Stepping inside, I flipped on the lights and sucked in my breath.

The sight of my old living room was like a punch to the gut. Here, too, as in the mansion, Lolly and Tad had not changed a thing. I picked up a framed photograph from the table beside the couch. There was my mother, her dark brown eyes molten with joy as she crouched down to hug an elfin version of me and a coltish version of Julia tight in each arm. I could almost smell my mother then, all warm sugar and vanilla and a hint of something citrusy and tart, like lime. I set the photograph down carefully in the same spot and tried hard to keep myself firmly planted in the present.

Now where the hell could that recipe book be? The last time I looked for it was the day of my mother's funeral, and over the years I'd come to wonder if perhaps the blinding fog of sorrow had prevented me from finding it. *Maybe*, I thought, *just maybe, I'd simply overlooked the book in my hurry to finally be out of that house for good.* Each time Lolly had contacted me over the previous decade, a part of me had hoped she was calling because she had found the book. But Lolly had never mentioned it.

My mother's book was more than just a place she stored her favorite recipes, though since she was an accomplished baker and chef, her book would have been precious to me even if that's all it were. But I knew that my mom had used the recipe book as a journal as well, a place to write down her thoughts on the day, her daughter, and the family of which she took such heartfelt care. The image of my mother bent over the book each evening, her pen marking the pages with careful, flowing script, her dark hair falling around her face like a privacy curtain, was ingrained in my memory. I suppose in some small way it had been a relief to not find the book ten years earlier—I hadn't really felt ready to read my mom's private thoughts so soon after her death. Wouldn't it have been breaking her trust to do so? But those recipes! The meringues, the *empanadas dulces*, the coconut flans of my youth! I had tried to re-create them, but without the book the resulting desserts were pale imitations of the confections my mother had made with such precision, patience, and love.

And so I had long ago given up on re-creating and started reinventing. I began baking in college in the years after my mother's death, and, no, I didn't need a therapist to tell me it was a coping mechanism, a way to feel closer to her. Once I realized I would never be able re-create my mother's specialties exactly, at least not without her recipes, I had taken to interpreting my memory of those desserts with a modern twist. The pastries I created made me feel both closer to my mother and further away than ever. I had no family—I'd never known my father, had no siblings, and even the cousin my mom had once lived with in South San Francisco had long since moved back to Ecuador. To taste my mother's passion fruit meringue one more time would have made me feel a little less alone, if only for one or two bites' worth of time.

The shelf beside the carriage house's stove still held a few cookbooks—*The Joy of Cooking, Mastering the Art of French Cooking*—but there was no sign of my mother's recipe book. I opened every last drawer and cupboard in the kitchen and even checked the refrigerator. I sighed, leaning against the narrow, tiled countertop before working up the nerve to walk down the hall to my mother's old room.

Her bed was made up with crisp white linens, as though at any moment she might return and need a clean place to rest her weary body after a hard day's work. The closet was empty. After the funeral, I had kept a few of my mother's clothes and told Lolly she could donate the rest to her favorite cause of the moment. The bedside tables, too, were empty. I was peering under the bed when I heard the sound of a faucet running in the kitchen.

"Hello?" I called, making my way back down the hall.

There, filling a glass with water from the sink, stood Curtis, the St. Clairs' longtime driver, handyman, jack-of-all-trades—whatever anyone needed, big, dependable Curtis was your strong and silent man. He looked so much older than when I had seen him last. Now in his fifties, his ruddy forehead was lined with age, his eyes darker and more sunken than I remembered, his brown hair nearly overtaken by coarse gray. *Mom, too, would surely have had a few gray hairs if she'd lived past the ripe old age of thirty-four.* Before I knew what I was doing, I had thrown my arms around Curtis and buried my face in his broad chest.

"Annie." He sighed, patting my back awkwardly. "I thought I spotted someone walking up here, but then I figured I was just seeing things. You scared the bejesus out of me."

I pulled away. "It's just little old me, Curtis," I said, swiping at my eyes. "Not the Ghost of Empanadas Past."

Curtis shrugged sheepishly. "What are you doing back at the St. Clairs'? It's been a long time."

"Oh, you know, getting Lolly and the crew hopped up on sugar for old time's sake. I thought I'd try to find my mom's recipe book while I'm here. You haven't seen it, have you? Black, leather-bound, remarkably skilled in the art of camouflage?"

Curtis shook his head. "Sorry."

"It's okay. I'll live." Even as I said the words, I realized how disappointed I was. I hadn't understood until that very moment just how much my decision to cater the St. Clairs' party had been tied to the hope, the expectation, even, of finding that book.

Curtis walked me out to Becca's car. It cheered me somewhat to pass through the St. Clairs' gate with him by my side. I felt buffered for a moment from the pounding emotions of the previous few hours. Out of all of the people I'd seen that night from my old life, I was happiest to see him. After all, he was one of us—or maybe it's more accurate to say that I always thought of myself as one of *them*: the help. There were the St. Clairs—Lolly and Tad and Julia. There was the help—my mom and Curtis and a small army of other household employees. And then there was me, stuck somewhere in the middle, attending fancy private schools with Julia and living out in the carriage house with my mother. When it came down to choosing a side, I decided pretty early on that I would always have more in common with the Lucias and Curtises of the world than the St. Clairs.

At the car, when we hugged good-bye, I thought I spotted the glimmer of a tear in Curtis's usually stoic eye. *Jesus*, I thought. *What's with everyone and the waterworks today?*

"See you around, Annie," he called hoarsely, lifting his hand as I rolled down the car window and turned on the headlights.

Not if I can help it, I thought. But I patted his big hand and smiled before pulling out into the street and heading toward my tiny apartment in the Mission. I think I realized even then, in the cool darkness of the car, sealed off from the swelling orchestra of the city around me as it segued from the quiet mansions of Pacific Heights to the brutish housing projects in Western Addition to the still-bustling bars and restaurants of the Mission, that I would be back. That the St. Clairs' grip wouldn't be so easy to slip out of a second time.

2

Julia

It was only in the weeks precipitating my move back to San Francisco from New York that I found myself, for the first time in my adult life, needing to rely on an alarm clock to rouse me from bed. Previously, I'd always considered it a point of pride that I didn't require the jarring buzz of an alarm, or even the gentle notes of classical music, to alert me that the day had begun. My body simply knew. No matter where I was in the world, my eyes would flip open at 6:45 a.m. local time, my mind already racing through the list of things I planned to accomplish that day, my stomach rumbling for my usual breakfast of freshly cut fruit, Greek yogurt, a chocolate croissant, and green tea. In the weeks leading up to my return to my parents' home, I was ashamed to find my eyes opening leadenly later and later each morning, until finally, rebuked, I began setting the alarm on my phone. Even with its tinny melody in my ear, I lay in bed a few extra minutes each day, my body no longer one I took much pride in.

Lying there in my childhood bed, it required an enormous amount of effort to keep myself from sinking into the dark thoughts that seemed to be the only ones I was capable of thinking those days. *So this is depression*, I thought, my lips curling sourly at the word. As if in response, my body turned and curled, too, until my knees touched my chest and my hip pressed into the firm mattress. I'd always, secretly, while expressing much sympathy for friends who had bouts with depression and sleeping disorders and migraines, felt sure that such conditions were a choice. Either you decided you were happy, or you decided you were not. And to decide you were not? Wasn't that just laziness? I mean for *my* group of friends, of course, women who were thin and pretty and well educated and whose parents still took the whole lot of us out to dinners at posh restaurants whenever they visited the city. What right did any of *us* have to feel depressed? *You are*, as my favorite economics professor at Stanford liked to intone, *responsible for your own experience*.

But this feeling—this sense that I could not possibly get out of bed and face another long, tedious day of pretending to be okay when I most decidedly was not—was *not* something I had chosen. Irritated, I swatted this thought away. *Just be still and clear your mind*, I ordered myself, uncurling my body until I lay flat on my back. I didn't really believe such peace was possible, but despite everything that had happened, my faith in discipline had not yet waned. I watched the ceiling fan turn again and again and again. All week, the fan's loud, monotonous whir had given me dreams of breathing under water, swimming down into murky depths for a shimmering something just out of reach.

As I lay there, working to clear my mind—*an oxymoronic statement if ever there was one*—something remarkable happened. It wasn't that I actually managed to wipe away all thoughts of that horrible morning I'd spent in the hospital weeks earlier—those thoughts were never really gone for long. But for the first time since that day, my efforts to clear my mind were punctuated not only with dark thoughts, but also with light, fluffy, lemony thoughts. Thoughts, to be precise, of Annie Quintana's cupcakes.

The moment I'd bitten into that Meyer lemon cupcake at the benefit the night before, I'd been transported through time. Suddenly, I was seven years old and back in the kitchen with Lucia and Annie, standing on a stepstool at the counter and using an ice cream scoop to carefully transport batter from a large bowl to a cupcake tin, my mouth already watering for the finished product.

"Okay, Julia. It's Annie's turn," Lucia said gently in my ear, her Spanish accent blurring the edges of her words.

I nodded at Lucia, ever eager to please her, but glared at Annie as I handed over the scoop. *Why did I have to share? My scoops were perfect, just like Lucia's!* My anger with Annie could never hold long though. We were inseparable then, spending our afternoons hanging from the monkey bars at the playground, performing elaborate skits of make-believe, and digging in the garden. At night, we would sneak back and forth between the main house and the carriage house, devising whispered plans for the next day until Lucia or my mother would finally threaten to enforce our curfew. I suppose you could say we had a yin-yang friendship, each of us perfectly balancing out the other—at least until high school, when our careful, if naïve, equilibrium failed us miserably.

Taking that scoop from me, Annie hopped up on the stool with both feet at once and began spooning out the cupcake batter quickly, with joyful abandon, in a way that made me laugh hysterically, but also made me a little nervous. Lucia caught my eye and gave me a little wink, a gesture that never failed to make my heart sing. She'd been my nanny for as long as I could remember, and it was into her arms I ran when I was upset, tired, or hungry. Even at that young age, I sensed that my mother, who was very beautiful and very busy with her steady rotation of benefits and galas and dinner parties, was always a bit befuddled by my myriad needs—it seemed, somehow, that a space remained between us even when we hugged. With Lucia, that gap was closed; her soft arms enveloped me fully, filling my nostrils with her vanilla scent (which I much preferred to my mother's Givenchy perfume), and she was never the first to let go.

No one is perfect, of course, but Lucia managed to come exceedingly close. She seemed to know an endless catalog of songs—both English and Ecuadorean—that she sang in her soft, accented, slightly wavering voice. She always remembered to slice grilled cheese sandwiches straight across for me and diagonally for Annie. She had a way of listening that made me feel like I was the most important person in the world—she didn't own a sparkly watch at which to cast covert glances while I recited my times tables, and no telephones ever rang for her in my presence.

It was only as I got older that I realized, with a small swallow of shame, that those women who always called and interrupted my time with my mother were the very ones who would ensure I received invitations to all of the desirable parties, and that walking down the street with my elegant mother at my side made me swell with pride in a way walking with Lucia decidedly did not.

While my mother preferred to start her day with a glass of ice-cold water and a power walk by the bay, my father—from whom I'd inherited not only a stellar internal clock, but also a head for business, a near obsession with current events, and a serious sweet tooth—had joined me for breakfast every day that week. We'd taken to spending our mornings poring over the day's newspapers, reading to each other from the occasional article, and slowly working our way through an oversized croissant and a double slice of coffee cake, respectively. On the morning after the Save the Children benefit, by the time I finally compelled myself to get out of bed, pull on black pencil jeans and blousy cotton top, and make my way downstairs, my father was well on his way through a third mug of coffee.

Sonja, my parents' chef, strode out of the kitchen with my green tea as I entered the dining room. My father looked over his paper at me and gave a low whistle.

"I know, I know," I said, forcing myself to sound lighthearted. "One week after leaving my job and I'm already getting lazy. What's happening in the world? What do I miss when I oversleep by five minutes?"

"Oh, the world just kept on spinning. No harm done," Dad said, shaking the paper until a page turned freely. Tall, broad, and boisterous, my father was like the sixty-five-year-old human version of an eight-year-old golden retriever, big, love-filled brown eyes, bellowing voice, insatiable appetite, and all. At home, this personality manifested itself as a sort of boozy, blustery devotion to my mother and me, but I'd heard enough of his work-related calls to know that in business, Thaddeus St. Clair was a larger-than-life force with which to be reckoned.

"Shoot," I said. "It's always so disappointing to realize the world goes on without me." I poured myself a cup of tea, nibbled on a croissant, and stared at the front page of the *Wall Street Journal* without reading.

"That was a big sigh," my father said after minutes of silence had passed.

"What?"

"You just sighed, my dear. Loudly. If I hadn't already read that paper, I'd be worried about economic catastrophe."

Had I sighed? I couldn't remember. But the look of concern on my father's face was enough to make me avert my eyes for fear of the sudden torrent of tears that I seemed barely capable of holding at bay these days. And I'd never been a crier before!

I mentally added that to the list of ways my body seemed to be telling me it was no longer functioning under my control. Each time over the previous few weeks that I had found myself blinking back tears I'd felt equally devastated and annoyed. *St. Clairs*, I admonished myself, *don't* dwell. *We don't* dwell *and we don't* cry. My mother and father were each, in their own way, comprised of stoic stock that could be traced back to the industrious gold-prospecting outfitters found on the uppermost branches of our family tree. My parents, I knew well, rarely let their emotions get the best of them. For all their faults, I admired them greatly. Each was remarkably successful: my father had parlayed inherited millions into more millions through savvy new technology investments; my mother had raised millions, *literally* millions, for various charities and social programs in the Bay Area. The path to such success seemed clear: strategize, focus, and don't take no for an answer. Needless to say, we'd never been the sort of household in which A minuses were greeted with a smile and a sticker.

"Julia?" my dad prompted, eyeing me.

I straightened in my seat and waved vaguely at the air. "Oh, I'm fine. The wedding, you know. Silly stuff."

Dad nodded sagely and cleared his throat. "A three-hundred-person event is nothing to sneeze at. But if anyone can handle it, you can." He paused. "And if it turns out you can't, I'm sure your mother would be more than happy to take the reins."

I forced a laugh, and my father cocked an eyebrow at me. *Shit*, I thought. *When exactly did I become so terrible at hiding my emotions?* I placed a heaping spoonful of berries in my mouth and tried to chew with gusto.

"Unless, of course, it's Wesley you're concerned about?" he asked, a hint of fatherly protectiveness edging into his voice. "Did something happen?"

"No! No, Dad. Everything with Wes is fine. Wes is great."

I had met Wesley Trehorn a year and a half earlier at a holiday party in Manhattan thrown by a friend of mine from business school. Wes was thirty-five and handsome like a man, not a boy, with the broad-shoulders-square-jaw-and-black-glasses look I loved—*your Clark Kent fetish*, Jason, my Columbia friend, had joked. But it was not love at first sight, though I was as charmed as anyone by the combination of his sweet, Southern boy manners and sharp intelligence. It was more like love-at-third-date, which was when Wes revealed more about the company he was in the process of founding, a company that would build small, inexpensive, nearly indestructible computers he believed would be powerful educational tools for children in third world countries. I'd heard hope and passion in his voice and saw ambition in his eyes as he spoke, and felt a slow turning sensation in my chest as though my heart were settling into a new, more tenuous position.

Some of Wesley's attributes were ones I recognized in myself as well—I, too, was ambitious, some might say to a fault. After I'd graduated from Columbia with my MBA, I'd joined Lane Thomas Ventures, a top VC firm in New York City, and had quickly proven that I'd inherited my father's uncanny ability to identify early on which high-tech start-ups would be successful. But it was the small differences between Wes and me, more than the similarities, that made me fall in love with him. He was like Julia St. Clair 2.0—ambitious to a fault, yes, but his ambition was to *do good*. Still, he wasn't some bleeding heart liberal. I could not have tied my life to someone who didn't believe in the importance of daily showers and a good suit, no matter how sweetly he drawled. No, even as Wes was envisioning the way his company could change children's lives, he was also envisioning the way his company would change his own. He had big plans for the fabulous life he would build for himself, and it didn't take long for his plans to become ours.

After breakfast with my father, I took a wedding magazine out to the patio and flipped through it idly. Photograph after photograph after photograph of perfect, smiling brides. Even in the photographs of real weddings, the ones that showed *actual* brides posing on their *actual* wedding days, the brides looked almost absurdly joyful. *Smug,* I thought, dropping the magazine down to the ground beside my lounge chair. Where were the brides who, yes, loved their new husbands, but who also dared to show a sliver of the uncertainty they surely must be feeling? Was it possible that all of these women knew exactly what their futures held? Or was it that they didn't know, but didn't mind the not knowing? Surely I wasn't the only control freak to face the end of a wedding aisle?

The morning air was still cool but the sun was bright so I closed my eyes as I reclined in the chaise. The sun painted flickering red patterns against my eyelids and I felt my mind begin to wander. Within moments, I was back in that hospital bed, awakening groggily to a middle-aged nurse standing over me. Someone was sobbing, a low and primitive sound. *The expression of sorrow,* I thought, *has been the same since the beginning of time.* A vast, hollow ache filled my stomach as I realized the cries were my own. I rolled over onto my side, my eyes swollen with tears, my heart splintering with grief.

"Is there someone I can find for you in the waiting room? Let them know you're awake?" the nurse asked, patting my hand. She was a blur of floral-patterned scrubs and long dark hair, her eyes drooping and sad.

I shook my head, unable to speak. What the nurse really wanted to know was if there was someone else who could comfort me, but the person in the waiting room was just a paid caregiver, a large woman named Yvette or Yvonne or maybe Ivana, who I had hired to drive me to and from the hospital.

The nurse's brow furrowed with concern as I pressed my trembling lips together. She had stopped patting my hand and now just gripped it, squeezing it tightly every so often. "Do you want to sleep a bit more?" she whispered, bending near my ear. I closed my eyes and in her Spanish accent, heard Lucia's. "I can give you something to help."

I nodded, grateful for her kindness, the sympathy in her voice. Hot tears snaked down my neck and into my gown and there was nothing I could possibly do but let them fall.

On the patio, my eyes fluttered open. I looked at the clock on my phone. Nine a.m. I sank back against the chaise and sighed, pressing my palms into my eyes. *Is this what the next year is going to be like? Lying around crying on the patio at all hours of the day?* Anyway, could it really take that long to plan a wedding with Lolly St. Clair, Master Party Planner, at the helm? What the hell had I been thinking, quitting my absolutely perfect job? Well, I knew exactly what I'd been thinking about when I'd given notice three weeks earlier, and it had only been in part about the wedding. *Anyway*, I thought, admonishing myself, *I need to stop obsessing over* why *I did it*. All that mattered was that I *had* done it; I'd packed up and left New York and was here now. Living in my parents' Pacific Heights house. Crying on the patio.

I tried to look on the bright side. I had plenty of time to take the long runs I loved through the Presidio and down by Marina Green and Crissy Field and up in the Marin Headlands. And there was always yoga (but, to be honest, I hated yoga—all that *oming* and *light within* gobbledygook). *Okay.* So then there were the parties. Already since my return, the party invitations had been piling up on the desk in my bedroom—cleverly designed invitations from people I had known a lifetime ago, or who knew my parents, or hardly knew any of our circle at all, but desperately wanted to. My life was full of these sorts of *circles*, but, I wondered, since Annie Quintana, had I really had a true best friend? *Wes*. He was a true friend. My best friend. But now he was halfway around the world, overseeing the opening of a manufacturing plant in China.

Wes. I had to tell him what had happened. He'd been away the entire month surrounding my hospital stay and had barely been in town two consecutive nights ever since. On the few occasions I had seen him, the timing just hadn't seemed right. But he was going to be my husband, for God's sake. *Well*, I thought, indulging in a rare moment of procrastination, *I will* tell him. *Of course I will. I have to. Later.* But right now? Right now, it was clear that I was in desperate need of another cupcake.

It takes a person with a serious sweet tooth to hide desserts in secret stashes. Mine is that serious. The previous night, after trying one of Annie's cupcakes, I'd immediately walked into the kitchen, taken a mocha-flavored cupcake from a tray awaiting circulation, and hidden it behind a jar of wild-grain rice on a lower shelf in the pantry. Now, I walked to the kitchen, shut the pantry door behind me, retrieved the cupcake from its hiding place, and, feeling only the slightest twinge of mortification for my little covert cupcake operation, took a large bite.

I had, I'll admit, effected a certain style—a method, if you will—of cupcake eating. To begin, you remove the cupcake liner carefully so as not to unnecessarily crumble the cake, and set it aside. You then turn the cupcake slowly in your hand, taking bites along the line where cake meets icing, your mouth filling with a perfect combination of both components. Once you've come full circle, you gently twist off the bottom half inch of cake, a move that takes considerable finesse and leaves a delicate sliver of cake—the ideal size for lying flat on your tongue and allowing it to slowly dissolve, building anticipation for that final bite. To finish, you are left with the center cylinder of cake and icing, the cupcake's very heart, sometimes filled with a surprising burst of custard or jam or mousse, sometimes not, but always, *always*, the most moist, flavorful bite of the entire cupcake. Take a breath before diving into that final, perfect bite; it is to be savored for as long as possible. Finally, of course, you scavenge the crumbs from the cupcake liner you set aside during step one, then ball the liner into your fist and overhand it into the nearest receptacle. Make the shot? You get another cupcake.

But I've gotten ahead of myself. Back to that very first bite of hidden cupcake in the pantry: a soft cap of vanilla buttercream giving way to light, creamy mocha cake. I kept eating, turning the cupcake slowly in my hand. This was not rich, one-bite-and-you-couldn't-possibly-have-more chocolate. This was refined, complex chocolate cut with a hint of coffee and what else . . . *Currant? Salt?* A grown-up, masterful cupcake. It was perfect. I leaned back against the shelves in the cool, dark pantry and felt myself relax.

Annie could make a fortune on these things.

I straightened, licked each of my fingers clean, and snuck one last nibble out of the bottom of the delicate white cupcake wrapper before balling it in my fist and shooting it into the pantry trash can. *Swish.* There I was, out of cupcakes—but with a very good idea in their place.

Of course! I kicked myself for not thinking of this the moment I tasted my first bite of lemon cupcake the night before. Wasn't I known for spotting a sure bet from a mile away? And here I was, taking more than twelve hours to realize the business opportunity that was staring me right in the face! Talk about going soft. One week off the job and already I was losing my edge.

I practically ran to my mother's study to find Annie's phone number. *This is exactly what I need*, I thought, pressing the number into my cell phone. *Something to distract me, something to pour myself into while I get through this . . . this year.* I walked out on the patio again and pulled the door shut behind me, listening as the phone rang in my ear.

"Hello?"

"Annie, hi! It's Julia."

Silence.

I cleared my throat, then clarified, "Julia St. Clair."

"Yes, I know. Hi."

The chill in Annie's voice was impossible to miss. *Was she really still stuck on a series of events that took place a hundred years ago?* I wondered. Of course, this had been fairly apparent the night before when she'd stared at me coldly all through our conversation and then left abruptly when Jake Logan appeared. I decided to ignore her rudeness and press on.

"Do you have a minute to talk?" I asked.

"Well, I just left the bakery and now I'm headed to the park with a few dogs, so . . ."

"This will just take a minute. Really. I have an idea I'd love to run by you."

More silence. But I was nothing if not persistent.

"It was great to see you last night, Annie," I said sweetly, trying a new tack.

I heard her sigh. "Is this urgent, Julia? Talking on the phone while walking three dogs with bulging bladders down an incredibly steep street toward a park is like trying to race the Iditarod with one hand tied behind your back. It would be much easier if we had this little chat another time."

I had the distinct sense that if I agreed to this, the next time I phoned Annie, my call would go straight to voice mail. It was time, I realized, for my business voice.

"Then I'll make it quick," I said, and immediately began pacing the patio. "Your cupcakes are the best I've ever tasted, and I've eaten more cupcakes than I care to admit. That's a compliment, but more importantly, it's a fact. I'm confident that with your skill and my operations experience, together we could open a cupcak-ery that would have a line out the door from the time we open in the morning until the moment we close at night. I can provide the capital to get us started. This is what I do, Annie, and I do it well: I invest in businesses and I drive them to be successful. I'll be in San Francisco for nearly a year—plenty of time to get you off the ground and seeing returns, at which point I'll bow out and you can take full ownership of the shop."

When she didn't answer right away, I continued hurriedly. "I know what you're thinking: a cupcakery? Does the world need another? The post-9/11 comfort-food era and Carrie and Mi-randa's little trip to Magnolia Bakery for cupcakes on *Sex and the City* definitely sparked a surge of interest—but let me tell you, I've tasted Magnolia's cupcakes and the cake is dry and the icing is practically grainy with sugar. Those cupcakes couldn't hold a candle to yours! Besides," I stammered, feeling the hollow rush of her silence in my ear, "anyone who knows anything knows to order the banana pudding at Magnolia, not the cupcakes." I was rambling, something I never did, or at least never used to do. Why was I trying to impress her? *It's just Annie*, I told myself. *Calm down.*

"My point is, people clearly want cupcakes—that desire won't wane anytime soon, I promise—and yours are the best. So let me do this for you." I paused, readying the final line of the pitch that I realized I'd already crafted in my head: "Your talent is ut-terly wasted working for anyone but yourself."

I swallowed. There was a beat of silence. And then:

"Well, gee, Julia, thanks so much for swooping into town and picking up the pieces of my *wasted* life. Whatever would I have done without you?"

"What? No, that's not at all what—" I sputtered.

"I'm going to decline your generous proposal. And I really have to go. Good-bye."

I pulled the phone from my ear and stared at it, shocked. *What just happened?* Leaning against the patio railing, I searched the still-green hills of the Marin Headlands across the bay to the north, trying to make sense of the conversation I'd just had.

Annie's voice had been so hard, so remote, and so angry. If it hadn't quite contained the cold ring of hatred, it bared at least the chilly tone of strong dislike. I was sure that she had never sounded like that when we were growing up. I remembered her as brave and independent, clever and warm in a way I'd always envied. Now she sounded hardened, more sarcastic than funny; her words were clipped and designed to sting.

Of course, I had some idea of what Annie was so pissed off about. Our senior year at Devon Prep had been especially hard for her, and I knew I hadn't made it any easier. As I thought about that time, I felt myself descending swiftly through a series of emotions—defensiveness, regret, and finally, with a heavy, sandbag thud: sadness. I crossed the patio and sank back down onto the lounge chair. *Sadness!* All my life I'd been proactive in my pursuit of happiness, and now suddenly I felt dogged, cloaked even, by sadness. I couldn't seem to shake it. The whole point of the cupcakery venture was to get my mind *off* of the past—distant and recent—and move forward. Put one foot in front of the other and just keep walking until I was out of this funk. And here I was, being dragged back into the thick of it by Annie Quintana.

It was selfish of her, really. And ungrateful. I hated feeling like I needed her, but there I was practically *begging* her to take my money and my expertise so that she could finally embark on her dream career—or at least, I assumed it was her dream career. And she'd said no all because of some silly misunderstanding that had taken place a decade ago! I quickly flipped through the series of events that had corroded our friendship. By the time we'd each left for college, I remembered, we were barely speaking. And then Lucia had died; after that, complete silence.

Oh! I thought with a start. *Is Annie's anger somehow related to her mother's death?* In the fall, after I had left for Stanford and Annie for Cal—or, no, I suppose that wasn't right, Annie's acceptance to Cal was still suspended at that point and she was living in the carriage house, waitressing, and taking classes at City College—my mother had walked into the kitchen one morning and found Lucia collapsed on the floor. She'd called an ambulance straightaway, ridden with her to the hospital, tracked down the very best doctors, and later paid for all of her medical bills. Still, despite my mother's best efforts, Lucia slipped into a coma before either Annie or I reached the hospital. She died several days later without ever waking. Her death had gutted me—I'd taken weeks off school and then slogged through finals in a stunned haze. Really, Annie should have counted herself lucky she wasn't at Cal yet and could deal with her grief at home, in private.

At the funeral, Annie and I had mostly kept our distance from one another but I do remember sharing a tearful hug at some point during the service. And then, nothing. A few weeks later, she left for Cal and basically fell off the face of the planet. *Does she blame our family for Lucia's death?* My mother in particular was hurt by Annie's chilly behavior over the last ten years. After all, Annie had lived with our family for most of her life—she was like a second daughter to my mother. A niece, at the very least.

My phone rang in my lap, startling me out of these thoughts, and I picked it up without checking the caller ID, hoping against odds that it was Annie calling with a change of heart.

"Hello?"

"Crap. I must have dialed the wrong number. You're no saint."

It was Jake Logan, with an old joke. In spite of my mood, I laughed. "That's Ms. Julia, to you," I said airily. "What on earth do you want?" Jake and I hadn't spoken much on the phone since our mutual breakup during our freshman year in college, but we'd seen each other at various parties thrown by the Devon Prep crowd over the years and had maintained an easy, drama-free friendship.

"Ah, yes. It *is* you, isn't it?" he said. I could practically hear his mischievous smile through the phone. "Good! I just woke up and was afraid I dialed the wrong number."

"You just woke up? It's ten o'clock!"

"Please, no judgment. I'm calling with a very attractive offer. It appears the sun is out, which as you know is simply inappropriate for a June day in San Francisco."

"True," I said, matching his mock-businesslike tone. "Do go on."

"To spite this defiant sun, in defense of our poor burned-up fog, and in celebration of the return of San Francisco's prodigal daughter—that's you, Saintie!—I propose we sit inside all day and drink. Balboa Café, for old time's sake. You in?"

I squinted out at the bay, considering. A drink at ten in the morning with an ex-boyfriend was not exactly my style. And yet. Wes was halfway around the world. Annie clearly wasn't speaking to me. When I spent time alone I thought only of hospital beds and a suddenly, heartbreakingly unknowable future. So where, exactly, had "my style" gotten me after all these years? And, really, what harm could there be in having one drink with Jake? I was supposed to meet my mother at the florist's in an hour, but she could handle that appointment in her sleep, couldn't she?

"I'll be there in thirty," I said, feeling the flutter of—what, exactly? Relief? Trepidation?—well, something other than sadness in my chest.

I walked down the long, steep slope from our house in Pacific Heights toward the flat stretch of the Marina neighborhood that housed the Balboa Café and many of the other bars that I had frequented on my trips to the city during college at Stanford. I'd never been much of a drinker and usually nursed one vodka-soda over the course of a night, taking tiny sips until I was left with only melted ice and a vaguely metallic lime taste. Lately, though, I'd started to enjoy drinking more and more. The first couple of drinks tended to make me feel morose and self-pitying, but the third? The third made me feel suddenly lighter, as though nothing that had happened over the previous couple of months was really worth worrying about at all.

Even with the panoramic view of city carved into steeped slopes and shining bay and green expanse of hills to the north, the walk made me miss Manhattan. When I first moved to New York, I'd been surprised to find that despite what everyone said, the city was *cleaner* and had *fewer* scary homeless people than my hometown. In San Francisco, sidewalks and streets appeared messy and leaf-blown all year long and buildings needed to be painted annually to combat the damage of salty winds and months of dust. There were entire neighborhoods that seemed in perpetual need of a hose-down. Still, there was something undeniably magical about this city by the bay. It was, and always would be, my home. Annie and I had that much in common, at the very least: we were San Francisco girls, born and raised.

Jake was sitting at the dark wood bar with his back to me when I entered Balboa Café. A girl a few stools down leaned toward him, her blond ponytail dangling over her shoulder as she laughed at something he said. Her friends exchanged knowing glances at the sound of her flirtatious laughter, and soon the whole group had burst into a fit of giggles. I paused in the doorway, watching them. *Why do women with muffin tops insist on wearing low-slung jeans?* I wondered, irritated. *Is it really too much to ask for a couple extra inches of fabric to protect the innocent public's eyes from their unsightly bulges?* I sighed, reminding myself I didn't care one bit if Jake flirted with a girl who couldn't have been older than twenty-one and whose pale pink Hanky Panky thong was pulled *above* the layer of fat on her lower back. And yet, gazing at the two of them, I felt a territorial buzz start up behind my eyes. It was a feeling I'd had before.

By the time I entered my senior year at Devon, I had long established myself as the school's queen bee in every respect. Of course, I didn't think of myself that way at the time, but looking back, it's easy to see that's who I was. I had the best grades, led a pack of pretty, popular friends, and had a closetful of clothes any girl would have killed for. When I noticed Jake Logan of the shipping Logans, captain of the football, swim, and baseball teams, and most certainly headed to Dartmouth in the fall, flirting with *Annie* in the hall—Annie, whose social circle at that point consisted of two pimply, tweezers- and sunshine-adverse girls whose names I always confused—I know I should have been happy for her. Instead, almost without thinking, I turned on the charm. Okay, maybe it wasn't *entirely* without thinking. In any event, Jake and I were officially dating by the end of the week.

"Julia!" Jake called from the bar, stirring me from these unproductive musings.

I crossed the room, enjoying the disappointed flush that crept up the back of Hanky Panky Girl's neck as I did so, and perched myself on the stool beside Jake. He leaned over to kiss me on the cheek.

"Glad you made it. Vodka tonic?"

"Please."

He ordered me the cocktail and watched with an amused twinkle in his aquamarine eyes as I took a long drink.

"You okay?" he asked.

"Sure," I said. "Fabulous."

He held his beer up to his lips and shook his head. "I don't know," he said, gulping. "Something's different."

I shrugged. "I'm engaged."

Jake laughed. "Well, I know *that*, Jules. It's not the rock—it's you. You seem . . . I don't know. Different."

"No, I don't," I said sharply. I drained my drink and Jake ordered me another. We'd moved on to other, lighter topics of conversation—Caroline Sistenberg's recent stint in rehab for a Vicodin addiction that developed after she blew out her knee skiing in Aspen that winter, the new Peter Carraway restaurant opening in Jake's building in North Beach, whether I should switch to a martini for my third drink—when I suddenly found myself asking, yelling, actually, truth be told, "And anyway, would it be so bad?"

"Would what be so bad?" Jake asked, surprised.

"If I were different! If I'd changed. People change, Jake. Sometimes for the better." I had no idea why I was saying this. I wasn't even sure I believed it. And anyway, I *hadn't* changed—I was exactly who I'd always been. Except, really, I *was* different now, wasn't I? I suddenly envisioned that the only thing left of the old me was a painted, external shell. *This*, I thought angrily, trying to rein in my wayward thoughts, *is why I shouldn't drink.*

Jake shook his head. "I never said change was bad, Jules. I was just checking in on you. I didn't mean to upset you."

"I'm not upset!" I said, but my face burned. I looked down at the martini that had appeared on the bar in front of me. "Maybe I should go."

"Oh, c'mon, stay," Jake said. He gave my shoulder a playful

little push. "Let's talk about something fun." He squinted at me. "I know! Have you met Linus Tarrington's new girlfriend yet? She's one of those awful girls who are always wearing sequins and preening for photographers at events. And do you know where she grew up? *Fresno*."

"Oh God, really?" I asked weakly.

"The worst part is I think she really has her eye on *me*. I have this theory that she's planning on leapfrogging her way through our crowd and right into Gavin Newsom's bed."

"Jake, no!" I said, feeling the beginnings of a smile work its way onto my lips.

He leaned in conspiratorially and held out his hand. "I'll bet you a hundred dollars she dumps Tarrington right after opening night at the opera."

"Poor Linus!" I said, shaking Jake's hand and laughing. At last, the martini spread its warmth through my veins.

And so I stayed. Over the course of the next several hours, we got very, very drunk. I remember wondering, when Jake finally walked me out to find a cab, whether I would tell Wes about this little sojourn down memory lane. Why would I? I decided. Really, there was nothing to tell. Just old friends catching up over drinks.

I recited my parents' address to the cabdriver, hoping I wasn't slurring my words. In the harsh light of day—and it was, uncomfortably, still quite sunny out—I was acutely embarrassed by the impropriety of being drunk on a Sunday afternoon. As I settled in the seat and pulled out my cell phone, I was surprised to see that I had just missed a call. I put the phone to my ear and tried to ignore the taste of bile that crept into the back of my throat as the cab raced, seemingly, straight up into the sky, peeling through every stop sign along the way.

Hi, Julia. It's Annie, the voice mail message began. *I've reconsidered. Let's do it. Let's open a cupcakery together. Call me.*

My mouth fell open and I slammed my fist down excitedly into the torn leather seat, and when neither action seemed to adequately express the surprising lightness that had suddenly swelled like helium in my chest, I found myself yelling, "YESSSSS!!!!!" into the cab, forgetting for a just a moment to care one bit what the cabdriver, or anyone else for that matter, might think of me.

July

3

Annie

LATER THAT WEEK, once June had given way to July, I walked toward Valencia Street Bakery through dense morning fog, still questioning my decision to go into business with Julia. At that point, of course, I had no idea just how far—and how dangerously—the cupcakery would plunge us into the past. I suppose if I wanted to—and, believe me, I often did—I could blame everything that happened moving forward from that point on Becca's expert needling. Becca and that too good bottle—okay, *bottles*—of Sonoma Cabernet.

The day after the Save the Children benefit, after I'd received that annoying call from Julia and had walked my three canine charges back to their respective homes, I'd headed to Becca and Mike's apartment on Capp Street for Craptastic Sunday. Having determined that the worst thing about moving in with her boyfriend Mike was that he refused to watch the steady stream of crappy reality television shows that she favored, Becca had invented Craptastic Sunday, a bimonthly event during which Mike vacated the apartment and Becca and I spent the better part of the afternoon emptying her DVR while simultaneously emptying a bottle or two—

and on that one occasion, three, but we later agreed that had been a terrible mistake—of wine.

"So how was it seeing Richie and Muffy McRicherson?" Becca had asked as she poured the first glasses of the afternoon.

Becca and I had been freshman roommates at Cal. At first, she'd been standoffish. That fall, her first roommate, a Midwestern girl, had dropped out in a fit of homesickness and she'd been left with a coveted two-room single, so she wasn't too pleased when I showed up at her door halfway through the year with a letter from student services clutched in my hand. Eventually, we'd bonded when, after making a pact to jog off the "freshman fifteen" we'd gained, we'd ended up, instead, sharing a joint behind the bathroom at the track and then an old-fashioned triple-scoop sundae at the ice cream parlor on College Avenue. After Devon Prep, Berkeley felt like a breath of fresh air; each year of high school had been more difficult than the year before, and by contrast, Cal, with its laid-back professors and the relative diversity of its student population, seemed like Utopia. Suddenly, I was surrounded by interesting, smart people who didn't base their opinion of me on the label of my bag or the tightness of my ass or the birthplace and occupation of my great grandfather. I knew there were people like that everywhere, including Cal, but it was much easier to avoid that crew at college without becoming a social outcast. In Berkeley, there were options. San Francisco was just across the Bay Bridge, but I felt entire oceans away from Pacific Heights. Nonetheless, Becca, whose parents worked at a post office in Sacramento and who had a quartet of loud, overly muscled brothers who scuffled like puppies during the holidays I spent with them after my mother died, had an unfortunate fascination with the St. Clairs. She seemed to think of the family as an alien species worthy of endless dissection and analysis.

"The party was exactly as I expected, with one glaring exception," I'd told her as I sank back into the couch, still flabbergasted by the call I'd received that morning from Julia. "The Ice Princess was in attendance."

"What? No! How did that go?"

"Weird. She's engaged, but she was flirting with a guy I used to have a huge crush on—her ex-boyfriend, actually. And she was doing this whole sweet-as-apple-pie thing to me that was just disturbing. 'Oh, Annie, your cupcakes are *amazing*.' Blah blah blah. It was one of those conversations that seriously makes me question if all compliments aren't inherently backhanded. I mean, isn't a compliment just someone's way of telling you they didn't think you had it in you to look so good or be so successful or, I don't know, pull off a sweater that shade of green?"

Becca looked at me, her head cocked to the side. "So you're telling me that bitch complimented you?"

"I know, I know. I sound crazy. This is what one night with the St. Clairs does to me. A decade of normalcy becomes a blip on the radar and I regress to being a self-doubting, self-loathing teenager." I sighed. "Never mind. Let's just watch some craptastic TV before Mike gets home twitching for *SportsCenter*."

"First of all," Becca said, "you forget that I knew you when you were a teenager, straight off the St. Clairs' yacht and fresh upon the Berkeley shore, and you were never self-doubting, self-loathing, or self-anything that I remember." She paused, her finger in the air. "Maybe self-deprecating. I'll give you that, if you really feel you need to remember yourself as self-something.

"And second," she continued, "I'm as fired up as any red-blooded American woman to watch some ripped, shirtless dude make out with The Bachelorette in a hot tub, but you seem a little distracted. And unless you're going to sit there and hurl clever peanut gallery comments at the TV, unless you can really put your game face on, I think we need to keep Craptastic Sunday on pause a little longer and just hash this whole St. Clair thing out."

I groaned. "C'mon, Becca. Do we have to? Julia has wasted enough of my time and energy today."

"Today?" Becca peered at me "What do you mean? I thought you saw her yesterday."

I looked down into my wineglass. I hadn't planned on telling Becca about Julia's call because I knew exactly what Becca would say. She would tell me I was crazy for saying no to Julia's business proposal, just like she had told me I would be crazy to say no to Lolly's catering request. But the thing about Becca, who taught math to tenth graders in one of the city's toughest schools, was that she was in possession of the most highly attuned bullshit detector I'd ever encountered. I could practically see it, flashing and beeping and vibrating behind her eyes as it honed in on me. It was an exercise in futility, really, to attempt to keep anything from her. And I did loathe exercise.

"Julia called earlier today," I admitted. "She wants to open a cupcake shop with me and she said she'd put up the money to get us started. But before you say anything, I already told her no. It would be too uncomfortable. I couldn't bear to work with her."

Becca's mouth dropped open. "Okay, you are now officially off-your-rocker insane," she said. She whipped her long, chestnut hair in front of her shoulder and began twisting it furiously until it coiled tight against her head. "I mean," she said, looking like a crazed, lopsided Princess Leia, "I think it would suck to work with Madonna and have to look at her bizarro mutant biceps and hear her faux-British accent day in and day out, but if she were willing to, gee, I don't know, *make all of my dreams come true*, I could probably learn to deal with her track suits and icy disposition."

"How is it that this is the first time I'm learning of your beef with Madonna?"

"Nice try. We're discussing you and Julia."

I shrugged. "What can I say? I feel like a second-class citizen when I'm with that family. Come on, Becca, you know what Julia did to me. If she's funding my dream bakery, it's not really my dream anymore because it means I've become a St. Clair employee, which is more like my nightmare."

"But your mom was a St. Clair employee. And she loved them, didn't she?"

"Look where it got her."

There was silence as Becca took this in.

"It's not like they killed her, Annie," she said finally.

"You say tomato . . ."

"Annie!"

"What? She basically died on their kitchen floor."

"That's not the same thing," Becca said. "You know that *where* she died and *how* she died are not necessarily related."

I poured myself another glass of wine, ignoring the slight shake in my hand as I did so. "Objectively speaking, yes, I know that. But it's tough to be objective when you're talking about your dearly departed mother."

"Fine, I get that. As long as you can admit that those feelings are irrational."

"Did I ever tell you what Julia said to me at my mother's funeral? She said, 'Well, at least now you're totally free. You can be anyone you want to be.' She presented this bit of wisdom like a gift, like I should thank her. I wanted to sock her."

"Okay," Becca said slowly, quietly. "But still. It's crazy talk in crazy town to let these feelings get in the way of your dreams. Unless, maybe, owning your own bakery isn't your dream anymore?"

My desire to own my own bakery was as strong on that day as it had been the day the seed was planted during my first pastry class at the San Francisco Culinary Institute five years earlier, and Becca knew it. The question was only whether or not the trade-off of linking my life with the St. Clairs in order to achieve my dream was worth it. The answer, I realized, was yes. Even if it meant allowing Julia back in my life. I took in the prodding smirk on Becca's face. She loved winning. It was, perhaps, the only thing she and Julia St. Clair had in common. Me, on the other hand? Sometimes I wondered if I had a competitive bone in my body.

"You know what, Becca?" I'd said then. "There are moments when I really, really hate you." The victorious grin that had grown on her face was highly contagious, just as I'd suspected it would be.

At five in the morning, the kitchen of the Valencia Street Bakery was a warm, dark, cavelike place: my private domain. I always found myself lingering in the doorway for a moment when I first entered the kitchen, savoring the silence and the way the edges of the appliances blurred with the still-gray air. Then I began my work. The two hulking ovens hummed and clacked and whooshed, the room swelled with warmth and the smell of butter and yeast, and the kitchen grew slowly brighter as though a veil were being lifted up and away from the dented steel counters and filling pastry racks.

At six, Lorena, my assistant baker, and Carlos, the dishwasher, arrived bleary-eyed at the back door. I unlocked it, returned their mumbled hellos, and watched as they shuffled through their predictable morning rituals. Carlos, a skinny twenty-year-old who lived at home with his parents and five siblings, flipped on the radio and hoisted himself onto the counter next to the sink, blinking himself slowly into consciousness. Lorena, neat as a tack in a teal button-down stretched taut over her enormous bosom, her graying black hair pulled into a tight bun at the nape of her neck, immediately strode through the swinging door into the café and returned to hand out three steaming mugs of coffee.

She stood, stout and serious, studying the prep list and taking admirably large gulps of the scalding hot coffee, before tackling the first duties of her day: mixing muffin batter and preparing pastry fillings. As Lorena switched on the stand mixer, Carlos dove into the Sisyphean task of scrubbing the mountain of crusted trays, tins, and bowls that had already stacked up in the sink. Lorena, Carlos, and I formed just the latest of a string of close-working kitchen teams I'd been a member of over the years, but we were more well-oiled than most, having been together long enough to iron out some of the kinks that come with working ungodly hours in tight quarters. But really, even the smallest, hottest, most adversarial kitchens in which I'd worked over the years—where Spanish bounced rapid-fire off the appliances—inevitably came to feel like some strange version of home. Eventually, though, someone always moved on—to a better gig, another kitchen, or a new city. This time, I realized with a pang, that someone would be me. I just hoped Ernesto, the owner of the bakery, would promote Lorena to head baker. She'd been working in kitchens for thirty years, and what she lacked in creativity she made up for in diligence and dependability. As tempted as I was to poach her for the cupcakery, I didn't have the heart to leave Ernesto and take his best assistant baker, too.

At six thirty I heard the jingle of keys in the café's front door, and a moment later Ernesto himself popped his head into the kitchen.

"Morning all," he trilled. Ernesto was a triller, the kind of man who was as chipper at six thirty in the morning as he would be when he locked up at ten that night.

"Banana-chocolate," I said, passing him a tray of perfectly golden muffins.

He faked a swoon against the door frame. "These are going on the top shelf. Ay, the aroma! The customers won't stand a chance."

"As long as you save them some." Ernesto's habit of "sampling" the goods sometimes made me feel more like his personal chef than his head baker.

"How can I serve something I haven't tried myself?" Ernesto called from the front room. I could hear him sliding the display case open. "It would be . . . what's the word? Unethical. And, you know, cruel. To me. Smelling these gorgeous little darlings all day long without being able to taste them. Cruel and unusual. Torture!"

I rolled my eyes, but couldn't help feeling pleased. I had to admit it was nice to have a boss who loved what I made. Over the years, I'd had every type of boss out there—the one who thought I used too much butter, the one who thought I used too little, the hairy one who was always trying to make out with me in the freezer, the one who never once in the two years I worked for her tasted a single one of my recipes, but fired me the day I asked for a raise. And now here I was, working for my dream boss, a boss who gave me free rein in the kitchen and had clearly formed an unhealthy, if flattering, addiction to the pastries I created, and I was going to quit? For the first time since college, I was in a place where I was one hundred percent sure that I would be able to pay my rent the next month—and even the month after that!—and I was about to throw all of that security away. I pressed my fingers into my temples to ward off the impending headache.

Still, Becca's words circled back through my thoughts, a not-so-gentle reprimand. Since when had I become such a slave to security? Since when had my dream to be my own boss morphed into merely working for my dream boss? Sure, the route I was headed down meant I was going to have to work with Julia, but wouldn't the end result of owning my own bakery make the hassle of seeing Julia day in and day out for ten months be worth it? *She's only around until May when she'll get married and move on to her next dilettantish distraction,* I told myself. *You just need to make it until May.*

Around noon, Ernesto popped his head back into the kitchen. "Oh, An-nie," he called, singsong. "You have a vis-i-tor." He wagged his thick black eyebrows up and down. Lorena and Carlos glanced at me and I shrugged.

I wiped my hands against my apron—after all those years, I still could not manage to don an apron without feeling like my mother (a complicated feeling, to put it mildly)—and walked through the door of the kitchen into the shop. The five tables were all occupied and a few people lingered at the counter, awaiting their coffees and covertly tapping their feet to the Latin pop that Ernesto pumped through speakers from his iPod. It was the usual Wednesday Mission crowd: laptops, tattoos, and messenger bags. And there, leaning against the window in a Polo, jeans, and flip-flops, was Jake Logan. On cue, my silly little heart began to thwap around in my chest as though it were hoping to break out and bounce over into Jake's arms. *Traitor,* I thought, giving my heart a few imaginary rat-tat-tat backhand-forehand slaps. I ran my hand over the top of my head and down the length of my ponytail. I'd later see that I'd imparted a fine film of flour like a skunk's stripe down the center of my hair.

"Hey," I said, making my way around the counter to greet him. "What are you doing here?"

Jake looked up and grinned. "I'm here to see you, of course." He kissed my cheek, his hand resting on my shoulder. "Mmm, you smell good."

It felt odd to have Jake kissing me as though we were really truly grown-ups and not just slightly more pulled together (Jake) and curvier (me) versions of our high school selves. I noticed Ernesto watching us and shot him my best go-about-your-business-or-suffer-my-unending-wrath glare.

"Do you live nearby?" I asked. "I haven't seen you in here before."

"Nope, I live in North Beach. Never heard of this place until you mentioned it the other night at the St. Clairs'. I thought I'd swing by and see what all the fuss is about."

"Not much fuss, I'm afraid. Some coffee, some sweets. This might in fact be the most fuss-free destination in the city. Sorry to disappoint you."

"Now that I think about it," Jake said, shrugging and grinning simultaneously, "fuss is overrated. Want to grab a coffee? Catch up? Can you leave?"

I laughed, gesturing at the enormous espresso machine behind the counter. "You just walked into what is, essentially, a coffee shop and asked if I want to grab coffee somewhere else. We're clear on that, right?"

"Well, I'd ask if you wanted to grab a drink, but I don't know where you stand on the midday cocktail."

"Fair enough. I won't be finished for another hour though. Can you come back?"

"I'll wait."

I looked at him. I was still having some trouble adding up the pieces. Jake Logan—yes, the guy's first and last name seemed eternally bound in my head—had arrived unannounced at my place of work just to see me. If he were any other guy, I would have found his actions to be a bit too much, a bit stalkerish. But that would have been an Adult Annie reaction. Teenage Annie was internally screaming something along the lines of: *Oh. My. God. Jake. Logan. Is. Waiting. For. Meeeeeeee!!!*

Back in the kitchen, Lorena smiled at me.

"How do you know him?" she asked, eyes bright with the promise of gossip. Lorena, ever eager for my stories of the incestuous dating world of young bakers and chefs, swallowed gossip whole like the calcium pills she took to make her bones stronger.

"He's not a baker," I said, hoping to leave it at that.

"Oh," Lorena said. She thought for a moment. "Well, that's good. He's very handsome."

Carlos turned from the sink with a smirk.

"I'll let him know he has admirers," I said.

I rolled out the dough for ham and cheese croissants and worked on getting a grip. Away from Jake's blue-green gaze and heart-crushing dimples, it was a little easier to take stock of the situation and get my bearings. *Jake Logan*, I reminded myself as I twisted the dough into perfect crescents, *is very much part and parcel of that world you hated in high school and have been avoiding ever since.* I realized I had no idea what Jake had been doing in the six years since graduating from Dartmouth. *Maybe he does community outreach*, I thought hopefully. *Or maybe he's a pediatric resident!* He had that man-child vibe that probably made kids love him. Plus, that would explain the irregular schedule and casual attire. *Or maybe he just hangs out all day, using hundred-dollar bills as coasters for his scotch tumblers.* This, I had to admit, seemed equally possible.

As my shift neared its end, I went over the day's remaining tasks with Lorena, hung my apron on a hook by the kitchen door, and gave myself a surreptitious once-over in the full-length mirror Ernesto had mounted on the inside of the bathroom door. All in all, the situation could have been worse. My dark tangle of hair was pulled back from my face and I was wearing a paper-thin black T-shirt and jeans that showed off my hourglass figure—hips made for *baking*, not birthing, was my line of choice. My petite frame probably carried ten or fifteen more pounds than it should have (who was counting?), but the extra weight gave me boobs and an ass. So I had that going for me. Besides, everyone knows that a skinny baker is not to be trusted. And who was I to discourage anyone's trust?

I thanked whatever spirit had prompted me to dab on a little under-eye makeup and mascara at the crack of dawn before work that morning. There were times, I knew, when I looked like a complete and utter wreck by the end of my shift; by some minor miracle, this afternoon was not one of them.

"Have fun," Carlos called loudly as I pushed open the door to the shop. Lorena giggled.

I ignored both of them, half expecting Jake to be gone. But there he was, leaning against the window, studying his phone. I felt self-conscious under Ernesto's intrigued eye, so I suggested we walk to a nearby taqueria that served enormous burritos and thick-as-tar coffee.

"You had me at burrito," said Jake, holding the door open.

At El Farolito, we sat at a tiny bright yellow table and took turns sprinkling hot sauce over our plates. Merengue music, as exuberantly frothy and light as its confectionary namesake, meringue, pumped out of the speakers, interrupted every so often by the same DJ who had been on the station since I was a kid. It was the station my mom always had on while we rushed around the carriage house getting ready in the early hours of the day. Like her embroidered turquoise and orange blouses or the purple hand-knit sweater with its zigzag pattern and zipper, merengue music was one of the things Mom never lost her affection for in all her years away from Ecuador. The music in the carriage house was a stark contrast to the concertos that would spill out and swell up against the walls of the St. Clairs' courtyard when we opened their kitchen door each morning. Actually, I kind of liked that classical music, too. Once Lolly and Tad were out of the house, my mother would flip the stereo to the Latin music station. Sometimes, if the soulful guitar chords of an Ecuadorean *pasillo* came over the radio, I'd catch her swaying slightly at the sink, her eyes almost closed. Only then would I see a hint of the dark ocean of homesickness that must have churned inside of her.

When I saw my mom's face cloud over like that, or even when I felt she was paying a little too much attention to Julia—

which was, of course, her job, but you try explaining that to a strong-willed child and see if heads don't roll—I'd do a little girl-walks-into-doorjamb slapstick number I'd picked up from television or, better, launch into one of the many impersonations I'd been perfecting. *Luciadahhhling*, I'd rasp in one long word like Lolly, *little girls* need *ballet. How on earth do you expect Annie to find her* core? If comedy failed to lift the cloud from my mother's head, I'd ask her to bake me something sweet, and we'd sit cross-legged on the kitchen tiles together, licking the bowls and spoons clean.

My mother rarely spoke of her family. I figured that if she didn't want to talk about them, there must have been a good reason. Through bits and pieces, I gathered that my grandmother was a rigid, fervently religious woman who ran her household like an army base; rules were obeyed, or you were swiftly discharged. I couldn't imagine treating the bonds of blood so lightly, but then again when you had only one family member, even the slightest tiff felt reckless. My mother seemed so nervous the few times I asked her about my father that I eventually stopped trying. *These are conversations we will have when you're an adult,* mi monita bonita, she'd say, wiping her hands on her apron. My pretty little monkey. I began to envision a trove of vital information I would be allowed to open when I turned eighteen, like a bride unpacking the trousseau that would lend beauty and grace to her new life. I never considered that my mother might die before we had our "adult" talk, taking large chunks of critical information along with her.

This was what a little music did to me: it sent me slipping down a dark, slick tunnel to the past. And then as soon as I hit bottom, before I could uncover any answers, I'd be catapulted back to the present.

———

So," I said to Jake Logan, eyeing him over my burrito. "What have you been up to all these years?"

"Time for me to dust off my résumé? Let's see. After college I spent some years in New York doing the finance thing, but eventually I just couldn't take it anymore. I had an embarrassingly boring quarter-life crisis. You know, the kind that usually leads to law school or business school."

"But that's not where yours led you?"

"Nah. Grad school would have just been laying the tracks for the midlife crisis train. Instead, I moved back to San Francisco and spent a lot of time surfing, trying to straighten myself out."

"So . . . that's what you do?" I asked. "You're Surf Guy?" I'll admit it was tough to keep the sarcasm from eking into my voice. I'd been struggling to pay rent on my studio apartment, walking dogs during the few hours of the day that I wasn't baking my heart out for minimum wage, while this guy had been surfing? I realized with a thud of disappointment that we had absolutely nothing in common.

Jake laughed. "In all honesty? Yeah, I surf. A lot. But doing that for hours at a time, being out there on the ocean and looking back at the land gave me a lot of perspective. I ended up deciding to open a surf camp for underprivileged kids. I'm still working out the logistics, but I bought some land down in Costa Rica. We'll provide scholarships and get some kids out of the concrete jungle and into nature. I figure if it helps me to be out in the water, it will probably help them, too."

I took a deep breath. "Oh my God," I said. "You're one of them."

"Them?"

"You know. *Those* people. You're one of those people out there in the world, doing good things."

Like stage actors with impeccable timing, Jake's dimples arrived on the scene. "Does it make you think less of me?"

"A little."

We smiled at each other. The beginnings of crow's feet webbed out from Jake's eyes, giving me a sudden glimpse of the middle-aged man he would become.

"I promise I have much better pickup lines that involve fewer references to children," he said.

"Fewer, huh? You can't resist throwing one or two in there?"

"Hey, if it ain't broke . . ."

I wasn't stupid. A part of me knew, even as I sat in front of Jake enjoying every second of the flirty banter that flowed as fast as summer fog over Twin Peaks, that I should run the other way. I knew I was dealing with a real charmer, a man who was handsome and funny and smart and sweet. A man who, I had no doubt, got exactly what he wanted more often than not. And even though I was a confident, intelligent woman who had received my share of attention from men over the years since high school and could usually sort a dud from a dreamboat within two minutes of conversation, I had to admit there was something about Jake that I couldn't quite put my finger on.

Okay, it was worse than that.

I wasn't usually the type of woman who met a man and immediately started to daydream about marriage and babies. In college and in the six years since, I'd dated. A lot. But as soon as things got serious with anyone, I always found myself pulling away. I wanted love, I did, but I didn't want to rely on it, or anyone, for happiness. So whenever I sensed love inching itself my way, I shut down; being acutely aware of what I was doing didn't seem to make me capable of stopping myself. In the end, I always found myself alone again. Still, I gathered from those relationships that I was lovable. But could I love? A sustainable, lasting love? I told myself I could; I just hadn't found the right man. As the morning progressed and Jake eventually put his hand on mine and told me how sorry he was about my mom's passing, albeit nearly a decade late in his condolences, and then later, how delicious he'd thought my cupcakes were at the Save the Children benefit, my mind began to meander down a previously untrodden, happily-ever-after path of thought.

Was it possible that Jake was the key to my whole confusing childhood? Growing up poor among such wealth, an outsider among die-hard insiders, feeling out of place even in the one place that I was meant to feel at home—maybe there would be some karmic retribution if the end result was that out of all that teenage angst I found love? It would be so handy, wouldn't it? If a relationship with Jake provided enough heat to iron out all the unsightly wrinkles of my life?

Oh, get a grip, Quintana, I told myself, without much hope of success.

Once we'd balled up our burrito wrappers and tossed them into the trash, Jake and I walked several blocks from El Farolito to the home of Gus, a rescued shepherd mix that I walked a few afternoons each week. Jake sat on the stoop while I ran upstairs. As usual, Gus was waiting for me at the door of his apartment; I could hear his tail pounding the floor as I turned the key in the lock. Once I got inside, he hopped around me, nipping delicately at my fingers, nails clackety-clacking at the floor, his tail an ecstatic black blur. I knelt down in front of him, pressed his floppy, expressive ears flat back against his head, and planted a kiss on the side of his long, black schnoz. He whined happily, his whole body shimmying. Gus was one of those dogs who had an entirely different personality at home, where his sense of security gave him the confidence to be joyous and goofy. Out on the street, the shelter pup in him came out and he turned skittish and sorrowful, his tan quotation mark eyebrows pressing together to turn his forehead into a series of anxious wrinkles. Needless to say, I was gaga for Gus and his layered personality.

Downstairs, I could see right away that Jake loved dogs as

much as I did. I had to warn him not to try too hard with Gus; too much attention from a stranger would only make Gus more nervous out there in the big loud world. Jake managed to restrain himself for half a block, but soon was cooing down to Gus, running his hand down the length of his silky black-and-tan coat, and passing him a little piece of chorizo from a napkin that he'd somehow slipped into his pocket at El Farolito without me noticing. Gus pressed himself against Jake's leg and looked adoringly up at him as he gobbled the meat, his tail for a moment wagging as freely as it did at home.

"So, can I see you again soon?" Jake asked, looking up from Gus to me, his eyes crinkling against the sunlight.

YES! Teenage Annie screamed.

"I suppose that could be arranged," said Adult Annie, finally, if barely, staking her claim.

4

Julia

WHEN I HEARD Jacqueline, the maid, opening the door for Wes, I hurried out of my bedroom, but it was too late: my mother's throaty voice carried up the stairs to me as clearly as if she were speaking directly into my ear.

"Wesley darling, how wonderful to see you! Julia didn't even let us know you were back in town. She must be trying to keep you all to herself."

Wes's response was too low to make out, but I could hear the warmth in his voice, the drawl of South Carolina hanging in there after all those years. I loved his voice. I loved thinking about him in business meetings all over the world, his honeyed, down-home vernacular and his gracious manner unexpected from a successful American businessman. I loved introducing him to people and watching their reactions when this big, sweet, slow-moving guy began talking about wireless Internet boosters and the socioeconomic complexities of third world countries. He had a pull, a magnetism, that people seemed unable to resist, least of all me. He was not really the sort of man I thought I would end up with, but I suspected I loved him for that reason, too.

"Well, surprise or not, I'm very glad you're here," my mother was saying as I descended the stairs. Her hand, I could see now, rested conspiratorially on Wes's arm. "Julia's been moping around this house night and day for weeks. Your visit couldn't be better timed."

"Mother, you're exaggerating," I said as I crossed the foyer to join them. "Wes knows I don't mope." I kissed him on the lips. "Hi."

"Hey there," he said, hugging me tightly so the side of my face pressed into his crisp linen shirt. He was one of those men who managed to make even off-the-rack clothing look perfectly tailored to his broad frame; the combination of that stylish, yet unfussy wardrobe and his debonair good looks created an overall impression of confidence without cockiness. There was something so unquestionably *manly* about him, and seeing him still gave me butterflies even after all our time together. I wasn't so head-over-heels to not realize that some of the spark between us was undoubtedly flamed by the fact that we had yet to actually live in the same city as each other, and had in fact only seen each other, at most, once every couple of weeks for the entirety of our relationship. Even now that we were finally living on the same coast, we were unlikely to see each other with much more frequency in the year leading up to our wedding. Wes owned a condo in San Francisco, but spent most nights at a hotel near his company headquarters in Silicon Valley and probably caught the majority of his sleep on airplanes, living out of a suitcase as he traveled nationally and internationally to raise funds and establish manufacturing operations. He'd already warned me that the months ahead would be no different; he'd be away from the Bay Area more often than he was there, determined to get his business ducks in a row so he could properly enjoy our wedding and subsequent honeymoon in Fiji.

When he released me, he looked over at my mother and said, "With all due respect, Mrs. St. Clair, Julia's right—I don't think moping is in her DNA. She must have her mother's dynamite genes to thank for that."

It was just like Wes to find a way to take my side and still manage to charm my mother. I could see the tiniest hint of a flush make its way across her smooth cheeks, her lips working to not break into too pleased a smile. "Wesley darling," she rasped, "it's *Lolly*. If that doesn't quite roll off the tongue just yet, I'll be forced to make matters worse by insisting you call me Mother. I don't think either of us want that, do we?"

"No, ma'am," Wes drawled, laughing. "Lolly it is."

"So, tell me, what do you make of this whole cupcake scheme?" she asked. "Here I thought my daughter and I were going to spend the year planning a fabulous wedding, and instead she's starting a business with her old friend Annie."

"Mother!" I cried. Wes looked at me with quizzical amusement, his brows raised high above his square-framed glasses. "I haven't had a chance to tell Wes about the shop yet. He just walked in the door!"

"For heaven's sake, haven't you two heard of telephones? What's with the secrecy?"

"I wanted to give him the news in person." I glanced at Wes. "I'll tell you all about it at lunch."

Wes's dark eyes twinkled. "You know me—if there's one thing I like better than surprises, it's talking new business ventures over a heaping plate of food."

"Where are you going?" my mother asked, pulling a tiny, wayward thread from the cuff of her white blouse.

"Rose's." I glanced at my watch. "We should get going. Our reservation is in ten minutes."

"Union Street was a zoo this morning. Curtis will drive you

so you don't have to deal with parking," my mother pronounced. She shook a finger at Wes. "The chopped salad followed by the roasted turkey on brioche. Don't let anyone talk you into ordering anything else."

"What's all this about a cupcake shop? You're taking up the domestic arts? Business school to baked goods . . . you're liable to give me whiplash!" Wes joked as Curtis eased the Bentley out of the courtyard, through the front gate, and into the street.

I tried not to bristle at Wes's teasing tone, but now that we were alone I felt on edge. There was so much unsaid between us, so many half truths that had built up so quickly. I leaned my head back against the cool leather seat and took a deep breath. If I could have foreseen the repercussions the conversation that followed would have over the course of that year, I would have avoided it all together. Instead, I plowed blithely forward, hoping that full disclosure in the seemingly innocuous area of cupcakes would act as a smokescreen for the nondisclosures in other, darker areas of my life.

"I'll be on the business end of things," I explained. "Annie will do the baking. You know the Save the Children benefit my mother threw? Annie made the cupcakes for it and they blew me away. It's crazy she doesn't already have her own bakery. Those cupcakes are going to take this city captive."

"If anyone can tap into the pulse of a city, it's you, baby," Wes said. "Sounds exciting." When he leaned over and kissed me, I felt myself relax a little. He seemed to notice this change and smiled. "You look good. I think being a small-business owner will agree with you."

"Well, nothing's official yet. We still have a lot of details to hammer out. And, about that 'small' part . . ." I shot him a good-natured warning look.

He laughed. "Oh, with you at the helm, there's no chance this business will be small for long. You could out-strategize Mrs. Fields, Auntie Anne, and Little Debbie combined any day of the week and twice on Sundays."

"Those old broads?" I scoffed. "They'll never see us coming."

We both looked ahead at the bay view as Curtis nosed the car down the steep slope toward Union Street.

"Still," Wes said. "I have to admit I'm a little surprised. I knew you and Annie grew up together, but I didn't realize you two were still close."

I'd told Wes about my childhood with Annie and Lucia, and he knew that Annie and I hadn't been in touch in years. I'd always implied this was due to a general drifting apart over time, and had avoided going into specifics. "Oh, we're not close any-more, but we're still friends," I said breezily. *Where's the harm in one more white lie?* "We've had our differences over the years, but I think if I can avoid bringing up some of the sore spots, we'll make excellent business partners."

I felt grateful when Wes didn't press me for details. His inher-ent patience, not at all indicative of a lack of curiosity or empa-thy, both heartened and baffled me. *If I took things one day at a time the way he does,* I admonished myself, *maybe the unknowns in life wouldn't drive me so crazy.*

As we turned onto Union Street, a sharply dressed couple with a toddler daughter in tow exited an ice cream shop that Annie and I used to frequent when we were kids. The father swung the little girl onto his shoulders, and a long chocolate drip from her ice cream cone immediately fell down his forehead.

Wes tapped on the car window. "That's us, baby, give or take a few years. Except I'm willing to bet there will be cupcake crumbs on my forehead instead of ice cream." He looked at me with an expression so heartbreakingly eager and kind that it was all I could do to quickly smile and look away before my true emotions overcame me.

I kept my gaze pinned to the window until we reached the restaurant and I felt confident that I'd regained my composure, if only temporarily.

5

Annie

STILL FEELING A tingle of electricity from my afternoon with Jake earlier in the week, I hopped off the 22 bus at Broadway and Steiner and began walking toward the St. Clair mansion. Julia and I were meeting to discuss the first steps we needed to take to get the cupcake business off the ground, but in all honesty, I didn't have a clue where to begin. The process seemed overwhelming—there was retail space to be found, equipment to be purchased, permits to obtain, employees to hire and manage. It was enough to make my head throb. But I figured Julia's experience with those logistical things was the singular bright spot of having her involved. No, not singular. There was, after all, the not-so-small matter of money.

I squinted down the street. It was one of those gray summer days for which San Francisco is famous and the fog gave the sky an oddly bright, bleached-out look. When a damp breeze swept up the hill from the bay, I pulled the belt of my crimson coat a bit tighter, unconsciously slowing my pace as I neared the St. Clairs'.

Each house I passed seemed bigger than the one before it, an architectural hodgepodge of the finicky tastes of the rich over the past century—there were the dark, shingled Craftsmen, the Queen Anne Victorian wedding-cake houses with intricate, pastel-painted curlicue details, the elegant Italianate homes with tall windows of thick, antique glass, and the sleek, contemporary ones where you'd be hard-pressed to locate a front door. I'd walked by this particular row of Pacific Heights homes hundreds of times before my eighteenth birthday. The Lorensteins, with their three boys, Irish setter, and Portuguese au pair, had lived in the towering glass, concrete, and steel structure with the dramatic waterfall-like fountain running down its side. The Chens, an older couple who lived alone in a squat brick mansion with white shutters, had had the pristine landscaping in their side yard tended to weekly by a muscular young gardener named Raul who, if Julia and I timed our walk-by ogling just right, would toss us ice-cold Cokes from his cooler. At a certain point in time, my mother and I had probably known more people on that block than anyone else—we knew the parents, the kids who went to the neighborhood playground and later Devon Prep, the housekeepers and nannies and drivers who were my mother's friends and confidants.

Mom had loved living on this block. The views, the magnificent homes, the well-dressed neighbors, the suburb-within-a-city feel never lost their luster for her. Everything remained new and sparkly and surreal for her, but as I grew older, I began to realize just how much was lost in translation. Where Mom saw glamour and beauty, goodwill and gaiety, I saw bulimic fourteen-year-olds and a perilous social ladder littered with casualties and boys who already behaved as if they owned, had somehow *earned*, the world. I'd known I was different from the other kids at the small, private elementary and middle schools Julia and I had attended, but it was only once I entered the halls of Devon Prep—to which the St. Clairs had shepherded my acceptance and paid my tuition—that I understood just how differently I was viewed. I don't think it was so much that I was of Ecuadorean descent as that I was the daughter of the St. Clairs' hired help. For example, I was pretty certain that if I'd been the first-generation American daughter of some Ecuadorean mining magnate, or even just the daughter of an exiled Ecuadorean politician, I would have received many of the same glittery party invitations I saw pinned to Julia's bulletin board. But my family didn't own a vineyard in Napa, a second home in Pebble Beach, or even a chalet in Tahoe. We didn't have season tickets to the opera; I didn't ride horses in Marin; there wasn't a wing named after us at SFMOMA. I lived with those people, but I wasn't a member of their club. We didn't speak the same language.

There were only two occasions on which I tried to explain the truth about Devon Prep to my mom. Both were during our senior year, and the first was right before the annual all-school spring dance that Julia had been obsessing over for months. As class president, she needed one hundred signatures for her petition to hold the dance at the Palace Hotel's opulent Garden Court and she enlisted her top minion, Caroline Rydell, to strong-arm the underclassmen into signing. And by strong-arm, I mean boobnotize. Julia, whose own chest fit into classy B-cups, knew that Caroline's D-cups were the way to freshman boys' hearts. I heard Caroline had gathered one hundred signatures by first period. I didn't go to the dance, but I'm sure the Garden Court was a fantastically over-the-top venue, with its domed glass ceiling and sparkly chandeliers. I'd made the mistake of watching *Carrie* in the weeks leading up to the dance, and let me tell you, there is no quicker way to get a social outcast to decide not to attend a school dance than the sight of Sissy Spacek covered in pig's blood. I'd tried to explain to my mother how I felt about my classmates, but when I saw her wounded face, I dropped it and just told her I didn't want to go because I had a stomachache. I decided I needed to buck up and let her believe in my happy, golden childhood and my lifelong friendship with Julia. She had worked so hard to give me that life.

Later that spring, I was compelled to try again. This time was more serious: I needed to tell my mom my side of all the rumors that had been spread about me. But almost as soon as I began, I saw a flicker of something dark in her eyes that was all too easy to interpret as a sliver of doubt.

"How will anyone believe me if my own mother doesn't?" I shouted, hurt to the point of anger.

"Annie, I'm just listening." My mother's face was pained. She reached out to me and I pushed her away.

"You're not listening, you're *deciding*!" Suddenly, all of the anger I felt toward Julia and my classmates and teachers at Devon Prep funneled down into one hot point of fury that I directed at my mother. "You're deciding, just like you've always decided everything! *You* decided to run away from home. *You* decided we were going to live at the St. Clairs'. *You* decided I needed to be friends with Julia and go to Devon Prep. And look where your decisions have gotten me! You think you know what's best for me, but you don't! All you know is how to kiss Lolly's ass and keep your head down so you don't get in trouble! You don't know what it's like to grow up here! You don't know anything about my life! You don't know anything about me!" I'd ignored her little gasp and the tears that sprang to her eyes, swatted her hands from me, and stormed out of the carriage house.

Almost immediately, I felt remorse. The worst part was that I didn't even believe half of what I'd said. My mother hadn't run away from home—she'd been kicked out. She didn't spend her days kissing Lolly's ass—in fact, over the years, Lolly had become as close a friend to my mother as any in her life. And *of course* my mom knew me—she knew me better than anyone in the world. Which was why, I suppose, the look I'd seen for just an instant in her eyes stung me so badly. Each time over the next few months that I found myself walking to her room to apologize, the memory of that look I'd seen on her face surfaced and reignited my anger. It was a long, lonely summer without my mother's company and with all of the unknowns about my future hanging over my head.

On the August day that my diploma from Devon Prep finally arrived in the mail—I had not been allowed to attend graduation that spring—I decided it was time to cut through the impasse. Crossing the courtyard from the carriage house to the mansion, diploma in hand, I felt that odd anxiety-induced tension straining at the muscles in my legs. I hoped that the diploma would be an olive branch of sorts and planned to invite my mother for milk shakes down on Union Street, an end-of-school-year tradition that she had instated when Julia and I were kids. That June—suspended from Devon Prep, my acceptance to Cal still under review with no hope of news anytime soon—the end of school had come and gone without my mother mentioning the tradition. Already, the summer was drawing to a close and we'd barely spoken to one another for months, and it was all the fault of my temper and pride.

When I walked into the St. Clairs' kitchen and showed the diploma to my mother, she fingered its edges with her small brown hands and sighed. It was a hard sigh to interpret, but before I let its ambiguity stoke my anger I quickly asked her if she wanted to walk down to Union Street for milk shakes.

She lifted her gaze from the diploma to me, her face softening. "That sounds wonderful, Annie," she'd said.

Even as the words came out of her mouth, Julia strode into the kitchen, her long blond hair freshly straightened and impossibly shiny. She shot me a saccharine smile. At school she was cool, dismissive, and curt; but at home all summer she'd been acting demure, nearly deferential. The juxtaposition tired me; in her presence, I felt almost physically ill. But I had no desire to fight with her. The events of that spring, the rumors and accusations, had deflated me, knocking the wind out of my proverbial sails. I held my breath, hoping, against odds, that my mother would wave good-bye to her so that we could be on our way. I knew my mother well enough to know that this would never happen. Out of respect for her job or actual love for the girl she'd had a significant hand in raising or some complicated combination of both, she was perpetually vigilant—*overly* vigilant, I thought— to include Julia in every activity.

"Annie and I are going to get milk shakes!" she said. "Will you join us?"

And Julia had looked at me carefully, almost calculatingly, and said yes. My heart sank. With Julia accompanying us, I would never have the chance to apologize to my mother. The next week, with no reason to hold out hope for word from Cal, I accepted a waitressing job and began taking classes at City College. The distance between my mother and me hardened into something rigid and sharp and crackling, like the torched top layer of crème brûlée. Our stilted interactions began to seem more and more like the norm. Still, I knew with all of my heart that at any moment I would conquer my pride, crack the wall between us, and make things right with her. And I kept on believing that up until the day, weeks later, that she died.

6

Julia

I COULD SEE Annie had a bee in her bonnet from the moment Jacqueline led her into the kitchen. She seemed jumpy, biting her lip, her cheeks still shining from the cool, sodden air outside. Instead of taking off her red coat, she pulled its belt tighter around her waist. Her small, heart-shaped face—with her light brown, wide-set eyes and honey-colored skin—was framed with her wild dark hair above and the coat's fake fur collar below; a clump of missing fur on the lapel gave her the look of a mangy, yet plump, street cat.

"Oh, hi!" I said brightly. "I didn't realize that was you at the door. I figured you'd come in the kitchen, like old times."

"Nope," said Annie, eyes flashing. "I came in the front door, like new times."

"Okay." She clearly planned to make this meeting as difficult as possible. "Either way, I'm glad you're here." The maid, meanwhile, was standing awkwardly in the door frame, and now cleared her throat. I gestured in her direction. "Jacqueline can take your coat, if you like."

With some reluctance, Annie slid her arms out of her coat, revealing a sunshine-yellow, houndstooth-print, seventies-style jumper that contrasted humorously with the pinched look on her face. *Where does she find these outfits?* I wondered, hoping that wherever it was, she washed those "vintage" numbers before wearing them. I smoothed down my own milk-white cashmere sweater and nodded toward the kitchen's built-in breakfast booth where my laptop sat open and aglow.

"I thought we could work in here," I said. "It's about as close to the espresso machine as we can get without sitting right on the counter."

Annie paled. She opened her mouth and then shut it. "Fine," she said at last. The craggy treads of her leather boots crunched loudly against the tile floor as she strode past me.

Oh, of course she doesn't want to be in the kitchen! I realized, feeling my stomach flip. I'd had ten years of chocolate croissant nibbling and fridge grazing and coffee sipping in my parents' kitchen to distance it mentally from the place where Lucia had collapsed, but for Annie, the feeling of shock and loss must still hang in that room as though her mother had just died yesterday. *Thirty rooms and I decide this meeting should take place in the kitchen?* I felt myself reddening.

"Oh, Annie!" I said. "I should have thought . . . I'm sorry."

"For what?" she asked thinly.

"For this." I made a sweeping Vanna White gesture over the kitchen's center island. "Should we move? What a way to kick things off. I'm so sorry."

Annie's eyes narrowed and I could tell she was thinking that I'd done this on purpose—that I'd wanted to upset her. She looked at me like she could see right through me, and her steady gaze gave me a rare jolt of nerves.

"It's fine," she said, settling into the booth.

"Okay. If you're sure." I turned away to fiddle with the espresso machine, talking over my shoulder all the while. "So what have you been up to all these years? I feel like we didn't really have a chance to catch up at the party. Obviously, you're a baker. A master of all things cupcake." I set a plate of Sonja's chocolate-dipped macaroons and two nonfat vanilla lattes on the table and slipped into the bench across from her.

"That's it really," she said, taking a sip. "Lots and lots of baking."

"My mom told me you studied pastry."

She nodded, her dark, flyaway—*almost feral*, I thought unkindly again before I could stop myself—curls shaking around her face. "At the San Francisco Culinary Institute."

"How fabulous. It sounds like you've been leading a very romantic life. Very *Chocolat*."

Annie sighed. "It would make it a little easier to roll into work at five a.m. if I knew Johnny Depp was going to be there."

I laughed and then stopped abruptly when I heard how loud it sounded in the room. "Are you seeing anyone?"

Annie hesitated for a moment before saying, "Not right now."

"Oh, I see. You're playing the field. How fun!" I said. "People are getting married later and later in life. I wouldn't even be thinking about marriage yet if I hadn't met Wes. You know what they say: it's all about meeting the right person. And it only takes that one."

Annie pressed her lips into a sarcastic smile. "Yes," she said, "there is a remarkable amount of clichés on the topic."

I flushed. Why was I trying so hard, beating back every potential moment of silence with inane chatter? It was the sort of behavior that irritated me to no end when others displayed it, and here I was polluting the already fraught air between us with my overly energetic voice. Annie was clearly becoming more and more annoyed; her fingers—which were still surprisingly childlike, small and plump—drummed steadily along the side of her latte glass.

The truth was that ever since she had agreed to open a cupcakery with me, I'd grown increasingly attached to the idea. Each morning that week, I'd awakened a little earlier, plans for the shop buzzing through my mind. My emotions still felt dangerously close to the surface, a huge, essential part of myself still felt irrevocably changed, but I could already sense how these very concrete, pressing thoughts of budgets and marketing plans and branding strategies would help me cling to some semblance of the person I'd been, a person whom I had liked—or at least respected—quite a bit. That very morning, in fact, I'd awakened at 6:45 on the dot, no alarm needed. I couldn't risk the chance that Annie might back out now.

"Shouldn't we get down to business?" she asked, as though reading my thoughts.

"Yes!" I said, straightening. "Of course. Let's start with the contractual details. My thought is that I will make an equity investment of start-up capital and will own fifty percent of the business for one year. In the months that I'm actively involved leading up to my wedding in May, we'll split ownership and cupcakery profits fifty-fifty; after May, you'll become the sole proprietor by buying out my share of the business at a fifteen percent premium according to a payment schedule that will be linked to the cupcakery's success." I didn't need this fifteen-percent return but feared that if I didn't include it, Annie would balk. Better to keep things businesslike than to let on that the return on investment for me would be related to mental stability, not money.

"If the shop does well, which I'm sure it will," I continued, "the schedule will be such that you'll buy out my investment over the course of about three years. On the opposite end of the spectrum, if the cupcakery were to fail, you wouldn't be required to repay me anything."

"That seems generous," Annie said, eyes narrowed. I could hear her foot anxiously tapping the floor below the table.

"Not really. This isn't charity," I said hurriedly. "Like any business investment, there's risk and the possibility of reward. The risk is one I'm more than willing to take after tasting your cupcakes and doing a little market research."

Still, Annie seemed skeptical. "And all of this is in the contract?"

What does she take me for? A criminal? "Yes, in explicit detail." I handed her the document. "You should have a lawyer look it over so you feel completely comfortable proceeding."

Under the table, Annie's foot was still at last. "Sounds fine," she said. "I'll have a lawyer friend look it over."

"Good. Let's move on to lighter topics." I swept my fingers along the laptop keyboard. "I've already scoped out a few retail spaces on Chestnut, Union, and Fillmore streets. The one on Fillmore was most recently a restaurant, so the kitchen is—"

"Wait," she interrupted. "Fillmore Street? I don't want the cupcakery to be in Pacific Heights."

"Oh," I said. I took a slow sip of latte, leaving a glossy peach rosebud on the glass. I'd envisioned the latest generation of Devon Prep girls strolling down the bustling shopping street, dropping into the shop on a daily basis to fritter their sizable allowances on cupcakes and coffee. Now I realized that that very clientele was probably Annie's worst nightmare. Still, those girls had money, and Annie's ample psychological baggage shouldn't take priority over the cupcakery's bottom line. "Where were you thinking?"

Without hesitating, Annie responded: "The Mission."

I sighed.

"The Mission," she repeated, jutting her chin into the air in a manner I remembered well from childhood. "It's perfect."

I took a bite of a macaroon, stalling as I worked to formulate a response. I was not one to pussyfoot when it came to matters of business, but I knew that Annie—who, stereotype or not, *did* seem to have a quintessentially *Latin* temper—required a certain deft approach. "It's just," I began carefully, swallowing a final bite of cookie, "we're aiming for a very specific clientele. A three-dollars-and-fifty-cents-cupcake-eating clientele, to be precise."

"Three dollars and fifty cents!"

"I ran the numbers. Three dollars and fifty cents per cupcake with a nice discount for a dozen. People spend forty dollars on a cake that feeds twelve, so why not forty dollars for a dozen cupcakes? These aren't just any old cupcakes."

Annie looked at me and shrugged. "Okay, fine. I'll leave the pricing up to you. But the Mission is nonnegotiable." She popped a macaroon into her mouth and chewed fiercely.

Now, I bristled. "Nonnegotiable? Annie, come on. We're just getting started—*everything* is negotiable."

Annie's nostrils flared. I resisted the urge to reach out and brush away the crumbs that littered her large chest, thinking, as I clutched my hands in my lap, that a good tailor could have done wonders for the way that silly yellow jumper buckled and gaped around her curves.

"Have you ever even *been* to the Mission?" she asked, still chewing. "You haven't lived in this city in ten years so I probably shouldn't assume you know anything about the neighborhood. The Mission is filled with trendy new restaurants and shops. More so than some of the older neighborhood residents would like, in fact. The hipsters, the dot-commers, the over-priced-baked-goods eaters—that's where they live. And if they don't live there, then they *go* there for cutting-edge cuisine. It's a culinary hotspot—*the* place to open a cupcakery."

Her argument made some sense. I'd heard about the positive changes that had been happening for years in the Mission, though admittedly I wasn't sure I'd ever been to the neighborhood. I reminded myself that this was Annie's business; I would reenter my old, more conventional—and lucrative—life come

May and she would be left running the cupcakery on her own. I held up my hands. "I'm not saying no. Let me just research the market a little more, and in the meantime we can check out what sort of spaces are available and see what the rent looks like. If it makes sense, we'll move forward. Okay?"

Annie sat back against the upholstered bench, looking a little surprised that I was so easily swayed. "Okay."

"Crisis number one averted." That false chipper ring had edged its way back into my voice. "Next item on the agenda is nailing down a timeline. I know it's tough to say without a space in mind, but if we start small, I think we can push ourselves to get this business up and running in three months."

"Three months!" Annie said. "Really? But there's so much to do."

I shrugged. "You'd be surprised how fast money can make people move."

Annie was biting into a second macaroon as I spoke and now slowly lowered the cookie to the table. Her eyes narrowed. "Did you really just say that?"

"What?" I asked, my mind racing back over what I'd said. The thing about money? It was a throwaway comment. Did she have to dissect everything?

"That I'd be surprised how fast money can make people move?" she said. "Please tell me you realize how that sounds."

Oh, enough, already! This meeting was beginning to exhaust me. "I'm sorry if that statement makes you uncomfortable," I said evenly. "Frankly, I thought it was only us WASPs who were supposed to be patently incapable of discussing money."

"I can discuss *money*," Annie spat. "It's your sense of entitlement that turns my stomach."

My mouth dropped. "Annie! Why must you act so mean?"

"Probably," she said, "for the exact opposite of the reason that you act nice: it's hard for me to be fake."

"No! I act nice because, because," I sputtered, "because I *am* nice! But you—you're not a mean person. I *know* you're not. So I'd really like to know why you act like you are."

She shrugged. "I'm the kind of person who doesn't sugar-coat anything but cake." I got the distinct sense that she was enjoying seeing me riled up. "Anyway, I think the question of whether or not you're a nice person is still very much up for debate."

For the first time since Annie had walked in the door, I allowed silence to fill the room. It seemed clear that any attempt to move forward would have to come from me. I thought back to what had happened between us all those years ago, a series of events that I still had trouble remembering as anything more than one minor misunderstanding after another toppling against each other like dominoes. And, anyway, in the end, what harm had been done? Annie had graduated from Devon and eventually gone to Cal just as she'd wanted. Still, it was clear she needed some coddling.

"Annie," I said at last, placing my hands on the table. My three-karat cushion-cut diamond engagement ring shone brilliantly below the kitchen lights; my fingers, compared to Annie's, were long and elegant—the hands of an adult. "In reflecting back on those years in high school, I realize I was not always . . . considerate of your feelings. I wasn't a good friend to you. I see that now. I'm sorry."

"You're sorry for being *inconsiderate*? Julia, it's not like you forgot to RSVP to my sweet sixteen party." Annie released a sharp little laugh. "We were best friends and then you tried to ruin my life. Cal nearly revoked my acceptance!"

"That had nothing to do with me!" I refused to be steam-rolled into taking responsibility for something that had been completely out of my control.

"Julia," she said, enunciating my name as though she were

speaking to a toddler. "Our senior year. Those rumors. You started them."

I sighed. As much as I wanted to end the conversation then and there, I feared doing so would push Annie—and the cupcakery—out of my life forever. "Listen," I began, trying again. "Senior year went by in a blur for me. I honestly hardly remember it—between working on my Stanford application and my valedictorian speech, I feel like I barely had time to breathe that whole year. But I am truly sorry for what happened and whatever part you think I played in it."

Annie's hair quivered. "Whatever part I *think* you played in it?" she repeated. "What does what I *think* have to do with anything? This isn't some philosophical debate. In this instance, there is one truth, and what either of us thinks about that truth does not alter it from being *the* truth!"

Suddenly, as I watched her hands clench into fists and felt the icy charge in her voice, tears sprang to my eyes. I quickly blinked them away, but not before Annie looked down, alarmed. She knew me well enough to know that, unlike her, I wasn't one to wear my heart on my sleeve. Annie had always, I remembered, cried nearly as easily as she laughed—her emotions had seemed irrepressible when we were kids, every thought and feeling scrolling across her face like sun and shadows across pavement. Now, it seemed almost like we had changed places; I couldn't control my emotions, and Annie, who used to be so empathetic, eyed me coolly, as though from a distance. What role had I played in her transformation? I shuddered to think.

"I'm not that person," I said quietly, deciding as I said it that I believed it was true, or at least that I planned to make it true. "Not anymore. I know you don't believe me now, but I'm going to prove it to you."

Annie shook her head and stood from the table. "I can't do this," she said flatly.

I rose with her. "Remember," I said, wincing at the pleading note in my voice, "my involvement in the business would only be temporary. I just want to help you get it off the ground, and then I promise I'll be out of your life. I'll get married and I'll find another job and you'll be rid of me. It will all be detailed explicitly in the contract. The cupcakery will be one hundred percent yours after I get married."

"But why?" she asked, staring at me. "Why do you want to do this?"

"I just—I think you're a good investment. You're so talented, Annie."

I could tell she didn't believe me. "Fine," she said finally. "But let's do ourselves a favor and keep our relationship about the cupcakery, okay? We don't need to be friends—we're starting a business, not a sorority. I'll look into spaces in the Mission, you can do whatever research you feel is needed, and we can circle back to compare notes. I'll see myself out."

"Okay," I said, surprised to hear the hurt in my voice. Business was exactly what I was looking for, wasn't it? "If that's what you want."

August

7

Annie

I HAD AGREED to let Jake Logan teach me how to surf. Yes, *me*, a grown woman born and raised in foggy San Francisco with about as much of a chance of becoming a beach girl as I did of becoming a Bond girl. But there was something about Jake that made me want to expand my horizons. I placed the blame fully on his damn dimples.

On a rare sunny afternoon in August, we drove through Golden Gate Park with the top down on Jake's yellow 1973 Mustang convertible (a vehicle I'd immediately christened "the Firm Banana"), two surfboards sticking up like antennae from the backseat. We pretended to be actors in some cheesy commercial promoting tourism in San Francisco, gesturing around wildly and throwing our heads back and fake-laughing with abandon as we cruised past the sparkling glass Conservatory of Flowers, the penitentiary-like observation tower of the de Young Museum, the Frisbee golf course frequented by Pabst Blue Ribbon–toting twenty-somethings, the middle-aged men racing toy boats across Spreckels Lake, the ever-fragrant bison paddock, and the Dutch Windmill at the far west end of the park. Nothing would have made me happier than if we'd just headed north at that point and pulled into the precariously perched Cliff House for an overpriced late lunch and cold beer overlooking the Pacific, but instead we crossed the Great Highway and pulled into the parking lot at Ocean Beach. I released a sigh of relief when I saw that the water was nearly lakelike that day; low, slow waves were like the doddering, geriatric version of the rough-and-tumble surf that usually pounded the shore.

Jake extracted the boards from the backseat and tossed me a wetsuit (an earlier mention of which was the only thing that finally prompted me to agree to this lesson; if I'd been forced to parade around in broad daylight in only a bikini, my own less appropriately placed dimples would have put Jake's to shame). I pulled off my Hawaiian-print baby doll dress and squeezed my bikini-clad self into the wetsuit as quickly as possible, a feat made all the more difficult by the fact that the suit seemed more appropriately sized for some much smaller ex-girlfriend. Jake shot me a raffish grin as I struggled with the zipper.

"Who'd have thunk—black rubber suits you."

"I figured that out years ago," I said, raking my hair into a ponytail. "Halloween. College. Cat Woman."

"Meow."

After a brief and humiliating lesson involving jumping up and then belly flopping down on the surfboard while still on sand, Jake deemed me ready to hit the water. Even with the wetsuit, booties, and hood, the glacierlike water turned my limbs leaden with cold. I quickly learned that it took every ounce of my inconsiderable upper body strength to paddle up, over, and past those waves that had appeared so small and unassuming from the sand. When I finally caught up to where Jake sat bobbing nonchalantly on his board two hundred feet off the shore, I pulled the insulated hood off my head, gasping for breath.

"Well, that was fun," I said. "When's dinner?"

Jake laughed. "Don't worry, you're in the sweet spot now.

The waiting game is just as good as catching a wave." The spark in his blue-green eyes flared brighter than ever as he gazed back at the shore, but I could see how the rest of his body language had mellowed to a calmer state out on the water.

I maneuvered myself around until I sat up on my board beside him, facing back toward the coast. The feeling I had then was probably a bit like waking up with your head at the wrong side of the bed—the colors and shapes of the city where I'd grown up were utterly familiar, and at the same time almost eerily different from this new perspective. I bobbed beside Jake in silence, catching my breath.

"What do you think?" he asked finally.

"Not bad," I replied, shooting him a sidelong smile. The lift and fall of the ocean had a numbing effect on my thoughts. My mind, which all afternoon had been frenetically running over the fairly preposterous idea of myself on another date—our third now—with *Jake Logan*, finally began to quiet itself. Out there on the ocean, with the city as a distant backdrop, he was just Jake: a cute, fun guy who didn't serve as a constant reminder of a painful past I'd tried for so long to put behind me. I found myself liking this Jake, the one without the fancy surname, more and more.

Unfortunately, it turned out his thoughts were not running down quite such a history-free path. "So you and Julia," he said. "The dynamic duo reunited. How's the cupcake business?"

I'd told him about the shop over oysters at Foreign Cinema during our last date and he'd made me promise to let him buy the first dozen cupcakes when we opened. "So far, so good," I said. "We're working on renovating a space in the Mission with the hope to open in October. It took some convincing to get Julia to that part of town, but I think we're more or less on the same page now."

"Julia St. Clair hard at work in the Mission," Jake mused. "Now there's a sight I'd like to see."

Something in his tone made my mind shift a gear or two up from its short-lived relaxed state. Or maybe it was just the mere mention of Julia, who I still had some trouble believing had managed to convince me that going into business together was a good idea. When I didn't immediately respond, I felt Jake's gaze on the side of my face. He reached over and pulled my surfboard closer to him. I nearly toppled off it in the process, but one of his arms quickly encircled my waist, righting me, while the other turned my face toward his. In a moment, we were kissing, the water lapping gently at my thighs, the lowering sun working its way down my back.

Jake pulled away after several long minutes, but kept his steadying arm around my waist. "Lesson adjourned," he murmured, his breath shallow. "I've taught you all I know. Let's go home."

It was the best news I'd heard all day.

By the time we reached the shore, the fog had rolled in. We couldn't put the Firm Banana's top up because of the surfboards and even swathed in the plush towels Jake had brought along I shivered the whole way back to his apartment in North Beach. I barely had time to register the fact that the building's elevator opened right into his loftlike apartment, and that the view through the floor-to-ceiling windows stretched from Coit Tower all the way to the Golden Gate Bridge—now draped in ever-thickening fog—before Jake steered me toward a large freestanding fireplace that separated the living room and dining room. He flipped a switch on the wall and in an instant the golden light of the fire danced against the dark walls surrounding us. I stared into the flames, mesmerized, feeling a heady mixture of exhilaration and exhaustion, while Jake poured out two glasses of scotch. I don't know if it was the bone chill or the booze, but I found myself in an unusually quiet, content mood. If I'd let myself, I would have admitted that it felt good to be pampered. That sort of tranquil luxury wasn't something I wanted or needed every day, but after so many years struggling on my own to make ends meet, I was not above enjoying the easy comfort offered by Jake and his swanky digs. Soon enough, I'd be back safe and sound in my own apartment, but for the moment I was just tired enough to let my guard down and enjoy myself.

Jake stood behind me, his arms wrapped around my waist, his bristly chin resting on my shoulder as we both stared into the fire, rocking slightly. The apartment seemed to creak and yawn around us—cool and shadowed everywhere but the living, glowing swath of light in which we stood. There was brief mention of a hot shower, and then Jake's surprisingly warm hands were on my shoulders and he was peeling off my dress and bathing suit until moments later he guided me, naked but no longer shivering, into the bedroom.

8

Julia

IN THE DREAM, I was running from someone or something but had been injured and too slow to escape. Or maybe I was running in mud. Or water. The sound of whatever was behind me got closer and closer. I felt its breath on my hair, and then I was falling an impossibly long distance, a horrible mournful howling in my ears. And then suddenly I jerked awake, heart racing in the dense blackness of my bedroom. The house, save for the whirring of the ceiling fan, was silent. My cell phone clock read 3:30 a.m. I could almost feel the steady, rhythmic breathing of the slumbering city. Out on the bay, a foghorn blew low and long.

I rolled to my side and turned on the bedside lamp, blinking as the familiar room with its trellis-patterned, Tiffany-blue carpet and tassel-trimmed drapes flooded with light. Circling my ankles beneath the cool sheets, I stretched the cramps from my legs. There was no way I would get back to sleep now. I swung my bare legs over the side of the bed and pulled yoga pants from where they were folded neatly on a cream-colored chaise. Immediately, I felt a little better. I liked clothing that not only showed off my figure, but enhanced it as well, and the yoga pants were ones that promised to lift and minimize my butt. They made me feel streamlined and efficient, a lean, mean, multitasking machine.

If insomnia has a perk, it's the extra work hours it adds to the day. *I might as well try to get some things done.* Cupcakery or wedding, though? I decided to check my e-mail and let any new messages make the decision for me. When I saw an e-mail at the top of my in-box from the contractor I'd hired to work on the cupcake shop, I breathed a sigh of relief. Thinking about the wedding inevitably turned my thoughts to the enormous secret I was keeping from Wes, which in turn left me a sniveling, mentally paralyzed mess; the cupcakery, on the other hand, produced no such rush of emotions. So I'd found myself leaving more and more of the wedding details in the hands of my mother—something I'd never in a million years thought I would do.

The wood bar should run the length of the front window, I typed in response to the contractor's question, the brisk clacking of the keyboard working to untangle the final threads of the bad dream from my thoughts. It annoyed me to have to repeat these instructions (I was sure this information was crystal clear on the design plan taped to the wall of the cupcakery), but I had to admit that, all in all, Burt Vargas had proven himself to be a dependable, efficient contractor—a diamond in the rough.

A week earlier, Burt had presented Annie and me with photographs of a gorgeous swath of redwood—its pattern of rich, golden-brown wood grains almost like tiger stripes—that had been salvaged from an old Sonoma barn. Immediately, both of us expressed that it was perfect for the cupcakery's window bar where customers would belly up to nibble an afternoon treat and sip a perfectly poured cappuccino. As with every decision that was made with relative ease, I had done a little internal victory dance when we had so easily agreed.

Things had moved remarkably quickly over the past month.

After the fight in the kitchen, Annie and I had forged a truce of sorts in the interest of getting things done. What else was there to do? I couldn't change the past. All either of us could do was move forward.

Within days of that first meeting, Annie had found vacant retail space on a dodgy stretch of Twentieth Street in the Mission and, despite the unease I'd felt walking around that unfamiliar, almost foreign part of the city, I'd agreed to rent it, hoping that the relative proximity of well-regarded neighborhood restaurants like Delfina and Tartine would result in some spillover patronage. A careful design plan would transform the tight space, and Annie assured me the kitchen needed only a few straightforward alterations to get it up to baking snuff.

We'd agreed—agreed!—that we didn't want to join the trendy ranks of bakeries that were decorated all pretty-pretty-princess sugary and white. Just as easily, we resolved not to go in the direction of the other ubiquitous restaurant trend toward sleek, minimal decor. Instead, we decided on a decadent, almost louche design: burgundy, threadbare carpets tossed over beat-up wood floors, damask wallpaper, an over-sized lacquer chandelier, display cabinets lined in black lace. The concept was cupcake as forbidden fruit. The shop would be a haven for those looking to escape responsible adulthood, work, and the relentless whip-crack of Northern California outdoorsiness that nipped at the heels of urbanites. *Why hike the Headlands*, our shop would murmur seductively, *when you can belly up to the bar for cupcakes and cappuccinos?* It would be a den for overgrown children looking for an indulgence, something nostalgic, something simultaneously luxurious and youthful. Much like a pharmaceutical drug or being in love, Annie's cupcakes would make you feel better.

At least that's what they do for me, I thought.

Treat. We would call the cupcakery Treat. After all, this was San Francisco.

It hadn't all been easy. We'd had some setbacks, including an odd week when the construction crew complained of missing tools and the evening that I'd walked down the street from the shop to my Mercedes to find one of its rear tires slashed, but we were in the Mission—what did we expect? At the time, there didn't seem to be anything particularly foreboding about these small crimes. Throughout it all, our timeline remained intact and, as I'd suspected, steering our little team through a lengthy to-do list was providing much-needed shape to my days. Still, I was disappointed to find that sadness continued to burn in my chest like a sunbaked stone, that the throbbing ache inside of me could not truly be relieved by any number of delicious cupcakes. But all I could do was keep trying.

Special delivery!" my mother called, carrying a large wrapped box topped by an enormous ivory bow into the library several days after that night of insomnia. I looked up from the book I was reading and sighed. The unsubtle tactics of those hoping to obtain an invite to my wedding entertained me at times, but at other times, like this one, I felt exhausted—disgusted, even—by the whole thing.

My mother took one look at me and made a tsk-tsk noise before lowering the box down to the floor at my feet.

"It's our *way*, Julia darling," she said. "When there's an engagement, there are gifts. And your thank-you note will be gracious and heartfelt, I'm sure. If I've taught you one thing, please tell me it is etiquette."

Not kindness? I wanted to ask, thinking of my treatment of Annie all those years ago. *Not how to hunt down happiness even when it's faster and wilier than it's ever been before?* I wanted to ask, thinking of myself.

When I didn't respond, my mother eyed me. "Well," she said, her voice a touch softer. "Aren't you going to open it?"

The box contained a carving set from my great aunt Lucy. The sterling silver knife handle was intricately detailed with fussy little curlicues that would normally have made me cringe but today just made me feel lost. What life were these presents for? Holiday tables? Family dinners? How was it that so many people seemed capable of envisioning what I could not?

My mother patted my head as though I were an obedient dog. It was an oddly consoling gesture. For the first time, I wondered just how much of the truth she had deduced from my abrupt return home, my avoidance of all things wedding, my sudden passion for cupcakes.

"I'll put this with the other gifts in the guest room," I said, standing. My mother's hand dropped back down to her side. "It's a beautiful set," I added, summoning a smile. I knew the kind of smile I had. It was part nature, part nurture. It told the world that I was fine, I was happy, I was neat and tidy and nothing to worry about.

My mother returned it with her own dazzlingly bright version.

I placed the box at the top of a stack of gift boxes in the guest room at the end of the second-floor hall and then lay back on the bed and held my cell phone above me, swiftly tapping in a reminder to myself about the thank-you note. When I finished typing, I checked the time and called Wes.

"Two more weeks, beautiful!" he said warmly.

"Two more weeks," I repeated. I propped myself up on the bed so it would be easier to match his enthusiasm. Two more weeks until Wes was in San Francisco again. "I'm so excited to see you." I knew acutely just how strange it was that I hadn't told him yet about the events surrounding my hospital stay, but with each week that passed, it seemed more and more impossible to share the news. Still, I couldn't live like this forever. And I couldn't stand up there in front of three hundred people and recite vows with this secret between us.

"Well, damn, Julia, could you make me believe it?" Wes drawled. "You sound like a coyote just snatched your puppy clean out your backyard."

"What?" In spite of my blue mood, I laughed. "Sorry, Wes. I really do miss you. I guess I'm tired."

"You? Tired? I am talking to Julia St. Clair, aren't I? And here I've been under the impression you didn't get tired. That tired isn't in your DNA. Is this Julia of the six a.m. conference call? Ms. New-York-Marathon-in-Three-Hours-Twenty-Four-Minutes? My wheatgrass-slugging, kickboxing, number-crunching, business-building, sexy-ass fiancée?"

"That was back when I was busy. I have too much time on my hands now. Even with all I've been doing for the cupcakery, the day just goes on and on."

"Sounds terrible," Wes said, and I could tell he really meant it. We shared a distaste for unscheduled, inevitably unproductive days. "I still can't believe you just quit your job lickety-split like that. Don't get me wrong, I'm thrilled. Now we can be together in San Francisco. But you loved that job. I'm still shocked at how quickly it all went down. Lo and behold, I'm marrying an enigma. Is it wrong that that sort of turns me on?"

"Well, there you go. That's why I did it. To reignite your passion."

"No need! Burning strong, baby!" Wes gave a little growl, and I couldn't help laughing again. It felt nice. Wes was good at cheering me up, not that I'd often been in need of the cheer over the course of our relationship. He was a smart, kind, solid man, and I wondered sometimes, in the rare moments when my confidence flickered for just an instant, if I deserved him. What would he say when he knew the truth? Not that anything that had happened was my fault, I reminded myself.

Unless. Unless something inside of me—something toxic that had been festering there all along—had made this happen? There was, I realized, a distinct possibility that when it came right down to it I was not a good person. I knew Wes would deny this, but he wasn't inside my head with me. He only saw what I let him see. I hadn't told him yet that my old friend Annie apparently hated my guts, and that she probably had good reason to.

The truth was that sometimes I found it nearly impossible to keep the toxic thoughts from entering my head. *It's not like there is a finite amount of good fortune in the world*, I told myself when good news from a friend put me in a funk. *Just because something good happens to someone else doesn't mean something good won't also happen to you.* Caroline Rydell, for example, had recently called with the wonderful news that she was pregnant. But wasn't it only human to want other people's good fortune for yourself? Or did that make you a bad person? Annie, I guessed, would say that made me mean.

Maybe I should give yoga another shot. Or—I cringed—*therapy.* I shook my head, unable to bear the thought of either. *I just need to tell him.*

"Wes," I said abruptly. "When you envision you and me in the future—what do you see?"

He laughed. "Uh-oh! Cold feet already?"

"No, no. Nothing like that. I just miss you. Humor me."

"Okay, let's see. I picture us getting married—let's start there. After that, I see us sucking down fruity drinks and baking in the sun and rolling around naked in our honeymoon suite for a good two weeks. You with me so far?"

"At your side."

"Phew. How much further should I go?"

I swallowed. "A lifetime."

"A lifetime? Good Lord, Julia, just how cold are your feet?"

"They're perfectly room temperature. I'd just like to hear a story."

"A story. A little ditty about Wes and Julia. Got it. Okay, next, I see us settled into a nice house in San Francisco with a little yard. Don't worry, I see a gardener as well—I'm well aware that not one of our four combined thumbs is the remotest shade of green. But it will have to be a very ugly gardener because my ego can't handle one of those strapping, sensitive fellows that clips rosebushes and hauls enormous bags of fertilizer in the same breath.

"What else? I see us meeting up for sushi and cocktails at Umami after we've each spent long days in our respective offices . . . or bakeries, or wherever. I see a lot of very nice bottles of wine. I see brunches and the Sunday *Times*. I see us butting heads over the current state of world affairs and enthusiastically, creatively making up all over the house. I see myself dragging you to a lot of movies starring Will Ferrell, and I see you dragging me to a lot of movies that involve more reading than watching. I see myself pillaging your brilliant brain time and time again for answers to any number of business conundrums that I'll face along the way of building this company. I see us traveling—scuba in the Galapagos, island-hopping off the coast of Croatia, eating our way through Asia. I see us old and sage and happy—two clever silver foxes with full bellies and toothy grins and eyes shining with love that has lasted a lifetime."

Wes paused. "Are you still there?" he asked.

"Yes," I said. My heart was racing in my chest. "I like that story." *This is it*, I thought. *This is when I should tell him.*

"Well, I hope so, because it's ours. I can see it all as clear as

day. Forty years from now: You, me, and a gaggle of grandkids.
There can't be a happy ending without rug rats, right?"

Grandkids. I swallowed. "Right."

"Feel better?"

"Much. Thanks." *Really, after all this time, it would be terrible to tell him over the phone, wouldn't it?* "Listen, I've got to go.
Cupcakes and weddings and all that!" I tried to make my voice
sound light.

"Atta girl!" he drawled, all gravel and honey. "Back to the
icing-and-roses grind. You're my hero."

"Well, someone has to ensure our wedding is the event of the
season," I said. "I love you. Talk to you later."

I ended the call and immediately, before I had time to process
the turns our conversation had taken, the phone rang in my
hand.

"Julia?" a gruff voice said. "It's Burt Vargas. Your contractor?"

"Hi, Burt," I said, struggling to switch gears. "Everything
going okay?"

"Well, see, that's the thing." Burt cleared his throat, a long,
wet rumbling that twisted my stomach. "There's been a . . . an
incident. I think you better get down here."

9

Annie

When I arrived at the cupcakery, Julia was already there. She nodded when she saw me and glanced down at the plank of wood at her feet.

"Hey, Annie," Burt said, pushing up the rolled sleeves of his gray plaid button-down. "I was just telling Julia that I don't understand how this could have happened. My guys locked the place up last night, and when they got here this morning . . ."

We all looked down at the beautiful, tiger-striped redwood plank that was meant for the shop's bar. In fluorescent orange spray paint, someone had covered the wood with the words "YOU DON'T BELONG HERE." I felt my heart begin to pound in my ears. *Those words.* I looked up again and found Julia's eyes anxiously searching my face.

"There's no sign of a break-in," Burt was saying. "Doesn't make any sense."

Julia moved her gaze from me to Burt. "No sign of break-in," she repeated. She tucked her blond hair behind her ears, revealing obnoxiously large diamond studs, and turned slowly in a circle. "Did they do anything else? Is anything missing?"

"Nah, nothing. Just this graffiti. Probably some neighborhood kids getting their shits and giggles. You know how kids are. Do you want me to call the police?"

"Of course," I said. My voice sounded small.

Burt looked at me and nodded. He pulled out his phone and walked into the kitchen where "his guys" were hammering and yelling to each other in Spanish, leaving Julia and me alone in the front room.

"So much for welcome to the neighborhood," Julia said. "Personally, I would have preferred a nice bottle of wine. But I guess that's not really the style around here."

I'd been sidetracked by those words on the plank of wood, but now I turned to Julia. It was hardly a shock that she would take this opportunity to insert one of her breezy slights against the Mission. *"Around here?"* I repeated. "This kind of thing can happen *anywhere*, Julia. There's no need to implicate an entire neighborhood." Even as I said this, my mind was racing. *Those words. Those* specific *words.* Could it really just be a coincidence?

Julia gave a little shrug. She looked down at the piece of wood between us and nudged it gently with the toe of her alligator-skin flat. "Poor wood. It makes it through the building and then demolition of a barn one hundred miles away, only to be destroyed by stupid drunk kids in the Mission. Well, not destroyed, I guess. Burt says he can sand it down and it will be good as new. Or, you know, good as old."

I was hardly listening to her. "This is all too weird," I murmured. The memory of slips of paper fluttering slowly down to the ground around me clouded my thoughts. My tongue felt thick and dry in my mouth. "Those words . . ."

Julia kept her eyes trained on the wood. "I guess someone doesn't want us in the neighborhood."

I lifted my gaze to stare at her. Was she really going to pretend those words held no history for us? "Julia," I said. "Those

words: 'You don't belong here.' You know it's not the first time
I've seen them."

Julia blinked, hesitating for a moment, then shook her hair
back. "I'll call the alarm company and see if I can get them in
here sooner than next week. Somebody in the neighborhood is
clearly in a tizzy about gentrification"—her lips curled around
the word—"or whatever."

"Gentrification!" I cried. "But I *live* here. I've lived here for
six years—I'm not some outsider swooping in!"

Julia smiled ruefully. "Some might argue that living somewhere for six years does not disqualify one from being part of
the gentrification process."

I couldn't believe it. She was saying I was an outsider here,
too! Was there nowhere she would allow me to feel at home? I
took a deep breath and tried to match her gratingly calm tone.
"We're employing locals," I said, gesturing toward the kitchen
door through which the steady stream of workmen's chatter
still spilled. "We're creating jobs. We're improving foot traffic,
which will help other local businesses."

She waved her hand in front of her. "Oh, I know, I know.
You're preaching to the choir." She sighed. "All I meant was that
I think we need to try not to take the graffiti personally."

I read those fluorescent orange words on the redwood
plank again. "How can I not take this personally? How can
I look at those words and then look at you standing there in
front of me and not think that somehow, in some way, the two
are connected?" I shook my head. "It just makes me think I
should never have done this. I should never have let you back
in my life."

"Annie—" Julia began slowly.

"Just tell me you remember," I interrupted. "At least give me
that."

She hesitated, nudging the plank again with her toe. "I remember," she said at last, as nonchalantly as if she were agreeing with some comment I'd made about the weather.

I sighed and sank back against a table the workmen had set up in the corner, my eyes burning with some strange mixture of relief and anger at Julia's small admission. I wasn't crazy. I knew she remembered everything about that year. I knew she remembered the truth.

The rumors about me had all started when a series of thefts rocked Devon Prep during our senior year. First, Katherine de Verona's Birkin bag was stolen from the bathroom counter while she was in a stall. Then Lauren Pearlman's Gucci wallet was lifted from her backpack. Other students lost expensive coats, gold key rings, Tiffany charm necklaces.

One day a few weeks into those incidents, my friend Jody told me to meet her in the school courtyard during lunch. When I walked outside, I realized it was drizzling. Other than Jody, who sat at a small metal table in a corner of the courtyard near the rock garden, the usually crowded eating spot was empty. Jody looked up and blinked rapidly when I approached, then looked back down and began gnawing her fingernails with an anxious abandon she typically reserved for the Sour Patch Kid candies she kept in endless supply in her backpack.

"What's going on?" I asked, dropping into the chair across from her. Even for Jody, who was as socially adept as a possum, this rainy meeting was odd.

"It's Clayton Reardon," she whispered, still gnawing on her thumbnail and not meeting my eye.

"What? Come on, Jody, out with it. You're being weird."

When Jody looked up, a deep, acne-scarred crease had formed between her eyebrows. "Clayton Reardon," she repeated, only a fraction louder now. She glanced around and then leaned across the table toward me. "This morning in gym he told everyone he saw you unzipping book bags in the hall. People are saying that you've been stealing our stuff and pawning it to send money to your family in Ecuador."

I laughed and then, when I realized she was serious, stopped and stared at her in stunned silence. "What are you talking about?" I sputtered. "Stealing? My family in Ecuador? I don't know anyone in my family but my mother!" *And thanks to her insistence on assimilation,* I thought, *I barely speak a word of Spanish!* The accusation would almost have been funny if it weren't so damn bigoted.

"I know," Jody said quickly. Her pale face was pinched with discomfort. "*I* know. But that's what everyone's saying. I thought I should tell you."

I sat back in the chair, my mind racing. The rain was falling harder now and we both pulled up the hoods on our jackets. "Why would Clayton say that about me? What did I ever do to him?"

"Nothing." Jody resumed biting her thumbnail and seemed to retreat deeper into her hood. "But you know how they are."

By "they" she meant the rest of our classmates, and I understood as she spoke just how hopeless the situation was. Clayton Reardon's word was practically gospel at Devon. In the eyes of my classmates, I was now a thief. I took in Jody's darting eyes and renewed commitment to eating her fingers and sighed. "Thanks for telling me," I said. "You should go. No reason to be late for class."

We both knew that class didn't begin for another fifteen minutes, but Jody rose so quickly her chair nearly toppled over. She hoisted her enormous backpack onto her shoulders. "I'll see you later," she said. "Hang in there."

Once she was gone, I sat alone at the table until the bell rang, my face burning with anger and frustration, acutely aware that even the rain could not shield me from the countless pairs of eyes I felt staring down at me from the classroom windows surrounding the courtyard.

After school that day, I trudged up the St. Clairs' grand staircase. I couldn't have explained why I'd decided to talk with Julia about those rumors—it had been months, maybe even a year, since we'd shared anything close to the sort of honest, heartfelt conversations our friendship had once been built on. I guess it just showed how upset I was about everything, and how alone I felt.

I certainly wasn't intending to snoop. Julia's relationship with Jake Logan was still in its early days and it didn't occur to me he might be with her. I was just about to push open her bedroom door when I heard his voice coming from inside. And he was talking about *me*. My hand, mere inches from the door, froze. I stared at it, thinking of the split-second pause of a bird just before it plummets, shot dead, to the ground.

"Annie cracks me up," Jake was saying. "Has she always been so funny? I wonder if she's home yet."

"Anita Quintana?" Julia asked, using my full name as though she barely knew me. She gave a sharp little laugh, nothing like the belly laugh I was used to hearing from her. "Oh, Jake. Annie's the St. Clair family project. She's just the housekeeper's daughter. Our favorite little bushy-haired charity case. It's so sweet you're nice to her, but didn't you hear? She's the one who's been stealing everything at Devon!"

And just like that, I knew. Something in her voice told me concretely what I think on some level I'd been circling all afternoon: Julia had started those rumors about me. I didn't bother to listen for Jake's response, but turned and crept back down the stairs, my cheeks wet with tears.

Over the next couple of weeks the treatment I received from my classmates plunged from benign neglect to active hatred— boys hissed menacingly in the halls; pencils were tossed at my back in class; my backpack was continually overturned and emptied. And then came the day in April when I opened my locker to find it stuffed with little slips of paper with the words "YOU DON'T BELONG HERE" typed on them in capital letters. I tried to gather those slips of paper as they drifted to the floor around me, but passing classmates silently kicked them back fluttering through the air, until I felt trapped inside some awful, nightmarish snow globe.

Later that day, I was summoned to the principal's office and placed on temporary suspension.

"It's for your own good while we sort this whole thing out," Mr. Crane said, but I could see the accusation in his eyes.

When I arrived home early from school, the look on my mother's face—a heart-crushing mix of concern, loyalty, and disappointment—was the day's final, and worst, injustice.

Any sort of suspension required a note be sent out to the colleges I'd applied to, which meant that the Cal admissions department soon alerted me that it was closely reviewing the situation as well. I was never allowed to return to Devon Prep, but, unable to prove anything, the school did eventually mail me my diploma. It wasn't until after my mother had died that fall that a gym teacher caught the school's front office assistant, Ms. Sherman, brazenly lifting Chanel No. 5 perfume from a student's field hockey bag. It turned out Ms. Sherman had a taste, but not the paycheck, for designer goods. Oddly, I felt a little sorry for her. I remembered seeing her smoking cigarettes around the corner from school, looking miserable and too thin in starchy pants. It turned out that being surrounded by a bunch of kids who had all of the beautiful things she'd never been able to afford knocked her a little off her rocker. She couldn't have been the first person Devon Prep drove crazy. I hoped her lawyer played the insanity card.

And now, right in the middle of the cupcakery floor, those same awful words that had traumatized me so deeply ten years earlier had resurfaced. I really believed I had basically come to terms with everything that had happened so long ago, but now

I was thrust back into that dark, thorny place. Standing tall and straight under the bare bulbs of construction lighting, Julia applied a fresh coat of lip gloss. Just watching her made me nearly shake with anger. Her shiny, pearly nails irritated me. Her thin gold watch annoyed me. Her perfectly twisted scarf drove me practically certifiable. Noticing me staring at her, she paled.

"Annie," she said. "You have to realize it's just an awful, awful coincidence." I glared at her in silence and her steady gaze wavered. "If you won't even give me the benefit of the doubt," she asked, "how will you ever learn you can trust me?"

"If I don't give you the benefit of the doubt," I said sharply, "I'll never have to be reminded that I *can't* trust you."

Julia's lips quivered and then suddenly her eyes were filling with tears. I couldn't believe it. I'd seen her shed tears only twice through our entire childhood—the first, when Curtis accidentally ran over her cat, and Lolly, who'd been complaining about the cat hair on her Oriental rugs for years, swore that another pet would never again cross the St. Clair threshold; the second, at my mother's funeral. Now this was already the second time in a few short months that she was crying in front of me. I felt the heat of my anger drop a degree or two. Whatever she had going on in her life, whatever weird journey had made her decide that opening a cupcakery with me was what she needed to do right now, I could not begin to fathom.

Julia's a vampire, I'd vented to Becca the other day, *but instead of blood, she sucks the sense of humor right out of me.* And here I was, letting her feed on me again. When push came to shove, did I truly believe Julia had something to do with that graffiti? No. And did I really think she would ever check her pride long enough to apologize for starting those rumors back in high school? No. I refused to spend any more time torturing myself by waiting for something that would never happen. I looked around the shop as she swiped the smudges of mascara from below her eyes. We needed, I realized, to get back to focusing on the business.

"Well," I said, nodding toward the redwood plank, "at least orange complements our color scheme."

Julia blinked, then laughed shakily. "Small favors, I guess." She sniffed, looking around the shop. "It's coming together, isn't it?"

The dark wood floors, though currently coated with dust, gave the shop a richness it hadn't had before. The large, black-steel-framed front window and door were in place, as was the steel-and-glass display counter and shelving units. In the next week the front bar would be installed (assuming the graffiti snafu didn't set things back too long), the dark red Treat logo would be transferred onto the front window and door, the chandelier would go up, and work on the kitchen would be completed. I had already hired two assistant bakers and Julia had hired two women to help manage the register, cupcake counter, and coffee bar.

"We're moving along," I said.

Julia sighed, clearly relieved. She reached into her oversized leather bag, pulled out her phone, and checked the cupcakery's to-do list. "How are the recipes coming?"

"Fine," I said. I mentally ran over the menu I'd been creating. "It would be even better if I had my mother's recipe book . . . there's this *tres leches* dessert with rum syrup she used to make that could be an amazing cupcake. And her passion fruit meringue. Remember that?"

"Yes!" Julia cried. "It was heaven. We *have* to find that book. Why don't you come over later in the week and we'll turn the house upside down?"

I nodded. "I guess it couldn't hurt to look again. Maybe third time's a charm."

"And we should probably do a little taste test of the menu then, too."

I couldn't help laughing; Julia was all but licking her lips. "Very subtle. I like how you slipped that in."

"What?" Julia said, widening her eyes innocently. "I'll supply the cups of milk and flutes of champagne." She looked down at the list on her phone again. "How about the vendors—produce, flour, etcetera. You've been in contact with them, right?"

"Yup. I told you, Julia, I'll handle *all* of the baking-related stuff, including food purveyors. I know who to call and where to shop. That's my wheelhouse. You don't have to worry."

"Perfect." Julia typed a note into her phone and dropped it into her bag. She hesitated, pressing her lips together in a manner that made her look disturbingly like her mother. "Listen, Annie," she said, "that graffiti . . . it really is just a bizarre coincidence. You believe me, don't you?"

Her eyes still glistened faintly and as I looked at her, even knowing full well that she was the master of false sincerity, I felt my shoulders finally loosen and fall from the tense position they'd assumed from the moment I'd seen that graffiti. It was exhausting being angry with her all the time, and she really did appear, whatever her motives, to be trying to make things right. "Yes," I told her, realizing that, despite my better judgment, it was true. I actually did believe her.

10

Julia

"JULIA ST. CLAIR, if you miss one more wedding appointment I'm going to lose my mustard!" my mother's voice rasped through my car's speakers when I called her after I'd pulled away from the cupcakery. I couldn't help smiling at the mixed metaphor. It was one of my mother's favorites, passed down from her own mother and her mother's mother before that as though the words "lose my mustard" were as precious as heirloom jewelry. I suspected I'd let the saying die with my mother.

"I'll be there! I promise," I said as I navigated the streets of the Mission, turning onto Dolores Street with its palm-lined divider and stomach-roiling hills. I was in a good mood after the way my meeting with Annie had ended, even if our cupcakery was under siege by some Mission hoodlums.

"Just how late are you going to be, Julia? At least give me that courtesy."

I glanced at the clock on the dashboard. "Twenty minutes. Maybe less. I'm on Dolores."

"You're still in the Mission?" my mother barked. "Are you driving the Mercedes? Lock the doors. And please get off the phone and concentrate! I don't know why you didn't just let

Curtis drive you. That's exactly why we *employ* him. *He* would have made sure you were back safe and sound and on the dot."

Lock your doors. I had, in fact, locked the doors the moment I'd entered the car back on Twentieth Street, but even I recognized how these words sounded coming from my mother. "Stop worrying. I'll be there," I repeated. I ended the call and pressed down on the gas pedal.

And I really did intend to go to that meeting with the wedding photographer. I was as mentally prepared as I'd ever be to pore over the photographer's portfolio, discuss the proper ratio of formal portraits to photojournalistic shots, and determine which overpriced package was overpriced enough to handle the demands of a St. Clair wedding. But as I idled at a light a few blocks from the cupcakery, a slim woman in narrow jeans and a gorgeous, funnel-sleeved tweed coat walked in front of my car with a baby strapped snug against her chest. The road wavered. I pressed my eyes shut as a black wave of despair swelled and crashed inside of me, splintering my heart into a thousand throbbing pieces. A horn blared behind me and I managed to pull over through a blur of tears before I dropped my head to the steering wheel. I wasn't sure I'd ever felt so alone in my entire life.

After what felt like an eternity, I finally caught my breath. In the visor mirror I saw that bluish circles had appeared under my eyes and the skin on my cheeks looked sallow and dry. I noticed a freckle near my temple that I'd never seen before. *And on top of everything, I'm aging.* I sighed. What would my mother say if she saw my skin in this condition? Lolly St. Clair, who had a standing monthly appointment at the dermatologist and had every freckle, every mole, and every minuscule spot removed immediately upon detection? My mother accused these skin imperfections of being scouts for the Grim Reaper. *Who wants to see little calling cards from Monsieur Death all over her body?* she'd ask, shaking her head with disdain when telling me about a friend of hers who didn't take care of the spots that appeared along her décolletage.

Clearly, I was in no state to see my mother. But if I didn't go to the meeting with the photographer, where would I go?

The 500 Club was a dive bar on the corner of Guerrero and Seventeenth streets that Jake Logan recommended when I told him where I was. It was dark and nearly empty, without even the remotest possibility of anyone I knew walking in. In other words, it was perfect.

"We have to keep meeting like this," Jake said when he slid into the seat across from me. I could smell the sweet, earthy scent of the scotch in his hand as he leaned across the table to kiss my cheek. We hadn't seen each other since that day at the Balboa Café in June; the padding of a few weeks' distance between meetings contributed to an unplanned, casual vibe that I welcomed. "Which appointment are we dodging today?"

"Photographer. My mother can handle it, though. She knows what I want."

Jake's blue-green eyes narrowed. "Do *you*?"

"Hmm?" I sipped my drink and scanned the bar. An enormous, bearded man in a leather biker jacket sat on one of the farthest stools, a fluffy white shih tzu panting happily on the seat beside him.

"Do *you* know what you want?" Jake asked. "It doesn't take a detective to figure out that you're avoiding everything related to your wedding. Don't get me wrong—I love seeing this side of you. Down-and-out Julia St. Clair is"—he grinned—"very, very sexy."

"Easy, tiger," I said. I'd forgotten that sometimes he could be a bit much. When I drained my drink and set the glass back down, the arm of my sweater stuck for a moment to the table.

"Seriously, is everything okay?" he asked.

"Everything's *fine*." I sighed. I waved my hand at the bartender, but he shrugged and turned away. Apparently, there was no table service at the 500 Club. Jake took my glass up to the bar for a refill and when he returned, slid into the bench beside me. "Thanks," I said, wrapping my fingers around the ice-cold glass.

"You're welcome," he said. "Let's try this again. I feel like I need to act the part of a concerned bridesmaid here. Let's pretend I just plunked down two hundred bucks on some hideous yellow taffeta number that gives me pancake boobs and a mare's ass. You now owe it to me to tell the truth. Are you having second thoughts?"

"What? No," I said. My voice sounded a little high, even to my own ears. "Anyway, you know I would never make anyone wear taffeta."

Jake smiled. "I'm sure having your handsome first love back in the picture isn't helping whatever bit of turmoil you're finding yourself in."

"Ha-ha," I said dryly, but couldn't help looking at him with affection. He was like an exuberant puppy that somehow managed to appear adorable even when he was piddling on your brand-new carpet. Had we ever talked about getting married? I couldn't remember. *There's a bullet dodged*, I thought to myself. Still, he reminded me of a time when my life had seemed remarkably happy and simple. And that, I realized, was why I'd wanted to see him again. *If only life had turned out as easy as it had seemed it would be when we were students at Devon Prep.*

Of course, Devon Prep hadn't been easy for everyone. Crossing through those doors freshman year, I'd immediately sensed how difficult it would be for Annie to be there. It was a small school and I knew nearly all of the kids already; we'd shared intersecting childhoods of horseback riding, skiing, ballet, and ballroom. Even though the faces were all familiar, something new fell into place inside of me as I walked through Devon's doors that first time. I slowed my step, studying the girls with their plaid uniform skirts rolled just so to reveal several inches of smooth thigh, the boys with their ties loose around their necks, their hair spiked jauntily. I felt at once utterly on edge and perfectly comfortable in those halls—it was a feeling I bit into and savored, the sweet rightness of the whole scene warming my body. That night, I convinced my mother to take me to Union Square and we spent hours searching for the perfect coat—a sky-blue Searle peacoat with silver toggles that the girls in our class fingered breathlessly the next morning, wide-eyed with envy. The next week, two girls showed up to school in ivory and camel versions—they swore, of course, that they hadn't realized it was the same coat—but it didn't matter; by then, I was wearing a black cashmere capelet with my grandmother's enormous Tahitian pearl brooch on the lapel. No other girl stood a chance.

Looking back, I suppose it would have been relatively easy to pull Annie along with me as I negotiated Devon's ranks. And maybe I would have, but it honestly never seemed, right up until the end of our senior year, like the social politics at Devon really affected Annie—she remained her freewheeling, funny, outspoken self while the rest of us did everything in our power to fit in. I'd have been the first to admit that I needed friends and their validation like a bee needed pollen, but Annie? She was so independent, and at the same time so close with her mom. It wasn't like she needed me.

Right on cue for my little mental time warp, Will Smith's "Gettin' Jiggy wit It" suddenly filled the bar. I looked at Jake and laughed.

"Oh my God," I said. "What is this, high school?"

"I wish!" Jake said, wagging his eyebrows. It was the kind of music that the radio had played nonstop during our senior year at Devon—the year Jake and I first slept together. He was the first boy I ever slept with and he claimed that I was his first, too, but even then I knew better than to trust him in matters involving bedrooms and body parts.

Before I'd even realized I'd finished my drink, Jake had wandered off to the bar for another round. I took the moment to text my mother that something had come up at Treat and I wasn't going to make the appointment with the photographer after all. I knew she would consider receiving this information via text message adding insult to injury, but I was already feeling a bit too blotto to call her and risk having to actually speak with her on the phone.

The last thing I remembered clearly from that night was taking a shot of tequila—my *third?*—with ★NSYNC's "I Want You Back" blaring in the background courtesy of the fistful of change Jake had dumped into the jukebox. It was dusk by then but the bar hadn't flicked on its lights yet and everything seemed pleasantly out of focus, like looking through the old, warped windowpane of a Victorian. After the shots, Jake lifted a finger to my lip to wipe away some trail of liquor. Then he leaned in as though to kiss me, and I pushed him away, shaking my head and laughing. The alcohol made me feel almost giddy; my heart felt bigger, more expansive and inclusive, more capable of joy. After that, the night just melted away with me.

Sometime later, I woke up in a bed in a pitch-black room. I bolted upright, then groaned and clutched my throbbing head. Fumbling to find the lamp on the bedside table, I groaned again when I found it and light pierced the room. I was alone. And, thank God, fully dressed.

I looked around slowly. The room was tastefully furnished with dark, Asian-influenced wood furniture and a few oversized 1960s-era photographs of surfers and beaches. There were no personal photographs, and I'd never been there before, but I was sure I was in Jake Logan's bedroom.

I rose gingerly and made my way to the door. In the living room, Jake was stretched out on the couch watching *Top Gun* on a large flat-screen television. Diet Coke cans littered the black leather ottoman, and three surfboards leaned against a navy accent wall. It was the quintessential bachelor pad, if you happened to be a bachelor with a trust fund. Three walls of windows revealed the bay, black and still, Sausalito twinkling in the distance.

"Sleeping Beauty awakens!" Jake called, making room for me on the couch. "I'd nearly forgotten how gorgeous you are when you're vertical."

I grimaced, collapsed on the couch beside him, and waved away the can of soda he held out to me. He shot me an amused smile.

"I'm afraid," he said, "you've come down with a serious case of tequila-itis. The only known cure is eggs, coffee, and sleep."

I groaned. "What time is it?"

Jake glanced at the glowing cable box and laughed. "Midnight. You're a cheap date. Passed out by nine."

I hung my head in my hands, unable to look over at him. "We didn't *do* anything, did we?"

Jake, cruelly, let a beat of silence pass before he answered. "Would it be so terrible if we had?"

"Don't be an asshole," I said, feeling tears prick my eyes.

"Ouch. Don't worry, Jules. Nothing happened." He sat back on the couch, sounding petulant. "Anyway, it's not like you're married yet."

I looked at him, wondering how he could be so dense and still so endearing. "No," I said, softly. "But you are."

Jake looked surprised. He shrugged, rubbing the base of his left ring finger, where a tan line was still in the process of fading.

"Only in the eyes of law," he said at last, dimples flashing across his cheeks and then disappearing like stones skimming water ever so briefly before they sink.

September

dependent. Ogden, big and muscular with sandy-brown hair and a prominent nose that was bronzed and peeling like a ten-year-old's, appeared to be in his early thirties, but he barreled his way through conversation like a lonely old man who was thrilled to find himself with a captive audience beyond the usual fruit trees and dirt. He seemed incapable of not moving his mouth—if he wasn't eating, he was talking, though one didn't necessarily preclude the other. Each time he broke his monologue to take a breath, I'd make some minor, throwaway comment about something he'd said, just so he'd know I was listening. But before I could even finish the thought, he'd steamroll over me, passionately disagreeing with each and every benign comment I made. Finally, I gave up and let his words fill up the bouncing, jolting truck cab, feeling pummeled on all ends.

"Here we are!" Ogden said suddenly, wrenching the wheel to swing the truck off the road and onto a dirt driveway.

The abrupt turn sent me on a collision course for the door and I rubbed my shoulder as we bounced down the long driveway. We pulled up in front of a small, neat, buttercup-yellow cottage crowned with solar panels that sparkled blindingly below the bright blue sky. Before the dust had even settled, Ogden hopped out, walked in long strides around the truck, and pulled open my door. Apparently, the sight of the old homestead sent him into gentleman-farmer mode.

"Welcome to Gertzwell Farm," he said, and offered one of his large hands. "Time for me to show off the fruits of my labor."

Ah, I thought, climbing down. *Fruit farmer humor.* I stretched beside the truck and attempted some surreptitious butt kneading.

Gertzwell Farm covered more than sixty acres, of which we walked at least six. I got the sense that if it were up to Ogden we would have walked the entire property. In the hot sun, the soil looked too dry to support anything at all, but we walked down row after row of low, knobby, gray-barked trees studded with apples in shades of deep burgundy and pale green. Ogden pointed out fruit that had a beautiful, rosy, sun-kissed blush, and others that had a smattering of black freckles—a not aesthetically pleasing but harmless mold that apparently became inevitable when it rained in June.

"You can have black specks like these, or you can have apples that have been doused with twelve layers of pesticide," Ogden said. His voice was arrogant, but I heard a hint of defensiveness in it, too. "That's your choice. But if you have a taste for perfect-skinned, toxic apples, Gertzwell Farms isn't for you. We focus on flavor and sustainability, which, we've learned, go hand in hand." As he spoke, I imagined organic farmers up and down Sonoma stamping their feet like frustrated children when the air turned ominously heavy and wet in June.

Pears speckled and huge as dinosaur eggs weighed down branches in the next row. Ogden reached up and in one surprisingly graceful motion twisted a pale green orb off the tree, expertly leaving behind its precious stem to allow for regrowth, as he'd instructed me earlier. As he reached up, the unbuttoned cuff of his sleeve flopped back for a moment and I noticed an old scar snaking up the topside of his browned, muscular forearm. I wondered where it stopped. He pulled out a pocketknife and cut a slice of pear.

It was crisp and refreshing, more like an apple than a pear. "It's delicious," I said, letting its layers of subtle flavor reveal themselves before commenting. "Sweet, but still earthy."

"Earthy? Not really," Ogden said, his brow furrowing. He took a bite. "I think you're tasting a hint of citrus."

I managed to not roll my eyes, but just barely. I was beginning to get used to Ogden's contrarian, superior way of conversing, which wasn't to say I liked it. He was obviously one of those insanely annoying, ever-blithering foodies, which I realized was a ridiculous complaint coming from a baker who was shopping for biodynamic fruit. In any event, I couldn't deny the excellence of his product.

"It's a Twentieth Century," said Ogden. Somehow, he deigned me worthy of trying another slice. "My favorite Asian pear." Even as he spoke, I was concocting a recipe for a pear and cinnamon cupcake filled with a molten burst of vanilla-bourbon cream.

"The farm was my father's way back when," Ogden explained as we continued walking. "But he nearly ran it into the ground. He expected too much of everything and everyone. He wasn't what you'd call a nurturing type."

I looked over at Ogden, puzzled by this admission. *Not a nurturing type.* Was he giving me the history of the farm, or the history of his childhood? In his mind, they were probably one and the same. In the blaring afternoon sunlight, I noticed a few grays threading through the sandy-brown hair that tufted out of his shirt at the top of his broad chest. His eyebrows were thick and blonder than the hair on his head and were set low over brown eyes lined with lashes as long as a cow's. In another life, he could have been a football coach at some suburban high school, preppy and tan and gregarious instead of dirt-flecked and sunburnt and serious.

"Dad would spray these fields down with pesticides when the bugs hit, never bothering to question whether those tiny living organisms were needed by the land they lived on, whether they—the bugs, the land, the season, the fruit—were all tied together in some harmonic balance." Ogden released a dark, hard laugh. " 'Harmonic balance'—two words my father would not have used, together or alone.

"Anyway," he continued, "lucky for the land, he died young. That was about twenty years ago. Mom took over, got rid of the pesticides, moved some fields around. She was like a chess player, moving apricots to the back ten, sliding pears up to the southern slope. Within a couple of years, we had rich fruit with layers of flavor that were at once delicate and robust. But that's because we had become self-dependent, which is what every farm should be. The organic compost that feeds our trees is created right here on the farm. We use enzymes that are cultivated . . ."

As Ogden launched into what might as well be the tree-hugger national anthem—a little ditty I liked to think of as "Our Compost 'Tis of Thee, Sweet Poop of Piety"—my mind wandered. What was Jake Logan up to at that moment? We'd seen each other once every week or two since that surfing excursion, and the lulls in between our dates were punctuated by the ironic little gifts he sent me at Valencia Street Bakery—Mylar balloons with the words "Get well!" scrolled in drippy pink, a mixed cassette tape I couldn't listen to because I didn't have a tape player (who did? Jake Logan, apparently), one of those ridiculous baskets of fruit cut to look like an arrangement of tropical flowers. Compared with Jake, who was full of quirky surprises, Ogden seemed solid and predictable. Just your run-of-the-mill bore. Well, maybe not run-of-the-mill. It wasn't all that often I met a farmer. Still, he didn't have that spark in his eye I found myself looking for when I met a guy. I didn't need, or even want, to be with the best-looking man in the room, but the one who inevitably got my attention was the one whose eyes held a glint of something magnetic—humor, mischief, curiosity, a sense of adventure. It was harder to find than it sounded. Ogden, who seemed tiresomely earnest, was yet another man whose eyes did not have that spark. Jake Logan's eyes, on the other hand, could practically start a forest fire.

"Suddenly, we had the kind of persimmons that editors like to cut open and put on the cover of *Bon Appétit* magazine alongside a scoop of vanilla gelato," Ogden was saying. "The kind that makes your neighbors jealous. They started calling Mom 'the Land Whisperer.' That whole 'whisper' thing is trendy *now*, with 'the Horse Whisperer,' 'the Dog Whisperer' . . ." He paused here and looked at me pointedly. "I'm sure you know all about that dog guy with your little side business. But this was back when you didn't really want folks saying that you walked the fields at night, whispering sweet nothings to your trees—"

"I didn't realize you knew I walked dogs," I interrupted. The snide comment about my "little side business" had pulled me from my reverie. "You've been checking up on me."

He shrugged. "You have to understand that Gertzwell Farm is a growing brand at a crucial moment. We've got to be careful about who we sell to at this point. We only have so much fruit," he said, gesturing around him, "so if we sell to businesses that don't succeed, we're not doing ourselves any favors."

"I'm not sure I follow," I said, though I had a sinking suspicion that I did follow, and just didn't like where he was headed.

"Well, you're a baker. A somewhat unproven one, if you don't mind me saying. And a dog walker. The two professions don't exactly go hand-in-hand, do they? And now you're opening a . . . what did you call it again? A cupcakery? It's not exactly like selling our fruit to the pastry chef at Chez Panisse, now is it?"

I couldn't believe what was happening. Was I really standing in the middle of bumblefuck being dressed down by Ogden Gertzwell? It appeared I was.

"Listen," I said. "Not that it's any of your business, but I'm going to stop walking dogs the day the doors of Treat open. Until then, I have to pay my rent, and every little bit helps. It doesn't make me any less talented or committed. Anyway, if you've already decided you're not going to sell your fruit to a silly little cupcakery, why the hell did you drag me out here?"

"I haven't decided anything," Ogden said simply. He put his hands at the small of his back and leaned into them for a long stretch. His back cracked and two small birds skittered out of the tree overhead. "I'm just glad to hear this isn't some lark."

So I'd been summoned not to evaluate the farm, but to be evaluated. I was usually all for eccentrics—freak flags were, after all, my thing—but this guy was too much, even for me. "Maybe it's time we head back to the city," I said.

"Not quite yet," Ogden said. "I haven't finished telling you about what I've done since taking over the farm from my mother five years ago. I need to explain how biodynamic farming merges the scientific and the spiritual."

"I've read your Web site, Ogden," I said, shaking my head. "I can assure you it's sufficiently . . . verbose."

On the walk back to the truck, I enjoyed the first stretch of quiet I'd experienced since Ogden had picked me up in the city. A light breeze ruffled the leaves on the trees. A dragonfly soundlessly darted and hovered by my side for several steps. The sun warmed my skin and, slowly, melted away some of my exasperation. As we neared the truck, I saw an older woman sitting on the front steps of the cottage. Her long gray hair was swept into a ponytail and she wore a navy hippie skirt that dusted the ground, a white T-shirt, and a necklace of yellow beads. When she stood and smiled and waved, I saw she had Ogden's funny beak of a nose under bright, dancing, brown eyes.

"You must be Ms. Quintana," she said, kissing my cheek. "I'm Louise Gertzwell." Her skin felt soft and papery and warm, like a cupcake liner that's just spent a few minutes on the cooling rack. "I've been so excited to meet you ever since Ogden told me about your new business. Gertzwell Farm fruit in cupcakes!" she cried, clapping her hands together. "Isn't that something?"

"It is," I said. "It is *something*." I shot Ogden a needling grin and his cheeks reddened. Still, it wasn't this lovely, cupcake-liner-cheeked woman's fault that she'd given birth to a jerk. I turned back to face Louise. "Please, call me Annie. We just finished up a tour of the orchard. It's even more beautiful than I expected." From the corner of my eye, I caught a glimpse of Ogden's fleeting, satisfied smile.

Louise looked back and forth between the two of us. She sighed. "Oh, Ogden, honey! You told Ms. Quintana we're just thrilled to supply her shop with our fruit, didn't you? We talked about it just this morning, didn't we?"

I was surprised to hear Ogden emit a good-natured laugh. "We sure did, Mom, and it's all under control." An affectionate, amused grin spread across his face as he looked at his mother. It was clear from their body language—Louise gazing up at her son with gentle admonishment, his large body angled down toward her slight one—that they were not only a mother and son, but also friends. I thought of Ogden growing up on the farm with his mother as his closest companion, felt the reverberations of my own relationship with my mother in the easy, effortless way they spoke with one another, and experienced an all-too-familiar pang of loss.

"You know what, Louise?" I said. "I think Ogden was just about to tell me exactly how thrilled he would be to supply our cupcakery with fruit when we ran into you. Isn't that right, Ogden?"

Ogden looked at me, the hint of a smile still on his lips. His voice was calm and sincere when he answered, "Actually, yes. I think it's just the sort of partnership Gertzwell Farm's been looking for."

"Well," I said. For one rare moment, I didn't know what to say. Then I remembered. I walked over to the truck, swung open its heavy door, and pulled out the shiny box I'd stuck in the shade under the seat. I walked back to Ogden and Louise, took a moment to show off the deep red Treat logo sticker that was hot off Julia's fancy branding team's press, and then slipped the lid off. At the sight of the dozen assorted cupcakes, as bright and optimistic as party hats, Louise's eyes lit up.

"How wonderful!" she said, clapping her hands together again.

I handed her one of the red velvet cupcakes that I'd made in the old-fashioned style, using beets instead of food coloring. I'd had to scrub my fingers raw for twenty minutes to get the crimson beet stain off them, but the result was worth it: a rich chocolate cake cut with a lighter, nearly unidentifiable, earthy sweetness, and topped with cream cheese icing and a feathery cap of coconut shavings. For Ogden, I selected a Moroccan vanilla bean and pumpkin spice cupcake that I'd been developing with Halloween in mind. It was not for the faint of heart, and I saw the exact moment in Ogden's eyes that the dash of heat—courtesy of a healthy pinch of cayenne—hit his tongue, and the moment a split-second later that the sugary vanilla swept away the heat, like salve on a wound.

"Oh," he said, after swallowing. He looked at me, and I could see it was his turn to be at a loss for words.

I smiled.

Louise, on the other hand, was half giggling, half moaning her way through a second cupcake, this time a lemonade pound cake with a layer of hot pink Swiss meringue buttercream icing curling into countless tiny waves as festive and feminine as a little girl's birthday tiara.

"Exquisite!" she said, mouth full. And then, shrugging in her son's direction, her eyes twinkling, "What? I didn't eat lunch."

12

Julia

"JULIA, MY DEAR, you seem content," my father pronounced, apropos of nothing, from his end of the dining table one morning that September. I looked up from my tea to see him peering at me, looking quite pleased himself as he brushed coffee cake remnants from his hands.

On some level, he was right. With the sun-soaked chandelier throwing tiny rainbows across the table, a flaky croissant oozing chocolate onto my plate, and the soothing rustle of my father's newspaper in the background, I had been feeling—if not content, exactly, at least sufficiently distracted.

"Who wouldn't be happy with this perfect fall weather? I'd forgotten how dreary the foggy San Francisco summer could be."

"We both know it takes more than fog to slow you down," my father chided, releasing one of his hearty laughs. I shrugged, smiling, relieved that he didn't seem to expect more of a response from me. "I think it's that cupcake shop that's put a swing back in your step."

"It's keeping me on my toes, that's for sure."

"How so?"

"Oh, nothing really. It seems we have some neighborhood vandals to contend with. Nothing we can't handle."

Earlier that week our contractor, Burt, had arrived at the shop to find a deep key gauge in the new front door. To me, the gauge looked more like the work of an ice pick than a key, but the precise tool of choice seemed hardly worth splitting hairs over. The door had been repaired and repainted by the end of the day and, after filing yet another complaint with the police, none of us mentioned it again. I probably should have taken the incident more seriously, but frankly, to my newcomer's eye, the Mission seemed like the sort of neighborhood where that kind of thing happened all the time. I figured it was par for the course and added another zero to the maintenance column of the cupcakery's projected monthly budget. Anyway, it's all too easy to retroactively kick myself for not seeing the pattern that was developing; at the time, each incident seemed isolated and unworthy of too much concern.

"Be safe," my father said, lifting his coffee cup into the air in front of him, "but give 'em hell! Don't let it get to you." He lowered the cup to his lips and took a loud, satisfied sip.

"Of course not."

"You and Annie together are unstoppable. Any fool could see that a mile away. I'm just . . ." He hesitated, clearing his throat. I felt the skin on the back of my neck begin to prickle. It wasn't like my father to have to search for words, and I suddenly felt anxious about where this conversation might be headed. "I'm really proud of you, sweetheart," he said. "I'm glad to see you rekindling your friendship with Annie. I know it's not always the easiest thing for you to fully open yourself up to people, but there's such a thing as too much independence. It's not in our nature. Everyone needs a best friend."

I stared at my father as he took another long sip of coffee. I bristled at the thought of him, or anyone, really, observing me like this, formulating theories about me. "I do have a best friend," I said. "I have Wes."

My father shot me an indecipherable look but didn't say anything.

"Well, who's yours?" I asked, irritated.

"I have two," he answered without hesitation. "Kip Shanahan, of course." Kip was my father's Stanford roommate and my godfather—a loud, good-natured orthopedic surgeon who shared my father's affection for Kobe beef and Bordeaux. "And Curtis. He knows all my secrets."

"What about Mom?" I asked quickly. I had no interest in hearing my father's secrets.

"Three!" he bellowed, laughing. He cast a comically exaggerated nervous glance over his shoulder. "I meant to say I have *three* best friends! And you'll never get me to admit I ever said otherwise."

"No," I said, laughing. "I meant, who is Mom's best friend?"

"Oh. Your mother's best friend? That's a tough one. She knows absolutely everyone, of course. Ten years ago I would have said Lucia. Now, I'm not so sure. I guess she's had trouble filling the slot lately."

I was quiet as I took this information in. I'd always known that my mother and Lucia were friends, but I'd never assigned quite such a level of importance to the role Lucia had played in her life.

"Those were good years in this home," my father said softly. He picked at the crumbs on his plate, suddenly subdued. "We had a solid run."

The shift in my father's mood was unsettling, but he was right. There was a period of time when our home felt perfectly in sync. My mother had Lucia, my father had Curtis, and I had Annie. It occurred to me, as it somehow never had before, that I had caused the first fissure in those happy times by abandoning my friend.

"Do you remember that Thanksgiving when we invited Lucia and Annie and Curtis to join us?" my father asked. "It must have been fifteen years ago. I can't for the life of me figure out why we didn't do that every year. It was a wonderful holiday."

This nostalgic streak was so unlike my father, the faraway look that momentarily glazed his eyes so different from his usual alert, jovial gaze that I didn't know how to answer. I felt a twist in my stomach and kept my eyes trained on the table. I didn't like the idea of age changing my father, making him a softer, vaguer version of the strong man he'd always been. He must have noticed my discomfort because he laughed, and the familiar, booming sound relieved me.

"Don't look like that, my dear," he barked amiably. "All I'm saying is that I'm glad to have you back! The house feels better with a little more life in it. And please keep in mind that just because you don't remember that particular Thanksgiving doesn't mean I'm a dotty old fool."

I didn't answer, but the truth was I *did* remember that Thanksgiving, just not in the same sentimental, soft-focused light that my father seemed to.

Our family had a tradition of spending the long Thanksgiving weekend at the Four Seasons in Maui, but for some reason my mother decided we would stay home that year. I had no idea why we were breaking with such a faultless tradition— I'd always loved returning home from Hawaii to endure San Francisco's rainy winter months with a nice bronze glow and sun-brightened streaks in my long hair—but my mother had insisted on Thanksgiving at home for once, and had extended the invitation to Lucia and Annie and even Curtis. Looking back, I suppose the change of plans might have had something to do with the fact that Annie and I were in eighth grade, safely ensconced in our small middle school yet less than a year away from entering the decidedly more adult world of Devon Prep.

Who knows—maybe my mother had a crystal ball that told her that our happy little home dynamic was about to irrevocably shift. I wouldn't have put it past her.

As it turned out, our strange little six-some spent nearly the entire day in the kitchen together. We were drawn there, of course, by Lucia, who had devised a Thanksgiving menu so aggressively American you would have thought she was born in Massachusetts, not Ecuador. By the time I made it downstairs that morning, the air was already thick with the mouthwatering aromas of sweet potatoes and cranberries and turkey and pumpkin pie. I expected to find Lucia alone when I pushed open the kitchen's swinging door, and so was surprised to see my mother perched on a stool at the center island, slowly chopping herbs between sips of ice water.

"Hello, darling," my mother rasped, waving the knife in the air. "Isn't this fabulous? The Four Seasons could learn a thing or two from our Lucia—if I ever let them get their greedy paws on her."

Lucia's hair was pulled back into a neat bun at the nape of her neck, but her dark cheeks were blotchy and her hands fluttered in constant motion from one task to another. I could see she was teetering on the edge of that rattled state she worked herself into whenever she was cooking for a special occasion. Still, she looked happy—those blotches on her cheeks seemed to flare more in response to my mother's compliment than any agitation she was feeling. She paused from work long enough to give me a tight squeeze; she'd always seemed allergic to the idea of a greeting or farewell that didn't include some physical demonstration of affection. Due to my recent growth spurt we'd had to renegotiate how our bodies fit together for these hugs and had settled into a new configuration in which Lucia's chin rested for a moment on my shoulder, her brief kiss grazing my jawline. When she released me, she gestured toward a heaping platter of pastries and an enormous crystal bowl of cut fruit on the counter.

"Good morning, *mi amor*," she said, holding eye contact for a long beat before turning back to the stove. "Eat breakfast and then I will put you to work. Your first job is to wake Annie or she will sleep all day long."

I dropped into the breakfast booth in the corner of the kitchen, stabbing drowsily at pieces of melon with my fork and half listening to the steady flow of conversation between my mother and Lucia.

"And how is Mrs. von Dreiden?" Lucia asked. She'd managed to slide the cutting board of herbs away from my mother without her seeming to notice and had begun expertly gliding her knife in a silent rolling motion through the green stems. "I haven't heard much of her lately."

I perked up. Judith von Dreiden was part of my mother's social circle and her daughter was a couple of years behind me in school. There were few topics that intrigued me more than adults' opinions of one another.

"Oh, I saw Judith last week," my mother said. "She had the usual litany of complaints—fatigue, sore joints, headaches. I can't imagine how long her visits with her *actual* doctor must be considering how long she'll rattle on about that nonsense to me—she must have him on a special retainer! I keep telling her she needs to take up a cause—it's not healthy to think about yourself too much."

"What a shame. She is such a nice lady," Lucia said. She transferred the cut herbs from the cutting board to a small bowl. "Maybe she can join you on a committee at the museum? She collects art, doesn't she?"

My mother thought about this for a moment. I expected a biting comment from her, perhaps something about the "housewife disease" she was often accusing her friends of suffering from—symptoms included acute laziness and addiction to shopping. Instead, she shrugged and said, "She does love art. It's a good idea, Luce. I'll ask her."

The back door to the kitchen swung open and Annie trudged into the room, her hair tangled and her eyes still sticky with sleep. Her step faltered for a moment when she saw all of us, but then she grunted a greeting and shoved me playfully deeper into the booth so she could slide in beside me.

"At last, our fourth wheel," my mother said jauntily. For a woman whose daily life always seemed to me to pitch steadily forward on a wave of brisk, self-propelled momentum, she seemed unusually relaxed and cheerful today.

"*Buenos días, mi amor,*" Lucia said, crossing the room to hug and kiss Annie. "Happy Thanksgiving."

"Morning, everyone," Annie said. "I hope you're all feeling particularly thankful for my big hair and unbrushed teeth today."

"Gross!" I said, laughing.

Lucia looked at my mother and shook her head, lifting her hands in front of her. "I take no responsibility for this. I know I taught her better."

"Oh, our work here is done, Luce," my mother answered. "These young ladies are responsible for their own actions." She shook a finger at Annie, who was biting lustfully into an oversized muffin. "Just promise me you'll reintroduce yourself to some soap before we sit down to eat this afternoon."

Annie grinned, and, though Lucia and my mother generously ignored the crumbs that dropped from her mouth as she did so, I fell into the sort of fit of uncontrollable giggles that only Annie seemed capable of eliciting from me.

We were still in the kitchen a couple of hours later when my father and Curtis returned from the driving range. It was barely eleven a.m. and my father was really more of a martini man, but he reached into the fridge and pulled out four beers. The sight of my mother's thin hand clasping a beer bottle was enough to set Annie and me giggling again, and Lucia and Curtis and my father all seemed to be having a hard time keeping a straight face at the sight as well.

"Just look at you all!" my mother rasped. "You'd think you stumbled into Mother Teresa sipping gin at the racetrack!" She tipped the beer bottle back for a long drink and we all erupted into laughter.

As much time as we each spent with one another, it was rare that we found ourselves all together in the same room. Curtis was his usual man-of-few-words self, but Lucia set him to work mashing potatoes and he appeared to loosen up a bit. I'd noticed that Annie always seemed to gravitate toward him, teasing him relentlessly and badgering him into conversation; he tolerated her needling that day in his typically unflappable style and even cracked a smile every so often.

As the morning wore on, I found myself feeling increasingly disconcerted by our strange six-some. Looked around, it dawned on me for the very first time that two of the four adults in the room were on our family's payroll. Did they even want to be there? I looked at Lucia, my heart aching with love for her. While my parents and I enjoyed ourselves, was she glancing at the clock, wondering when her workday would be over? I suddenly felt sick. Lucia was *paid* to ask my mother about her friends. Curtis was *paid* to join my father on the golf course on a national holiday. Worst of all, Lucia was paid to love me. I watched her pull Annie tight to her side as they passed each other by the fridge, watched Annie wriggle away, feigning irritation, and felt the unfamiliar tremors of jealousy and loss rattle within me.

Later, we all showered and changed into more formal clothes for the Thanksgiving meal and reconvened in the dining room.

After Lucia set the last steaming dish on the table and took her place beside Annie, my father lifted his wineglass.

"To being home for Thanksgiving," he said, adopting the serious voice he used for such occasions, "and to the countless ways each one of you contributes to making this house a home we all want to be in today. Your efforts are always appreciated."

I noticed Lucia and Curtis exchange an indecipherable look, and felt a stinging in my eyes that I blinked quickly away.

"Here, here!" my mother rasped, apparently oblivious to any undercurrents of discontent at the table. "Happy Thanksgiving!"

We clinked glasses and dug into what would turn out to be the one and only Thanksgiving we all celebrated together. The next year, with little discussion and zero fanfare but with much relief on my part, my mother, father, and I boarded our usual flight to Maui for turkey among the coconut trees.

13

Annie

IT HAD BEEN a very long time since I'd baked anything in the St. Clair kitchen, but rummaging through the cabinets for the various tools I needed felt disturbingly familiar. Some of what I found in those cabinets was new—a spotless stand mixer, for example; other things, like the set of scratched steel mixing bowls Julia handed to me from an upper shelf, were objects that I remembered my mother using regularly. I was trying hard to interpret my mother's lingering presence in the room as something positive, something to be savored, but it was hard not to feel overwhelmed by darker, more melancholic thoughts. Julia and I had checked every one of the many cabinets and each corner of the pantry, but my mother's recipe book still hadn't turned up, not that I'd entertained much hope by then.

"Finding everything?"

I looked up from where I was crouched at a low cabinet to see Tad St. Clair grinning down at me. I hadn't crossed paths with him yet, having ducked out early from the Save the Children benefit that June, and I was surprised by how little his looks had changed. His hair had already turned white by the time I left for college; other than a slightly paler undercast to his perpetually tanned skin and a couple of extra inches at his waistline, Tad was exactly the same. He pulled me up into a warm embrace complete with a couple of hearty whaps on the back.

"Wonderful to see you, Annie! Just wonderful!" he boomed. "You've been sneaking in and out of here as stealthily as a cat these last couple of months. Glad I've finally caught you!"

"It's good to see you, too," I said. I meant it. Tad was always a benevolent, if sporadic presence in my childhood, swooping into the kitchen early in the morning to tuck a newspaper under his arm and press hard kisses to our foreheads before hurrying out to the enormous black Bentley that Curtis had idling in the courtyard.

"Annie's going to bake a new recipe she's working on for the cupcakery," Julia said from where she leaned on the white marble island at the center of the kitchen. She glanced up from the cell phone in her hands. "We're deciding on the menu today. She brought a few kinds that she baked at home earlier if you want to weigh in."

Tad opened the box on the counter and gazed down at the cupcakes. "Weigh in, indeed," he said, patting his stomach. Still, he pulled out a mint-chocolate cupcake with dark chocolate icing that glowed richly under the kitchen lights and took a huge bite. Few things in life made me happier than watching someone aggressively devour one of my desserts. Julia's meticulous, OCD-like manner of eating a cupcake, on the other hand, drove me crazy. By contrast, my method of eating a cupcake was quite straightforward—step one: gobble it down one large bite at a time until there's nothing left. That's it. I was forced to practice dainty nibbling all day long as I tasted various recipes and cupcake batches, so when I sat down with a cupcake to eat for the pure pleasure of eating, I meant business.

"Annie!" Tad said when he was finally done chewing. "Where have you been hiding yourself? This is a show-stopping cupcake. I don't have a clue what I'm eating, but it definitely gets my vote."

I laughed. "You haven't tried any of the other flavors!"

"How could they possibly be better than this one? Lucia, my dear, you are without a doubt the best baker in San Francisco."

I opened my mouth, but didn't speak.

"You mean *Annie*," Julia said quietly, looking at her father.

"Hmm?" he asked.

"*Annie* is the best baker in San Francisco. You said Lucia."

Tad waved the hand that held the cupcake in front of him, sending a sprinkle of dark crumbs down to the counter. "Annie! Of course I meant Annie. I'm sorry." He seemed flustered for a moment, looking around the kitchen. "But Lucia's baking skills are . . . were . . . second to none. Do you remember that cake she made for my fiftieth birthday? I'll never forget it." He said this in a wistful voice that did not sound at all like him. Julia and I exchanged puzzled glances.

"Anyway, girls," Tad said, squishing the cupcake liner into a ball in his hand, "please remind me again—when is Treat's opening party? I want to be sure I don't miss it, and you know how Lolly likes to stack our social calendar."

"Dad!" Julia said. "It's October fifth. I've told you a million times. I sent you the invitation by e-mail. And the *printed* invitation is on your desk. I even entered it on your online calendar."

Tad looked indignant, running a hand through his floppy white hair. "Since when do you have access to my online calendar, young lady?"

Julia looked at me, rolling her eyes. "Since forever, Dad. Since the world began."

"And on the seventh day God said, 'Let there be online calendar access!'" I said cheerily.

"I see," Tad said, an amused glint in his eye. "Fine. Then I shouldn't miss it, should I?"

"You better not," said Julia.

Tad turned to me. "She's very bossy, isn't she?"

"Oh, I know," I said. "She should be leading armies in a jungle somewhere, bamboozling impoverished peoples into relinquishing previously untapped natural resources."

Tad laughed. "Well, try not to let her drive you crazy," he advised. "She is, unfortunately, often right. Which makes her more like her mother than any of us would care to admit."

Julia watched her father silently.

"It was good to see you, Annie. We're all very glad to have you back in the fold. I'm off to lunch now, but I'll see you October sixth."

"Fifth!" Julia cried.

"I'm kidding!" Tad said, hiking up his pants. "Sheesh!"

After he left, Julia was quiet for a bit while I finished gathering all of the ingredients I needed. I'd brought a small crate of Gertzwell Farm's Twentieth Century pears, and they glistened like Christmas balls in a strainer in the enormous farmhouse sink.

"Did he seem weird to you?" Julia asked finally.

I turned off the faucet. "Weird how?"

"I don't know. Different."

"I haven't seen him in more than ten years, Julia. I'm probably not the best judge." I was tempted to leave it at that, to move on to the task at hand, but Julia looked pale and I could see the shadow of bluish circles under her eyes. "Are you worried about him?" I asked.

"Maybe. He's my dad, you know?"

"Yeah," I said, though of course I was the last person to ask about how one was supposed to feel about one's father.

The door opened then and Curtis walked into the kitchen. His step faltered when he saw me, but then he nodded and waved.

"Hi, Annie. Didn't expect to see you here." He took in the kitchen's state of disarray, looking from one end of the room to the other, his craggy face impassive. "Hi, Julia."

"Hey, Curtis," we both said, and the synchronicity of our two voices in well-worn harmony, the feeling of both of us hanging out in the kitchen with Curtis, was enough to twist my stomach. All we were missing was my mother. Impulsively, I stepped forward to hug him. He still had the same smell he'd always had when we were kids—a sharp peppermint scent mixed with the faint cling of cigarettes, though I'd never seen him smoke.

Curtis gave my head an awkward little pat and then rocked back on his heels. "Have you seen Mr. St. Clair?" he asked Julia in his stiff way. *Curmudgeon Curtis*, I thought, but resisted the urge to poke fun at his formality. Some things never changed.

"He was just in here," Julia said. "Why?"

"I've got the car ready. He wanted to go to the driving range."

Julia's brow furrowed. "Maybe he forgot? He wasn't dressed for golf."

Curtis shrugged. "He must have changed his mind. I'll find him." He wandered off into the hall with a vague wave.

I looked over at Julia, but she was studying her phone. She seemed distracted and sad and, I realized, hadn't read from her ever-present cupcakery to-do list once that day. *Don't get involved*, I warned myself. A big part of me wanted to ignore her obvious sadness and pretend that everything was fine. Since when did I care if Julia St. Clair was having a bad day? I had to admit that over the past months of working together—watching her take the odd hiccups we faced (a second deep key gauge in Treat's just-repaired and freshly painted front door was our latest setback) in stride—the wall between us had slowly been coming down, one solid gold brick at a time. I figured the wall was at about shoulder height by then, low enough that I could see Julia's facial expressions, but still not the rest of her body—and who knew what sudden moves she was capable of? She'd been an athlete *and* a queen bee, after all. A dangerous combination. And so even though I was tired of carrying around that ancient grudge—bored of it, really—I still got the sense that where the St. Clairs, and Julia in particular, were concerned, I needed to be careful. Who was going to look out for me if I didn't look out for myself? I was on my own.

But really, when it comes right down to it, aren't we all on our own? Even Julia St. Clair? As I watched her flick through her phone, pausing every so often to run her hand distractedly down the length of her glossy blond hair, I realized that in all the time we'd spent together over the past couple of months, I hadn't heard her talk to, or about, a single friend. Or even her fiancé, for that matter. Where was he, anyway? Hadn't he returned from yet another business trip recently? I'd thought his return would improve her mood, but, in the moments she let her guard down, I still saw that shadow of sadness behind her eyes. I had no desire to try on Julia's shoes, and not simply because they looked like the kind of designer flats that bit into your ankles and slowly sawed off your pinky toes. But before I knew it there I was, putting myself in her Miu Mius.

"Julia!" I said, tossing a pear at her. She looked up from her phone and caught it easily, as gracefully athletic as ever. "I think it's time."

"For what?" she asked.

"For you to learn how to make the world's best cupcake."

October

14

Julia

I WAS SURPRISED to find myself jittery with nerves as Treat's opening party kicked off to a start. Work? Parties? Were there two things in the world that usually came more easily to me? After a lifetime under my parents' tutelage, I should have been the picture of calm efficiency and easy charm. Instead, I was plagued by an uncomfortable tightness in my chest. When I touched my finger to my forehead, it felt slick. *Me!* Of the perpetually matte T-zone! Maybe it was the fact that I was still mildly hung over from the night before—one too many glasses of wine at dinner with Wes, to whom I still hadn't, somehow, brought myself to tell the truth. Or maybe it was the fact that there were about fifty people crammed into a space zoned to hold half that number, and when it came right down to it, I was not a fan of tight crowds (there was a very good reason why I never jumped into the mosh pits at Pearl Jam concerts like my Devon Prep peers, and it was that I was never really in the mood to be *crushed to death*). Or maybe it was that the entire night I felt dogged by the disquieting sense that I was being watched—hunted, almost—fifty pairs of eyes trained on me, an attention that I would normally bask in, but tonight just added to my anxiety. Or maybe it was the simple fact that I was launching the first business I'd ever owned, and I hoped, mostly for Annie's sake but as a point of pride as well, that Treat would be a success.

Reasons aside, I found myself exceptionally thirsty, and the abundant champagne was doing a bang-up job of making me feel less anxious. At least at the beginning. It was only much later that I wished I hadn't drunk so much—and wondered if I would have been able to keep Annie and myself out of harm's way if I'd been sober.

Looking around at the start of the party, seeing how all the hard work we'd put in over the previous few months was paying off, I felt a surge of satisfaction crackle within me and hoped it would eclipse my nerves. I still couldn't believe how creative Annie was in coming up with the different flavors and embellishments for each cupcake; the finished products looked like huge jewels that sparkled appealingly in the counter display and on the black lacquer trays passed by the waitstaff. Annie had had her nose to the grindstone for days, as focused as I'd ever seen her, dicing apples and pears until they looked like nuggets of gold—*as well they should, considering what that fruit cost!*—and tasted like pure, sweet, warm explosions of flavor baked into the cakes. Annie's dexterity, precision, and speed with a knife had been a sight to behold. My contributions to the cupcakery's opening night were decidedly more mundane: I'd interviewed and hired the night's waitstaff, overseen the completion of the various construction and design projects, and ordered all of the noncooking supplies the shop needed. Treat glowed with sexy, low-lit energy; laughter and music filled the space; hip, beautiful people bit into cupcake after cupcake. If the shop had been in the Marina instead of the Mission, it was just the sort of place I would have visited frequently. But there was no use crying over *that* spilled buttermilk.

"Hey there, Cupcake," Wes said, appearing by my side and

wrapping his arm around my waist. "Congratulations to the boss lady!" He kissed my cheek and I allowed my eyes to shut for a moment, blocking out the crowd, the sticky-sweet air, the music that Annie had dug up from who knew where featuring a cool-as-a-cucumber Frenchman rapping rat-tat-tat over re-mixed John Coltrane jazz tracks. Part of me wished I could just slip out unnoticed into the night, tucked securely under Wes's strong arm. A larger part of me was disgusted and confused by this desire. If I weren't careful, before long I would find myself morphing into the type of soft-spoken, ineffectual girl-woman who was stepped on during business meetings.

"I'm not sure you should call me Cupcake anymore," I said, opening my eyes to look up at Wes. "It's like mixing business with pleasure."

"Tough tamales. I had dibs on that endearment long before you decided to rekindle your friendship with a baker. Where is Annie, anyway? I want to finally meet this mysterious child-hood best friend of yours."

I scanned the room, knowing it couldn't take long to spot Annie, who had chosen to wear a floor-length 1960s muumuu in a deep shade of turquoise that looked, I had to admit, strikingly lovely against her honey-toned skin. Her dark hair was piled on top of her head, giving her a couple extra inches of height, and spiked through with a gold, rhinestone-encrusted chopstick. Or at least I thought it was a chopstick, but who knew what you called the utensil once it pierced a mound of hair. Perhaps just a stick? Regardless, she looked stunning—like a colorful little bird that surprises everyone with its audacity and out-of-place beauty by landing right in the middle of a bustling city sidewalk.

As I suspected, Annie was easy to locate. She was leaning against the door to the kitchen, her upturned face flushed and radiant as she chatted with a man who had his back to me. Just as I was about to point her out to Wes, the man she was with planted his hand against the door behind her ear, leaned in, and kissed her on the lips. I stared at the man's back, feeling an uneasy shiver of recognition travel up my spine. *Jake Logan! Jake Logan and Annie?* When Jake pulled away, Annie's face glowed, surprised and pleased and somehow even lovelier than it had seemed a moment earlier. I turned back to Wes, irritation, anger, and then that old buzz of jealousy traveling through me in swift succession.

Isn't there some rule about friends not dating one another's exes? I thought, blinking down into my champagne glass so that Wes wouldn't catch on to my distress. This thought was followed quickly by a pang of concern. Annie's eyes were all moony and big when she looked up at Jake, but I knew for a fact that Jake— who sailed through life on a steady breeze of charm and limitless credit cards—wasn't good for someone like Annie. Sure, Annie put on a jokey, blithe front, but over those last few months I'd learned, or perhaps remembered, that in truth she was a hard-working, focused woman. She deserved a man, not a boy. And certainly not a boy who was married to someone else.

Suddenly, my parents swooped into view, double-kissing Wes and then me in a lightning-quick motion perfected by years of practice.

"Congratulations, Julia darling!" my mother rasped. She held up a pumpkin spice cupcake from which she'd taken one tiny bite. "My compliments to the chef and her spectacularly clever business partner on a smashing debut."

"Hear, hear!" thundered my dad, knocking his half-eaten chocolate cupcake against my mother's. He beamed at me.

"Thanks," I said. I shook my hair back, determined not to let the sight of Annie and Jake kissing cast a fog over the entire evening. "It does seem to be going well, doesn't it?"

"Absolutely. In fact, I bet if you spent half as much time on your wedding preparations as you have on this cupcake shop, we might have things sorted out on the whole biggest-day-of-your-life front," my mother said smoothly. "Wesley darling, did you know your bride-to-be has ducked out of nearly every wedding-related appointment I've made in the last few months? How does it feel to play second fiddle to tiny cakes?" She looked up innocently at Wes and took a nibble of her cupcake, lips curled back so as to not smear her lipstick.

"Now, Lolly—" my father began.

"Mom!" I interrupted, working to keep my voice low. Wes watched me with a bemused look from behind his black Clark Kent glasses. "This really isn't a good time to talk about the wedding."

"Well, of course it isn't!" my mother scoffed. "But desperate times call for desperate measures. Don't you think Wesley ought to know where your priorities lie?"

I stared at her, flabbergasted. Suddenly, Wes's hand encased mine. When he gave my palm a squeeze, I turned my attention from my mother to my future husband and melted as I always did when faced with the incomparable gift that was his kindness.

"Mrs. St. Clair—apologies, *Lolly*," Wes said, correcting himself even as my mother tsked at him. "If I didn't know I was second fiddle to cupcakes in the eyes of my beautiful fiancée, I really wouldn't know her at all, would I? The good news is that I love her sweet tooth just as much as all the other pretty white teeth in her pretty pink mouth. All I really want to do is marry the girl. Heck, we could get married right here in this shrine to sweets if that solves the problem of planning a big shindig."

I tried not to laugh outright at the look of horror that crossed my mother's face. She took a larger, distracted bite of her cupcake, looking wide-eyed from me to Wes to me again. When neither of us spoke, she dabbed at the corners of her mouth with a black cocktail napkin and sighed. "I see. Well, let's not be hasty. I'll just plan the wedding on my own. There's no need to resort to justices of the peace or drive-through chapels or *cupcake shops in the Mission*—no offense, of course, Julia darling. You two can stop your flower-child scheming, if you please, and leave this in my capable hands. I just hope you feel as strongly as I do about tiered floral arrangements, Chiavari chairs, and gold damask tablecloths."

"I'm sure Julia and Wesley trust your taste implicitly," my father said, winking at me. "I'm sure that's exactly what all this absenteeism was about in the first place." He placed his hand at the small of my mother's back. "Now you two will have to excuse us. It's our duty as both guests and guinea pigs to reacquaint ourselves with the young lady who was doling out those heavenly mint-chocolate numbers."

Once they were safely out of earshot, Wes laughed. "Our 'flower-child scheming'? What on God's green earth was all that about?"

I shrugged, smiling, and stopped a passing waitress to exchange my empty champagne glass for a full one. I took a long gulp of champagne, but swallowed quickly when I realized Wes was still watching me. He leaned down toward my ear.

"Baby," he said softly. "Everything okay?"

My spine stiffened. The concern in his voice was too much. It would only take a few more words from him before the stress of the evening finally broke me down.

"I really wish you all would stop asking me that. I'm busy, Wes! I've *been* busy for months and I *am* busy tonight. My mother is driving me crazy with this wedding stuff and I really don't need it from you, too. Why does everyone suddenly think this is an appropriate time to discuss anything but cupcakes? I would like to talk about catering opportunities and marketing plans! Can you do that or not?"

Wes's handsome face darkened. "No, Julia, I suppose I can't. Not right now anyway." He brushed his hands against his pant legs, as though he'd accidentally touched something unpleasant. "I'm going to track down a cupcake and leave you to it. You've got an event to manage."

As if I need you to remind me, I thought irritably as I watched him walk away. But my thoughts were starting to come more slowly now, taking a bit too long to arrange themselves into any sort of order. *Why did I just snap at him?* Already, I had trouble remembering.

When I allowed myself to glance back toward the kitchen again, Annie and Jake were still leaning against the door frame, gazing at each other and stealing little kisses. My eyes buzzed. *She should be mingling!* I thought crossly. *These people need to buy into her as much as they need to buy into the idea of cupcakes.* Why did it suddenly feel like I was the only one pulling my weight around here? I started to make my way over to Annie, but was quickly intercepted by a gangly, red-haired, vaguely familiar-looking woman.

"Hi, Julia?" the woman said, her apologetic smile revealing a horsey mouthful of large, unnaturally white teeth. "I'm Lainey? Lainey Pruott? From *San Francisco* magazine? We chatted at the Meals on Wheels holiday benefit last year?"

Shit! I pressed my shoulders back, trying to shake the blurriness from my vision and thoughts. "Lainey!" I cooed, dropping two swift kisses on the woman's cheeks. I gave her elbow a familiar squeeze to seal the illusion of warmth. "I'm so thrilled you made it! How are you? How's—" I searched my memory for the name of Lainey's husband, a writer for the *San Francisco Chronicle* who I'd also met at the party that winter. *Why did I have to drink so much?* One less glass of champagne and that name would have been on the tip of my tongue. My memory was usually a steel trap, a dependable strategic weapon in business and social warfare. But now I drew a blank. I remembered only that Lainey Pruott phrased everything like a question, making you unsure—right up until the day when you saw yourself quoted in glossy print comparing the city's homeless population to "a glaring blemish on an otherwise flawless five-carat diamond"— whether you were having a conversation or being interviewed. Context, it seemed, really was everything.

"Tim?" Lainey said helpfully. I could tell she was happy to supply the information, and flattered that I remembered either of them at all. I stole another sip of champagne to cover my relief.

"Yes, of course," I said. "Is Tim here as well?"

"Unfortunately, no. He had another obligation. But I promised to do reporting for the both of us. I know he's planning to stop by sometime in the next few weeks."

"Wonderful! We'll keep on our toes. Have you had a cupcake yet?"

"Um, three?" As Lainey giggled nervously, her lips spread back to her pale pink gums and revealed a smudge of chocolate lodged at the top of her right canine. "I know it's a very exciting night, but do you have time for a quick interview?"

"An interview?" I repeated. "Now?" Apparently, Lainey's irritating question marks were contagious. I cleared my throat. "Of course. Just let me grab my business partner, Annie Quintana."

"Why don't I talk to her later?" Lainey said hurriedly, pulling out a notebook. "Besides, you're the one our readers know. You've been gracing our pages since your debutante days. Julia St. Clair opens a cupcake shop! What a story, right?"

I shook my head. "Annie's the pastry chef. She's the heart behind this place." I glanced over to where Annie still stood beside Jake, laughing flirtatiously with him as if they were alone and not in the midst of her business's launch party. *Ungrateful.* The word flashed in my mind, followed almost instantly by a feeling of guilt. *But why should I feel guilty when I have done nothing but behave generously toward her for months now?* Guilt was the last thing I should feel.

Lainey smiled at me encouragingly, pen poised above her notebook.

"I do see your point," I said slowly. "Let's give your readers what they want."

An hour later I was enjoying that holy-grail state of inebriation: appropriately high energy paired with a comfortable, manageable plateau of dulled nerves. Considering the amount of champagne I'd imbibed, I felt I was handling myself admirably, and chatting easily, but with the proper modicum of restraint, with everyone who approached me. I didn't even mention that kiss I had witnessed when Jake came over and wisecracked about how someone must have slipped a Mickey in my cupcake. Despite his comment, I remained sure I was holding myself together quite well. I felt illogically pleased by this, like being able to run a business while sloshed was some adult rite of passage and I had come out the other side unscathed.

The party was starting to thin out, and for the first time all night, I began to feel I could breathe again. Wes reappeared at my side—where had *he* been all night? The man could talk to anyone.

"I met Annie," he said. "She's a riot, isn't she? You didn't tell me that."

"Oh sure," I said. "She'll joke you right out of your pants. The original man-eater."

Wes looked at me strangely. "Julia," he said, "I think you might be a little drunk."

"No, I'm fine." I looked down, picked a piece of lint off the bodice of my black cocktail dress, and held it out to Wes as though it was evidence of something. After a moment, he took it from me and let it drop to the floor.

"Why don't I take you home? My car is parked right up the street. I'm sure Annie can handle closing up."

"What are you talking about? I can't leave! This is *my* shop." The irritation I'd felt earlier swiftly returned. It was a feeling, I realized, I'd been experiencing a lot when I was with Wes lately. I was alone for weeks at a time, suffering in silent anguish, and he expected to swoop in and take care of me whenever it was convenient for his schedule? The fact that he didn't actually *know* I'd been suffering all that time was no excuse.

Wes was saved from the full force of my anger by the approach of a man I had noticed mingling all night with the crowd of chefs and bakers that Annie had invited to the opening. The man was sandy-haired and burly, out of place but self-possessed among the bespectacled, skinny-panted crowd. *Another journalist?* I doubted it, but summoned my most charming smile just in case.

"You're Julia, aren't you?" he asked.

"I am. Julia St. Clair. And this is Wesley Trehorn," I said. Not introducing Wes as my fiancé was a covert jab that I noted with satisfaction hit its mark precisely.

"Nice to meet you both. I'm Ogden Gertzwell." After a night of shaking hands with sycophantic strangers, I noted that Ogden's hand felt uniquely huge and warm and solid.

Ah, I thought. *The organic farmer.* I clicked my smile wattage down a notch. Annie had told me all about her day at Gertzwell Farm. In her particular Annie way, she'd described Ogden as a self-righteous bore who would be well served to figure out how to convert his long-winded orations into energy to fuel his farm. What Annie hadn't told me was how handsome he was. Or, if not *handsome* exactly, then hunky in that way guys could be when they had big noses and thick biceps.

"It's not every day I meet an Ogden," Wes said, giving the farmer's robust handshake a run for its money.

"Ogden of the delicious pears," I said, taking in his wide-wale corduroy pants rubbed bare at the knees, his plain black T-shirt hugging his broad chest, his calm, thoughtful eyes. "I hear we should be quite honored you selected us as the middlewomen between your fruit and the public."

A slow flush worked its way up Ogden's neck. He looked at Wes. "Ogden Nash," he explained. "My mother is really into punny poets."

"'I think that I shall never see / A billboard lovely as a tree. / Indeed, unless the billboards fall, / I'll never see a tree at all,'" Wes quoted theatrically.

As the two men eyed each other appreciatively, I worked hard not to roll my eyes.

"Have you seen Annie yet?" I asked.

"Seen but not spoken to," Ogden said. "She's quite the belle of the ball. It's been hard to get her attention."

We all looked toward the bar in the front window where Annie was laughing with her friend Becca. When she laughed like that, the usual sardonic posturing was swept from her face and she looked just like her mother. Growing up, it had always seemed to me that people came out of the woodwork to befriend Lucia—she'd had one of those open, sweet faces toward which people from all walks of life seemed to naturally gravitate. Annie, for all her sarcasm, had the same quality. She'd invited an eclectic group of friends and acquaintances to the party and each one—from this burly farmer with the dirt under his nails right up to my moneyed Lothario of an ex-boyfriend—seemed determined to wrangle some time with her. By comparison, my measly entourage of fiancé and parents felt pathetic. I drained the champagne in my glass quickly enough that it was possible to believe the sudden burning in my throat was from alcohol and not jealousy.

"Is there something in particular you want to say to her?" I asked Ogden, my voice almost singsong with teasing. "I'm very good at delivering messages."

Wes shot me a look.

"Oh, it's nothing," Ogden said. Even flustered he managed to hold himself very still. For a moment, I had a sense of the party flowing around him, like a river churning around a rock. "I just wanted to talk to her about the next delivery. We're seeing remarkable results with this new compost blend we're using. The Fuyus are coming in as big and glossy as tomatoes."

"Ah, the Fuyus," I said. I thought I kept the mocking tone in my head, but Wes shot me another look, his brow furrowed with disapproval.

"Persimmons," Ogden said. He cleared his throat. "We grow Fuyu persimmons."

"I see," I said. "You're a proud papa. I'll pass on the news to Annie."

Ogden was silent. He glanced again in Annie's direction. I had the distinct sense that she had been purposely evading eye contact with him all night. I felt something like pity for Ogden then, knowing firsthand just how cold Annie's cold shoulder could be.

"Well, okay," he said. "I've got a drive ahead of me so I should get on the road. Good night." He thought for a moment. "And congratulations. It seems like tonight was a big success."

"Great to meet you, Ogden," Wes said, clapping him heartily on the back. "I'm looking forward to trying those Fuyus."

I smiled and nodded but now the grasp I'd felt sure I had on myself was beginning to slip. The room seemed suddenly dim, the beat of the music too loud for the small space now that the crowd had thinned.

"Who turned down the lights?" I said to no one in particular once Ogden had left. "I didn't tell anyone they could do that."

"The lights are the same as they've been all night," Wes said, sighing. "Julia, you were very rude to Ogden." And then, almost to himself, he said, "I've never seen you like this."

I bristled. "Well, maybe you should leave then. I'd hate to disappoint you."

"I didn't say—"

"I know exactly what you didn't say," I interrupted, my tongue thick in my mouth. "My behavior may be a surprise to you, but *I* know *you* inside out. You couldn't surprise me if your life depended on it."

"Is that right?"

"Yes," I said, looking away.

"How sad," he said softly. "Maybe I shouldn't have come tonight. Didn't you say something about not mixing business and pleasure? You might have been on to something. Can you promise me you'll find your way safely home?"

"I promise." I'd meant to sound chilly, but the words came out childlike and small.

"Okay." He kissed my cheek, letting his hand linger for a moment on my shoulder before withdrawing it. "We'll talk tomorrow."

And then I was alone in the tapering crowd.

15

Annie

TREAT'S OPENING PARTY was turning out to be the prom I never had. I was decked out in a new dress, the music was pulsing, and I couldn't move a foot without bumping into a friend eager to shower me with a steady stream of praise. I deflected the first few compliments, but eventually I gave in and let the good vibes that were sent my way soak in. Sure, it was a decade late to aspire to being prom queen, but the people—*my* people—had spoken.

I'd invited practically everyone I knew to the party—Jake, Becca and Mike, Ernesto and Lorena and Carlos from Valencia Street Bakery, and numerous members of the interconnected circles of bakers and chefs and culinary world people with whom I'd worked and socialized over the years since college. It was the *This Is Your Life* of opening parties—everywhere I turned, there was someone from my past or present life supporting me. The only person missing, of course, was my mom. That month marked the ten-year anniversary of her death, but I tried not to dwell on that thought. Instead, I found myself imagining that she was somewhere in the room, trying each and every one of the cupcake flavors offered to her, her face radiant with pride.

There was even a moment that I could have sworn I smelled her distinctive vanilla-and-citrus scent; turning around, I realized I was only catching a whiff of a nearby tray of Key lime cupcakes, but the feeling of believing, if only for an instant, that my mom was close flooded me with a warmth that I carried with me for hours.

"This must be the famous Becca," Julia said, appearing beside Becca and me at the bar toward the end of the night. Julia's little black dress was typically classy but her words, I noticed, were atypically slurred. "I'm Julia St. Clair," she announced to Becca, sticking out her hand.

Becca shot me a look as she shook Julia's hand. "Why, hello, Julia St. Clair," she said, clipping her words with the hint of an English accent. "*Verrrry* pleased to meet you." I kicked her shin under the bar.

"It's so nice of you to make it tonight," Julia said. "This has been such an enormous labor of love for Annie and me and it's just wonderful so many people have come out to support us."

Labor of love? People? Us? Julia's words seemed strategically chosen to draw some line in the sand between Becca and the two of us. I would have thought Becca would have been too secure in our friendship to take the bait, but when I looked at her, I saw an angry glint in her eye.

"Oh, Becca knows I don't consider any party without her a party worth hosting," I said quickly. "Besides, with free booze and cupcakes, you couldn't have kept her away if you tried."

"It's true," Becca said. "If there's one thing I like even more than Annie's company, it's freebies."

"Well, you've hit the mother lode tonight," Julia said, releasing one of her carefully arranged smiles. "Did you try the pink lemonade cupcake yet? It's one of Annie's best. I'll track one down if you like."

I wondered if Julia had any idea how distantly she held herself, even when tipsy. *Loosen up!* I wanted to scream. *It's a party!* It seemed to me that she had painted herself into a corner with this persona of perfection, and she wasn't doing herself any favors. Why did she lock herself off like that? While I'd been having fun all night, she'd seemed tightly wound, her bare shoulders almost sinewy with tension.

"I'm actually more of a mocha gal," Becca said. "But thanks."

Looking back and forth between these two hardheaded women, I was struck by the sense that if Julia had actually been able to let her guard down and relax for a moment, she and Becca probably could have been friends. I felt sorry for Julia and the artificial life she seemed to have built for herself, but now that she had made her bed, I supposed all there was left for her to do was to lie in it.

When the last guests had left, and we had paid the waitstaff and sent them on their way, Julia and I drained the final dregs of champagne and savored a few final cupcakes. For the first time all night, Julia appeared to actually be enjoying herself. I walked around, turning off the lights in the kitchen and the shop one by one until the room was lit only by the streetlamp out front. If I hadn't been so surprised by the sight of Julia genuinely relaxed and happy, maybe I would have caught some glimpse of the shadowy figure awaiting us outside, but Julia's ridiculously sloppy attempt to eat a banana-toffee cupcake in her usual methodical manner provided an inordinate level of distraction.

"Why, Julia St. Clair, I do declare you're drunk!" I said, laughing.

Julia paused and frowned, but a split second later began giggling uncontrollably. "I am," she said, coughing and laughing as she looked down at the crumbs that had fallen on her dress.

"Drunk as a skunk." As if her body had been waiting for this cue all night, it suddenly lost its rigidity. She slumped forward, barely catching herself on the bar at the front window.

"Oh boy," I said. "You really are." I thought for a moment. "Maybe you should spend the night. I don't live far. Can you walk?"

This stoked another burst of laughter from Julia. "Can I walk? Can I *walk*? Can pigs fly?"

"Well, no, actually," I said. My shoulders, it turned out, were the perfect height for wearing her limp arm. "Let's go, Piglet."

"Heave ho, Pooh," she mumbled.

When we stepped outside, the cool night air seemed to revive her and I felt her straighten a bit at my side. Both of us must have seen the man at the exact same moment; our steps simultaneously faltered and then quickened in sync as we neared him, the only other person on the street at that late hour. Stocky in a black zippered sweatshirt and jeans, a dark cap shadowing his eyes, the man leaned against the shuttered bodega storefront next to the cupcakery and silently watched us hurry by. His footsteps immediately fell into an echoing rhythm behind us, the hard soles of his shoes crunching loudly against the sidewalk. My blood suddenly felt like it was pumping through my veins at twice its normal pace; my thoughts jumbled together indecipherably in my head.

"Hey!" the man called gruffly.

My heart leaped. I half turned around to face the man, but as I did Julia grabbed my arm and broke into a run. A group of twenty-somethings loitered on the corner at the end of the block. Julia sprinted toward them, dragging me along with her, apparently forgetting that we didn't all train for marathons in our spare time.

"Help!" she yelled. We didn't stop until we reached the group, and when we finally looked back, the empty sidewalk behind us glowed eerily below the flickering streetlight.

"Holy shit," I said, breathing hard. "That was scary."

The cluster of people on the corner had turned toward us. "Are you okay?" one of the guys asked, eyeing my flowing turquoise dress with an amused expression and swaying slightly as he lit a cigarette. The cloud of smoke and beer that clung to them turned my stomach.

Cars whizzed by us on this street, which was much busier than Twentieth. Even at that late hour, the sounds of traffic were punctuated by the laughter and chatter of people heading out, or in, for the night. "Yeah, we're fine. Thanks," I told the guy. At my side, Julia had turned a sickly shade of gray. "Let's go," I said to her. "My apartment's just a few blocks up the street."

As we walked, I couldn't help thinking of the graffiti that our contractor, Burt, had scrubbed out of the tiger-striped redwood bar. *You don't belong here.* After feeling so elated with the party, I now felt shaken and exhausted and confused all at once.

"You set the shop's alarm, right?" Julia asked in a strained voice.

"Locked and loaded." I usually followed up any discussion of the alarm with a comment about how I felt as safe in the Mission as in any other neighborhood in the city, but now I fell silent.

We walked the final blocks to my apartment in tense silence. It was only once I'd shut the locked steel gate at the front door behind us that I realized my teeth were chattering. The familiar carpeted flight of stairs now seemed impossibly long and I had to fight a strong urge to curl up right there at their base and fall asleep.

"I didn't know they had high-rises in this part of town," Julia said when we'd looped around what seemed like the tenth landing.

"I'm on the fourth floor—the top," I said. "You have a generous definition of a high-rise. I'll have to tell my landlady she should call my apartment a penthouse next time she lists it on Craigslist."

Once we finally reached my apartment, Julia made a bee-line for the emerald-colored velvet couch steps from the door. She was sound asleep within seconds, not stirring even when I slipped a pillow below her cheek. I collapsed on my bed and tried to regain some of the exhilaration I'd felt an hour earlier, but a feeling of unease kept me tossing and turning all night.

16

Julia

I awoke to blinding sunlight on my face, the sound of silverware against china, and the smell of coffee. My mouth tasted sour. I blinked and sat up to escape the relentless stream of sun. *Annie's apartment.* Each moment from the night before came back to me one at a time, like a puzzle being snapped together piece by piece. Annie and Jake kissing. Arguing with my mother. The interview with Lainey. Meeting Ogden Gertzwell. Fighting with Wes. The man who had lurked outside the cupcake shop, followed us, and then disappeared into the night. *Annie and Jake kissing.*

I spotted the open door of a bathroom across the living room and delicately made my way to it. Inside, I swished cold water in my mouth and swept the mascara smudges from under my eyes. I pulled a small hairbrush from my purse and ran it through my hair. My dress was remarkably wrinkle-free considering it had spent the night half wedged in a couch. *Thank God for wool blends*, I thought, settling my face into a composed half smile in the mirror. *And the minor miracle that is the Prada LBD.*

In the living room again, I took my first good look around. An overflowing bookshelf—IKEA, I surmised, cringing—separated the caramel-colored living room from what appeared to be Annie's bedroom. Between copies of Elizabeth Falkner's *Demolition Desserts* and Allen Ginsberg's *Howl*, I spotted an unmade platform bed with a quilt in vibrant shades of blue and an entire solar system of white paper globe lanterns hanging from the ceiling above it. The living room contained the now all-too-familiar emerald-green couch, an open laptop on a low coffee table—*how exactly had I slept through the annoying flicker of a computer light all night, considering I needed blackout drapes at home?*—and a full wine rack topped by iPod speakers and a photo of a school-age Annie with her mother, Lucia. I distinctly remembered taking that photo. It was at the San Francisco Zoo, beside the penguin pond. We had taken Muni all the way there, rejecting Curtis's offer to drive us in favor of the rare adventure and people watching that public transportation offered. Annie had shown me how to drop my change into the little metal machine at the front of the bus, and the tutorial had made me sullen for the rest of the bus ride, having deduced that Lucia and Annie were members of some club to which I didn't belong. I had this left-out feeling again, looking at that photo in Annie's living room. *The only reason you're not in the photo*, I chided myself, *is that you're the one who took it!*

"Hey, Julia. I'm in here," Annie called from around the corner. The kitchen was compact but sunny, with saffron-colored metal cabinets and spotless counters, the sort of kitchen someone who didn't have a splitting headache and a yearning for darkness might describe as "inviting." Annie was wrapped in a fuzzy white bathrobe, her hair messy and huge, her light brown eyes raccooned with mascara. The fact that she could pull off this look both impressed and bothered me. How hard was it to run a brush through your hair? I preferred to not look like I belonged on Hippie Hill in Golden Gate Park with a shopping cart full of blankets and cans, though I admitted, begrudgingly, that Annie did look more the part of bohemian beauty than greasy park dweller.

Squinting in the sunlight, I lowered myself into the other chair at the small white table and accepted the mug of steaming coffee that Annie offered. *So much for tea, fruit, and chocolate croissants*, I thought, my stomach rumbling petulantly for my usual breakfast menu.

"I'm making chocolate croissants," Annie said, as though reading my mind. She nodded toward the oven, and sure enough, a sweet, buttery scent filled the room. *How did I miss that?*

"Wonderful," I said. *But you still shouldn't be dating my ex.*

"Well," she said, "other than our little run-in with the world's creepiest man, I'd say things went pretty well last night."

I felt my eyes widen, remembering. "That was terrifying." I tried to recall the man's face, but it was blurred by drink and darkness. I cupped my hands around the chipped coffee mug in front of me and took a long sip, feeling its bitterness coat and dampen the putrid taste in my mouth. "But, yeah, otherwise, I think the party went perfectly."

"Now I just have to wring the champagne out of my liver and get in there and start baking. Doors open at ten."

I groaned. "What time is it now?"

"Seven. But don't worry, I've got it covered," Annie said, laughing. "You don't have to come in today. Tanya and Eduardo are already in the kitchen. Devi is coming in to cover the register."

Devi was one of the two college girls I had hired to help out in the front of the store. She was serene but savvy, an old soul with wide, almond eyes, skin the color of iced tea, and a glittering nose ring that annoyed me to no end but would probably make the Mission crowd feel right at home at Treat.

"I'll come in. I can't miss our first day," I said. "I just need to go home and change. But I'll be there, I promise."

"I'm not worried," Annie said.

We sat in silence a moment, breathing in the rich chocolate scent that was filling the room.

"So," I said, clearing my throat a little. My eyes still felt swollen and dry, but I blinked them into alert submission. "I saw you with Jake last night."

"Oh." Annie tapped her forefinger against her lips, thinking. "Well, we weren't trying to hide anything."

"Clearly."

She blushed. "I was going to tell you, but honestly, I didn't know what to say. We're not anything serious yet. I don't know what we are. I probably shouldn't even be saying 'we.'"

"But you like him?"

Annie looked at me steadily. "Julia, you know I've always liked Jake." As usual, I had the sense she was looking right through me. *What do you see?* I wanted, and at the same time had no desire whatsoever, to know.

"Well, that was when we were fourteen," I said. "I don't still like Gummi bears and scrunchies."

Annie smiled. "Are you comparing Jake to a scrunchie?" She didn't seem to be taking this conversation seriously at all.

"You know what I mean. This isn't high school. He's not the guy you think he is. I don't want you to get hurt."

Whenever Annie got excited or angry her nostrils flared like a horse's. Or, given her diminutive stature, perhaps more like a pony's. They began flaring now. I could practically hear her mentally stomping her tiny hooves.

"You don't want me to get hurt," she repeated. "That's very thoughtful of you."

"Annie, come on. Trust me. I know Jake really well. I know how fun and charming he is. But I also know he's married."

Annie's eyes flashed. "What?"

"He didn't tell you, did he?" I sighed. "That's probably because to him, marriage doesn't mean much. He treats everything too lightly. I don't want him to treat you that way, too." I worried that every word I said fell like a brick between us, building that decade-old wall back up, but I couldn't stop myself.

"Jake is married," Annie repeated slowly. The skin on her cheeks had grown blotchy in a way that reminded me of her mother.

"He married his college sweetheart," I said, swallowing a sip of hot coffee. "Gorgeous girl. One of those white-blond, lives-in-a-bikini, surfer types. I heard their wedding was absolutely beautiful. Jake invited me, of course, but I didn't think it was appropriate, me being his ex-girlfriend and everything. I didn't want her to feel awkward on her wedding day. I guess she's working as a stylist in L.A. now."

"So they're divorced?"

"No. Separated. As in, still married."

Annie's eyes narrowed. "And you're just voicing these concerns out of friendship. This has nothing to do with the fact that he's your ex-boyfriend?" she asked, incredulity dripping off her words like melted butter. "Nothing at all?"

"Nothing at all," I repeated. "Really." Even I could hear the lie. *Why can't I just tell her the truth? That some of this is jealousy and some of this is sincere concern? Would that be so terrible to admit?* I felt tempted to tell Annie everything then—what happened at the hospital, my secret meetings with Jake, the missed wedding appointments. I wanted, I realized suddenly, to be one of those girls who had a best friend with whom to share things. But I wasn't one of those girls, and probably never would be. I wasn't sure I could bear the messiness that came with such honesty.

Annie looked at me, waiting, but I couldn't bring myself to say anything more. Finally, she rose from the table and opened the oven, releasing a wave of hot, cloyingly sweet air into the room. The tray of glistening croissants dropped against the top of the stove with an abrupt clatter.

"Don't burn yourself," she said thinly, and left me to sit alone in the too-bright kitchen.

17

Annie

"HE'S *WHAT*?" BECCA screeched when I told her the news about Jake's marital status during Craptastic Sunday. The baking was done for the day at Treat, *The Bachelorette* was paused on the DVR, and a second glass of Cabernet Sauvignon glimmered dark and promising in my hand—it seemed as good a time as any to update my friend on the whole dating-a-married-man thing.

"It's fine," I said, shrugging, trying to keep my voice nonchalant. "Or it will be. They've been separated for six months. It's not like I'm the other woman or anything."

In truth, the marriage bombshell had really freaked me out. I couldn't believe Jake had omitted such a critical detail. Among other things, it made me doubt how seriously he took our relationship. Of course, I'd confronted him straightaway and had been both shocked and relieved when he didn't deny it.

"I don't know why I didn't tell you," he'd said. I'd appreciated, grudgingly, that he hadn't tried to take my hand, just looked me straight in the eye with his arms hanging a little forlornly at his sides. "Because I'm a moron, I guess. Kiley and I have officially been separated for six months, but grew apart a long time before that. This isn't a recent thing—I'm not hiding some deep, bleeding wound. I guess I don't talk about it because I feel like I've already dealt with it and moved on. But I should have told you. I hope you don't feel like I lied to you about anything."

In a lot of ways, I did feel like he'd lied to me, but I knew that he had never actually fed me any false information. Still, her name—*Kiley? What kind of name is that?*—landed on my ears like a second affront. Jake watched me take this new information in, the set of his face open and honest and apologetic. I realized, with both relief and irritation, that I wasn't ready to give up on him, or us. I warned myself to proceed with caution, and accepted his apology.

"Don't pull this shit with me again, Jake," I'd said. "I'm not a three-strikes-and-you're-out kind of girl. This is it. If there are any more secrets, you better tell me now."

Jake was silent for a moment before his eyes brightened. I could practically hear his dimples clamoring for release. "I ate a cupcake the other day, and it wasn't one of yours," he said. "I was at a party. Everyone was doing it. I promise I didn't enjoy it."

I looked at him, debating whether or not I wanted to follow him down this path away from a more serious line of conversation. I decided I did. I shook my head, feigning a look of disgust. "You dirty bastard."

"Can you ever forgive me?"

"I can," I'd said, and despite our swift retreat into humor, I'd felt a little disconcerted at how easy the words were to say.

I repeated Jake's explanation about his separation to Becca now: he and Kiley had gotten married straight out of college and had found within a few short years that they'd both become different people, people who weren't in love with one another. The divorce, which involved interpretation of a prenuptial agreement, was taking longer than either wanted. It was a plausible, if unromantic, story, and without talking to Jake's ex, it was the only one I got.

Becca wound her chestnut hair against the side of her head, her blue eyes studying me. I worried I sounded like I was making excuses for him.

"Reasons aside, he's a jerk for not telling you. Right?" she demanded. When she was indignant, her freckles seemed to flare up like little embers against her pale skin.

"Oh yeah." I nodded. "Total jerk."

Becca sank back into the couch and took a long sip of wine. "I guess he's lucky he's so hot."

"I know. It's very important that I continue to judge him solely by his cover."

"Excellent strategy," Becca said. "At the end of the day, it's not his honesty keeping you warm at night—"

"—it's his hot, hot bod."

We both laughed and I tried to cover the twinge of discomfort I felt with a sip of wine. It was easy to make light of my relationship with Jake, but if I admitted the truth to myself, I didn't actually feel so lightly about him. I was falling, in fact, quite heavily. And I had a growing suspicion the landing was not going to be a soft one.

"Anyway," Becca said, tucking her bare feet underneath her, "let's forget Jake for a minute and focus on shooting the messenger. Julia must have been smug as hell delivering that bit of news. I bet she acted all sweet and innocent, like she was just trying to help. Phony cow."

I felt another pang of unease. This was the moment I would typically dive into the conversation with some easy jibe, mocking Julia's snobbery or her ridiculous competitiveness. Today, though, I hesitated. I thought of Julia at the very end of Treat's opening party, how those glasses of champagne had made her relaxed, goofy—almost fun. Of course, the next morning her rigid veneer of composure had returned, but still. The memory of the two of us closing up the shop together, giddy with joy over the party's success, lingered, overshadowing even my annoyance about the insensitive way she'd delivered the news of Jake's marital status. And the next day, after that argument, we'd been shocked to open Treat's door to a line ten people long. I'd invited a slew of food bloggers to the opening party and it turned out a couple of them had already posted favorably about Treat's cupcakes and ambience. Opening the door to that line, and the even longer lines that followed it all week, I'd watched Julia struggle to keep her face cool and professional while her eyes sparkled with excitement and pride. And I'd known just how she felt.

"You know," I said slowly, staring ahead at the paused television rather than meeting Becca's penetrating gaze, "part of me *does* believe that she told me about Jake because she wants to protect me. I know it's more complicated than just that—the girl has serious issues—but I'm actually tempted to give her the benefit of the doubt on this one. I don't think having to be the one to tell me Jake is married made her particularly happy."

Becca looked baffled. "What are you saying?" she asked. "Julia got *precisely* what she wanted. She one-upped you. It's the exact kind of shit you've always said she pulled all the time when you guys were kids. Competing is her modus operandi. Right? She's bitchy and cutthroat and fake. Isn't that what you've always said?"

"Oh, come on—don't be snarky just to be snarky," I said, surprising myself. I guess it was one thing for me to say those things about Julia, and quite another for Becca to say them. "I'm telling you, it wasn't like that this time. Besides, remember: I'm trying not to let her suck the humor out of me."

Becca seemed on the verge of responding, but after a moment she pressed her lips tight together and sat back into the couch.

"What?" I said. "Just say it."

She shrugged. "I'm sorry," she said. "I guess I didn't realize."

"Realize what?"

"That you think of Julia like a sister."

I laughed. "Please excuse me while I throw up all over the table."

"You do! You're envious of each other and you drive each other crazy, but at the end of the day, you don't want to hear anyone else say a bad word about her. Julia is family. I just can't believe I never saw it before."

"Becca, I think that one psych class you took in college permanently scarred some critical part of your brain."

"Maybe, but you two are more alike than you think," she continued, undeterred. I was astonished to hear the sharp bite of jealousy in her voice. "You're sarcastic and independent. Julia's a control freak and independent. You're both loners pretending not to be. You're both probably lonely."

"Well, who isn't?" I asked. "If loneliness were the only criterion for being family, I'd be related to everyone in the world. And if I share genes with a lonely heart like, say, Jennifer Aniston, I demand to know how I missed out on the washboard abs and big, pearly whites."

"The pearly whites are man-made," Becca said with a faint smile. I could tell I'd hurt her feelings. How was it possible that Becca resented my relationship with Julia? Becca who had a great boyfriend, a clan of boisterous, bear-hugging brothers, and a mother who still regularly sent her care packages of Rice Krispies treats? She leaned away from me on the couch, her face tight. Up until that point, our friendship had been miraculously spat-free—I hardly knew how to proceed. The silence was excruciating. My thoughts turned to the silly slapstick routines and impersonations I used to trot out when my mom was feeling blue.

"So," I said then, nudging her thigh with my toe. "Have you heard the one about Jake being married?"

I'd be lying if I said that after Julia told me Jake was married I hadn't asked myself for the umpteenth time why I'd allowed all of our lives to become so entangled yet again. If I could have simply walked away from both Jake and Julia at that point, maybe I would have. And, looking back, maybe I should have; it certainly would have averted some of the danger we soon found ourselves facing. But Jake, despite everything, made me happy. And Julia? I imagined us divvying up our shared assets on the sidewalk of Twentieth Street like a squabbling couple that had finally admitted any attempt at cohabitation was futile. *Hey, Jules*, I'd say. *I'm outta here, and I've got dibs on the muffin pans.*

The problem, one of them at least, was that by then I was already in love, and Jake Logan, for once, had nothing to do with it. In the fast few weeks since our opening, I'd fallen head over heels in love with Treat. During the hours before daybreak when I worked alone in the kitchen, I'd pinch myself and repeat over and over again: *This is mine. This is mine. This is mine.* The slight creak of the front door when it opened. The sounds of customers' shoes on the wood floors and threadbare carpets. The cushiony thud of the glass cupcake case opening and clos-ing. The early mornings when vendors would deliver dry goods and dairy and fruit. The old-fashioned whoosh of the register drawer with each sale. The unbelievable feeling of fulfilling a dream, and having it all happen sooner, bigger, and better than I could have ever hoped. I was deep, deep in love.

As well as things were going, the shop was still brand-new, and without Julia, it could all slip away from me. Yes, I needed her money, but I'd long since realized her value lay in more than her bank account. Even over the radio in the kitchen, I could

hear her talking to customers, upselling them a few more cupcakes in a way that made them feel like it had been their own
idea to try a few chocolate cheesecakes in addition to their usual
Meyer lemon dozen. She had a way of listening and talking to
customers that warmed them up immediately; I'm sure her an-
gelic face and big blue eyes didn't hurt that immediate bond of
trust she seemed to establish with people when she set her mind
to it. Why was it that she could be so intuitive and relaxed with
strangers and yet couldn't translate any of those people skills to
her personal life? Her easy banter with people she'd probably
never see again struck me as incredibly sad. But, as Becca might
have said: *Sad shmad*. Julia was good for business. No shock
there. I only wished my mother could have seen how successful
Treat was becoming. And that our menu could have been graced
by one of the recipes it seemed she'd taken with her to the grave.
And so, like parents who stay together for the child, Julia and
I worked to keep our conversations focused on common goals.
Besides, I kept telling myself, *it's only until May*. By then, Treat
would have an established clientele and Julia would ride off into
the sunset with Wes.

"The vanilla-chocolate cupcakes sell out every single day,"
Julia was saying, reading from her laptop during our weekly
after-hours powwow on all things Treat. We sat at the shop's
front bar and I looked more at Julia's reflection in the darkened
window than I did at her actual face. I splayed my fingers on
the glossy redwood bar that bore no hint of the graffiti that had
covered it not so long ago. But, somehow, I could still see that
graffiti as clearly as if it had never been removed. *You don't belong
here*. The words glowed phantomlike, drifting up to the surface
of the bar when I least expected them to, words that had followed me from childhood to adulthood, words that struck me as
equal part criticism, warning, and threat.

"Up the count on the vanilla-chocolate," I said. "Got it."

"And we have to get the word out that we're available for weddings. We're not going to turn a profit selling one, two, even a dozen cupcakes at a time. We have to get into parties."

"Story of my life," I said.

Julia smiled and seemed almost hesitant for a moment. "I have a few new ideas," she said. "If you're open to them."

"Hit me."

"After-hours cupcake-baking parties. Girls' night outs, bachelorette parties—those kind of things. It could be a mess, but a lucrative one. And it wouldn't cut into our daytime selling hours, like kids' birthday parties would."

I wondered if this bachelorette party idea was some sort of veiled reference to her own wedding. It was easy to forget that Julia was engaged. She never spoke about her upcoming wedding. Would she have a bachelorette party? Did she have bridesmaids? If she'd made a single friend in the past decade, I'd yet to meet her.

"I like it," I said, not taking the bait on any hidden agenda. But Julia didn't seem to expect me to say anything more. She just nodded, typed a note in her laptop—*That bitch Annie won't throw me a bachelorette party*, perhaps?—and read the next idea from her list.

"A cupcake truck. Taco trucks do it, why can't we? We could drive downtown and hit the big office buildings during the lunch rush. If I was working in one of those buildings and a Treat truck pulled up during my lunch hour, I'd eat a cupcake every day."

I had no doubt that Julia could easily put back at least one cupcake a day without ever adding an ounce to her slender, toned frame. *Runners.* Was there any more annoying population in the world? Fifteen minutes into our meeting, she was already halfway through her second chocolate cupcake, eating it in her slow, disciplined, Julia-specific way. So far during that meeting I had wolfed down one coffee cupcake, telling myself the caffeine would rev my metabolism, and then consoled myself with sips of actual coffee while I watched Julia dive lip gloss first into her second. And still, her legs looked like toothpicks in her skinny jeans. *If I ate that many cupcakes,* I thought, *I'd wind up wearing them around my hips like dimpled holsters.* The cupcake cowgirl. Not as cute as it sounded.

"A cupcake truck. Brilliant," I said. "But I worry that we're still just getting things off the ground here in the shop. It's only been a few weeks. I already feel like I live here—which is fine, a cupcakery makes for a surprisingly lovely second home—but we probably shouldn't spread ourselves too thin."

"Oh, absolutely," Julia said hurriedly. "Couldn't have said it better myself. I just want us to know what's in the pipeline. We should have ideas nailed down for when we're ready to grow."

"Right," I said. "The nailing and the piping. I forgot that's why I keep you around."

Julia laughed. She snapped her laptop shut. "You're right. I'm getting ahead of myself. Let's just focus on the shop for now."

I could tell she was embarrassed. Don't ask me how I knew, because on the outside she was all easy-peasy confidence. Our shared childhood ran deeper in my veins than I cared to admit, though I still preferred to think of it as Stockholm syndrome rather than friendship. *I'm just identifying with my captor.*

"I meant to tell you I liked Wes a lot," I said, apropos of nothing. I guess I was trying to make her feel better. "We spoke at the opening party."

Even with his Southern twang, Wes had the rich, melodic voice of an NPR newscaster, and I'd been surprised by how much I liked him from the moment he introduced himself at the party. He didn't have any hint of that pretentious, upper-crust vibe I'd always assumed was Julia's type. Knowing he loved Julia made me attempt to look at her anew. Soon after, I started to notice that she asked me how I was doing every single day, and

not just in an offhanded, polite way, but in a way that convinced me she really wanted to know. She asked me questions
about baking that I was surprised to find I enjoyed answering. I
wouldn't have enjoyed those questions half as much if she'd been
blowing smoke up my ass, but I could tell she was legitimately
curious. I'd forgotten that when it was just you and Julia, and
no one else was around, she looked at you straight-on and with
full attention as though you were the only person in the world.
It was a quality my mother had had as well, and one, I realized
with a start, that she had probably instilled in Julia. All of Julia's
focus, her drive, her determination, zeroed in on you as you
spoke and you could almost *feel* her listening, digesting, empa-
thizing with your words. It was a remarkable skill and I could
only wonder why she didn't employ it more often. Probably, if
she could have, she would have.

But she still hadn't apologized for what she'd done to me in
high school, and until she did there would always be a partition
of ice between us that would not melt, leaving a slight chill to
our every interaction.

"He liked you, too," Julia said. "He said you were funny."

I could tell something about this troubled Julia, though I
could not for the life of me imagine what.

"Two girls, one fat, one thin, walk into a cupcake shop—"

"You've got a better repertoire than that," she interrupted,
taking the final bite of her second cupcake. I decided it wouldn't
kill her to hang out with a little smudge of chocolate cake on
her lip.

Meeting adjourned, I double-checked that all of the ovens
were off in the kitchen while Julia switched off the lights in the
shop. She set the alarm, and its frantic beeping hurried us onto
the sidewalk. We'd gotten in the habit of walking together to
Julia's car; she'd drop me off at my apartment a few blocks away
on her way back to Pacific Heights.

the simple fact that an unknown man was walking down the same dark street we were? Did that incident alone give us the right to assume the guy was up to no good? I convinced myself the whole thing was a misunderstanding—he was just a guy who lived nearby, he wasn't following us, he wasn't threatening us.

But now that he'd approached us in that way on the sidewalk, gruff and menacing, his hands jammed into his sweatshirt pocket like he was hiding something, I could no longer deny that his presence was a real threat.

"I've seen him a couple of other times, too," I admitted to Julia and Ramirez. "I think he's been hanging around the shop a lot." Julia looked at me, her eyes wide. "I thought maybe he lived in the neighborhood," I said to her quietly. "We don't have proof of anything. I didn't want to worry you."

"I'm afraid Ms. Quintana's right," Ramirez said. "We really don't know what this guy is up to. Nonetheless, there *are* some things you can do to take charge of your own safety. Don't leave the shop alone at night. Always have a buddy." Despite the circumstances, I couldn't help smiling at this. Julia and I had perfected the buddy system back in elementary school. "Tell your employees what's going on," Inspector Ramirez continued. "Keep alert. Buy Mace. Always carry a cell phone. Call us if you see him again or if anything else happens. Use common sense."

I stifled a laugh. This was quickly deteriorating into a public service announcement. Julia looked at me sharply.

"Take this seriously," she said.

"I am," I said, deadpan. "I plan to exercise my common sense to the full extent of the law."

Now it was Inspector Ramirez's turn to look at me sharply. "The worst thing you could do would be to take matters into your own hands. Don't confront this guy. If you see him again, I need you to call 911. Or," he said, handing me a card from his wallet, "call me directly."

I turned the card over in my hand, sighing. "Oh, I didn't mean anything. I cower in the face of violence. I can't even watch *Bambi*!"

Julia rolled her eyes and turned to Ramirez. "Thank you," she said. "Would you mind walking us to my car?"

We went through all the motions of closing up the shop again—turning off the lights, activating the alarm, switching the deadbolt. It was eleven p.m. by then and the street was quiet save for the occasional car whizzing by. Below the streetlight on the corner I saw a group of men huddled together, but none had the stocky build of our guy. *Our guy*. We had a guy now. Great. Inspector Ramirez walked us to Julia's car as promised and waited on the sidewalk until we'd locked the doors behind us and pulled into the street. I noticed Julia's knuckles were white as she gripped the steering wheel.

"It's okay," I told her. "That's the last we'll see of him. I'm sure your Native American huntress scream scared the crap out of him."

Julia breathed out a laugh. "Was that me? I thought that was you!"

"No way. Are you kidding? I scream like a little girl. You scream like a freaking entertainment wrestler. I thought you were going to put that guy in a half nelson."

Her tight grip on the wheel began to loosen. "Why is he hanging around? Everything else about the shop is going so well. I love walking through the door each morning. I feel so happy there all day. Really, it's the best I've felt in . . . a long time. And now I feel like he's poisoning it."

This was about as forthright as Julia got. I heard in her voice a hint of that sadness I'd seen dulling her polished edges at the Save the Children benefit so many months ago. I felt a strong— *sisterly?*—urge to reward her for this show of vulnerability, to show her that she wasn't alone. Maybe Becca was right. Maybe my relationship—my *friendship*, there, I admitted it—with Julia was different from any other because of all we'd been through together. All I knew was that, despite how miserable she'd made me over the years, it gave me no joy whatsoever to see her so unhappy now.

"I love Treat, too," I said. "And . . . I'm incredibly grateful for everything you've done. We can't let this guy rain on our parade." It was as Girl Power as I got.

Julia pulled up in front of my apartment building. She looked over at me and smiled. It was her real smile, not the perfect, composed one she usually displayed, but the one that was wide and sort of cockeyed. I hadn't seen it in years. As I was about to shut the door behind me, she leaned over the passenger seat and called out, "Buddy One!"

"Buddy Two," I responded, wincing and grinning at the same time at our ridiculous hokiness.

November

18

Julia

"Julia!" my mother called. "Oh, Juuuuuliaaaaa!"

I walked from my room to the top of the stairs and looked down. The odd angle made my mother look like a floating head, her body hidden beneath her smooth, round bob.

"There you are!" she said. "Why we didn't install an intercom system in this place years ago, I'll never know. Have you seen your father's Cartier watch? He can't find it anywhere. He'd lose his own head, if it weren't—"

"No," I said, interrupting. I hated when my mother talked about my father as if he weren't there. I could hear him speaking to Curtis in the kitchen at that very moment, their duet of deep, muffled voices as comfortingly familiar as an old nursery rhyme, so it was safe to assume he could hear us, too. "When did he wear it last?"

My mother threw up her hands. "Sunday, he thinks. He doesn't really know." Suddenly, she was striding up the stairs. I took a few steps back from the landing. Within moments, she stood in front of me, not in the least bit out of breath from the climb, her head lowered conspiratorially. "He also lost his Hermès cuff links a couple months ago. You know, the ones I got him for his birthday last year. Did he tell you that? He never used to be so careless! I'm starting to think I shouldn't buy him anything nice. Let him go to the opera with safety pins in his cuffs! That will teach him."

"Should we be worried?" I asked, ignoring her indignant tone. "It's not like him to be so absentminded." I thought of my father's desk, with his Montblanc pens lined up perfectly straight in the drawer, the monogrammed crocodile skin box that held a carefully edited, alphabetized stack of associates' business cards, the silver tray of mail that he read and discarded or appropriately filed daily. A place for everything and everything in its place.

My mother raised her eyebrows. "Oh, don't be silly. Your father is fine. Sharp as a tack. He does these things for the simple pleasure of driving me crazy."

"Are you sure?" I lowered my voice. "I've noticed a few things, too. The other day I found his car keys in the silverware drawer."

"Julia darling, when is the last time you saw your father drive himself anywhere? Curtis must have put them there."

"Well, there have been other strange things, too."

"And I'm sure there's a reasonable explanation for each of them," she said dismissively.

If there was one thing that irritated me more than anything else, it was when my mother didn't take me seriously. In high school, in college, in graduate school, in business meetings across the globe, people immediately took me seriously—but at home, when push came to shove, I was just a daughter. In the eyes of mothers, it seemed, daughters never truly grow up. I'd found, over the years, that this realization made me speak less and less openly with my mother. She didn't seem to notice, filling the air with opinions and anecdotes and advice until it seemed every room in the house was crowded with her words and there was barely room for anyone else to breathe.

She must have noticed my frustration because she added, "If it makes you feel any better, I'll keep an eye out for anything off-kilter. You have enough on your plate without worrying about this."

Which overflowing plate, exactly, is she referring to—everything that has been happening at Treat? The wedding? Or something else? Not for the first time, I wondered how much my mother had deduced about the true cause of my abrupt return home that summer. She raked her manicured fingernails through her white-blond hair, smoothing some imagined imperfection, her pale blue eyes trained on me.

"Julia darling, I hope you don't think these little foibles of your father somehow keep me from seeing the elephant in the room."

My heart skipped a beat. "Which elephant is that?"

"The *gown*, darling!" she rasped. "The wedding gown! I can handle the rest of the planning, but the dress . . . we simply must go shopping. And I'm not using the royal 'we,' my dear. I mean *you and I* must go shopping, with emphasis on the *you*. Time is running out! Only six more months until your wedding! A wedding gown can take *years* to make!"

The dress! Of course. I hadn't actually forgotten this critical piece of the wedding puzzle; I'd simply slid it, along with everything else related to the Big Day, into a mental folder marked TBD, and filed it somewhere between my return on investment predictions for Treat and the winter nail polish colors I'd seen in *Vogue*. I pulled out my phone and checked my online calendar. Every day had a block of time reserved for Treat, and I felt protective of that time now the way I used to only feel about the time I carved out for long runs, the early morning hour I spent reading the *Wall Street Journal*, and the rare weekend Wes and I would steal away, sans cell phones, to Woodstone, my parents' vineyard in St. Helena. Though I hated the thought of cutting my time at Treat short even for one day—the possibility of leaving Annie in the lurch, the likelihood of missed upsell opportunities with only Devi manning the counter—I knew from the look on my mother's face that it was unavoidable.

"Can you clear your schedule on December third?" I asked.

My mother nodded, pleased. "Anything for you." Then her brow wrinkled as much as it could, two little furrows forming on either side of the bridge of her nose. "But I'm warning you, if you don't show up—"

"I'll be there, Mom. I promise."

"Good." She spun on her kitten heel. "Tad darling!" she rasped, clicking rapid-fire back down the stairs. She had a habit of speaking in full sentences to people who weren't even within eyesight, assuming, I suspected, that the whole world stopped to listen whenever she spoke. "If you can't find the Cartier, you'll just have to wear the Tiffany!"

19

Annie

A WEEK BEFORE Thanksgiving, Jake and I had one of those ridiculously perfect dates that I'd previously thought were only the stuff of romantic comedies starring Kate Hudson. We ate dinner in a tiny North Beach Italian restaurant with a back patio all cozy and aglow below crisscrossing strings of twinkly white lights and full-blast heat lamps. It was the kind of night that makes it easy to forget the guy you're dating is actually married to someone else. The expensive wine coated my throat with warm notes of fig and vanilla. Mozzarella melted like cream on my tongue and a jumble of lacy and tubular wild mushrooms lent an earthy heartiness to a glistening plate of homemade pappardelle. The dessert—my litmus test for any restaurant, of course—was a flourless chocolate cake so dense and rich that most people would have put down their forks, happily satiated, after a few bites. But Jake knew to untangle his hand from mine when the waiter set the two plates down on the table. Within minutes, I'd finished my entire slice. *Be still*, I thought, *o heart of mine*, when I looked up to see that Jake had also scraped his plate clean. *Finally*, I thought, grinning at him, not caring that my teeth were probably stained a lovely shade of dark chocolate. *A real* man.

Oh! The conversation? It was okay.

I kid! We joked and opined and butted heads flirtatiously tit for tat all dinner long. At the end of the meal, as we sipped our last bit of wine and waited for the check to arrive, Jake nudged my foot. I smiled at him, but his gaze had an unfamiliar, serious set to it. I felt my heart clench.

"You never talk about your mother," he said.

I released the breath I hadn't realized I was holding. "Oh, I do," I said. "I talk about her all the time. I love talking about her. I love talking about her in a totally healthy, normal way."

Jake grinned, relaxing, dimples firing on all cylinders. "What was she like?"

I thought for a moment. "She was very *good*. She was a hard worker—one of those people who seem tireless, like they can function perfectly well on five hours of sleep." I drew circles on the base of my wineglass, trailing my short fingernails against the glass. "She was a wonderful mother. Of course, I never got a chance to know her as an adult, so my memory of her is probably kind of sentimental. Still, I'm pretty sure that everything she did, every choice she made, she made with my well-being foremost in her mind. She'd had a hard childhood. Her own mother was tough as nails and kicked her out of the house when she got pregnant at sixteen. That's when she left Ecuador and came here."

"She sounds brave," Jake said.

I nodded. "When I was young I always thought she seemed very shy when she spoke with anyone but me or Julia. Now I realize she was just a kid herself. A kid trying to navigate a new country, a new language, motherhood, being an employee. Can you imagine? Anyway, as we both got older, she started to lose that reticence. Her laugh became . . . *bigger*—not just more frequent, but louder, longer, more confident. I like to think I had something to do with that."

"I'm sure you did," Jake said. My heart seemed to swell suddenly and I looked down at my plate. After a moment, he reached across the table and put his hand on mine. His brown hair fell boyishly across his forehead. "How did she die?"

I swallowed. Ten years after my mother's death, it still felt like it had happened yesterday. *You should be able to talk about this without getting upset*, I told myself.

"She had a brain aneurysm. It was completely out of nowhere." I shook my head and released a strangled little laugh. "*Completely out of nowhere*," I repeated, sipping my wine. "I don't know why I said that. Like something can be *sort of* out of nowhere. Or just a *little bit* shocking. *Mildly* life altering."

"I'm sorry," Jake said, stroking my fingers. "If you don't want to talk about it, I understand."

"No, I'm fine. Thanks."

Our waiter deposited the bill in front of Jake and he dropped his card on it without checking to make sure they hadn't charged us for an extra bottle of wine, or three desserts, or the lobster instead of the pasta. I summoned the tiny reserve of self-control that is apparently pooled in some shadowy, rarely accessed part of my brain and managed to resist the urge to stop the waiter from taking away Jake's card before I had a chance to give the bill a quick once-over.

"Did you ever think of finding your father?" Jake asked, startling me out of an imaginary wrestling match with the waiter.

I thought for a moment. "You know, I must have at some point. Right? It would be weird if I never did. But I think I must have had the thought and dismissed it in the same moment. My mom never told me anything about him, so it's almost like he never existed. I'm just my mother's daughter. There's no one else."

Jake smiled and leaned back in his chair, his blue-green gaze warm. "I don't meet girls like you every day."

"What, you mean orphaned, first-generation American cupcake bakers with immaculate conception complexes? We're a dime a dozen."

"I guess I just haven't been looking in the right places."

"Kitchens," I said. "We hang out in kitchens. And mangers. You know, around Christmas."

We both had early mornings so we ended the night with a steamy make-out session in his car parked outside my apartment. Growing up as a city kid with few boyfriend prospects, I'd missed out on that whole teenagers-making-out-in-cars stage. Leaning into Jake under the moon roof, feeling his lips pressed warm and urgent against my neck, his hands tangled in my hair, the car seat heater jacked up to the level of hot embrace, I realized for the first time just how gypped I'd been.

Jake and I were still at the point in our relationship where every kiss electrified my entire body with anticipation and that greedy feeling of wanting more, more, *more*. By the time I shut the car door behind me and waved good-bye through its window, I was hopped up on life, buzzing and overheated, and not ready to return to my quiet apartment. I needed to talk to someone—not about Jake necessarily, but just to talk. I wanted to extend that feeling of connection, to take advantage of one of those fleeting moments when I didn't feel on my own in the world, but connected to everyone. *We all love! We all kiss!* my brain was ruminating at full speed. *We all bask in the glow of other humans' warmth! How pathetically wonderful!* The person I wanted to call, I realized, was not my best friend, Becca, but Julia St. Clair. Before I could overthink anything, I dialed her number. I had no idea what I planned to say.

She answered the call immediately. "You got my message," she said by way of greeting. Her voice was low and glum. I could barely hear her.

My stomach dropped, my runaway happy thoughts slamming

hard into the wall that was her tone. "No," I said. "What happened?"

"Someone threw a brick at Treat's front window. It's cracked, but not shattered; we'll need to replace it. The alarm went off. I'm at the shop now."

"Oh no," I breathed. "Are the police there?"

"Yes. The inimitable Ramirez is on the scene."

"Good. I'm walking there now—I'm just a few blocks away." I realized I'd started walking toward the shop the moment I'd heard Julia's voice.

"Okay. Be careful."

"Yup," I said, and immediately cast a nervous glance over my shoulder.

"Wait, Annie?" Julia said as I was about to hang up. "You didn't know about the window? That's not why you were calling?"

"No, I . . ." I hesitated. Why had I called Julia? Whatever feelings I'd had moments earlier were now completely inaccessible. "Honestly, I have no idea why I was calling. Baker's intuition?"

Julia laughed, and the sound relieved me. Everything was going to be okay. "You're bizarre," she said. "Now, walk faster."

December

20

Julia

SINCE THE INCIDENT with the window, things had been noticeably calmer at Treat. Well, maybe not calmer, exactly—the
shop bustled with customers each and every day, and I sometimes felt that I was working harder at this little cupcake venture
than I had ever worked at any multimillion-dollar deal in all
my time in New York. But the fractured front window had
been quickly replaced, and other than having to step over the
occasional sidewalk condom or crack vial on the walk from my
car to Treat's door each morning, or having to put in a call to
a painter to cover some relatively benign graffiti that appeared
on the front door every so often, it seemed that the Mission had
finally decided to cut us some well-deserved slack.

When I arrived at Treat that morning, Annie was already
hard at work in the kitchen with Tanya, one of the shop's two
assistant bakers, and Eduardo, the dishwasher with a thick coat
of black downy hair on his forearms who didn't seem to speak a
lick of English.

"Morning, everyone," I said to the room at large. "*Buenos
días*," I called in Eduardo's direction.

Annie shook her head, smiling. In the warm kitchen, her skin glowed bronze against the burgundy apron she wore, and her dark ponytail was streaked with flour. "Well, aren't you feeling multicultural this morning!" she teased. "What's up?"

"Just saying hello." I plucked an un-iced cinnamon-pear cupcake from a cooling tray and picked at it absently.

"You gonna pay for that?"

"Put it on my tab." The pear was light and sweet on my tongue. Farmer Ogden sure grew a mean organic pear—worth every pretty penny. I leaned against the door frame and took a few more small bites. I'd been mulling an idea over, but as I watched Annie move authoritatively around the kitchen, I found myself uncharacteristically hesitant. I never ceased to be amazed at how she was transformed in the kitchen. Outside of Treat, Annie's sarcasm was like a coat of armor protecting a woman who seemed a bit adrift in the world; here, in the kitchen, she was completely at ease, brimming with confidence and happiness and admirable competency. It was clear she knew how good she was at this, and I felt a prick of envy for the uncomplicated direction and shape that baking gave my friend's life. Looking down, I saw that the cupcake was dwindling quickly in my hand. Finally, Annie switched off the drone of the huge Hobart mixer and, turning around, looked startled to see me still there.

"Uh-oh, Tanya," she said, one hand still on the mixer switch. "I think the boss might be angling to can us."

Tanya straightened up from the corner stove, her eyes wide.

"Annie!" I laughed. "Don't listen to her, Tanya. She's cruel."

"Well, what is it, then?" Annie asked, hands on hips. "Did you run out of numbers to crunch?"

"Very funny, wise guy." Still, I didn't move. Why was I drawing this out? It really wasn't a big deal. "Can I talk to you up front for a second?"

Annie's brown eyes questioned me, but she wiped her hands on her apron and followed me into the still-dim shop. Through the window, Twentieth Street looked deceptively charming and unsoiled in the forgiving glow of early morning.

"Everything okay?" Annie asked once the door to the kitchen had swung shut behind her.

"Oh sure. No, everything's fine. It's silly." I felt myself flush. *Just ask her already!* I was behaving ridiculously.

Annie leaned against the counter, idly sliding the cupcake case door open and shut. "Listen, Julia," she said, suddenly straightening. "I think I know what's going on here."

"You do?"

"Yeah, and I'm afraid the answer is no. I simply cannot lend you any more money," Annie said, deadpan. "You've got to stop asking. It's getting uncomfortable."

I laughed and felt myself relax. "You're really on a roll this morning, aren't you?"

"Well, out with it already. I've got cupcakes to bake."

"Right." I took a breath. "Do you think Tanya could handle the kitchen on her own this afternoon?"

"Today? I guess. Why? Where are we going?"

"Wedding dress shopping. You, me, and my mother."

"An outing with Lolly dearest?" Annie grinned. "Sounds like a barrel of fun. Count me in."

I breathed. "Thanks." I hadn't expected her to agree so readily.

Annie shrugged. "No problem. I know how you rely on my fashion prowess. Can I get back to work now?"

Thirty minutes before we were supposed to leave for the bridal boutique, I looked up from the register to see Wes standing before me holding up a very expensive bottle of champagne.

"Hey, there, beautiful!" he drawled. "How 'bout a little bubbly?"

"Wes!" I cried. "What are you doing here? You didn't tell me you were getting back in town today!"

"I believe this is what some people call a surprise." His dark eyes flashed behind his glasses. "Surprise! Now are you going to make me show off my considerable vaulting skills or are you gonna come out from behind that counter and give me a kiss?"

The line was short enough that Devi could handle the customers on her own, so I untied my burgundy Treat apron, hung it on a hook by the kitchen door, and had made it half-way around the counter before Wes reached out, pulled me tight against his chest, and kissed me. Was the haven created by his arms the warmest, snuggest, most perfect place on earth? In that moment, I thought it just might have been. I kissed him back, my heart buoyant, and led him by the hand to the window bar.

"You should have called," I said, "I could have moved things around. I have to leave to go to an appointment any minute."

"I know. Wedding dress shopping. A little birdie with a very big mouth told me. Hence, the champagne. Thought you might need some preshopping lubrication."

"My mom called you? Why would she do that?"

"Your mother's mind is a mysterious place," Wes said, "but I think she was just excited. I get the feeling she's been worried about you."

He was quiet for a moment and I sensed he was giving me an opening to speak. I looked down at the bar and tried not to think about the cruel line of graffiti that had been rubbed and lacquered out of the wood. After a moment, Wes pulled me to his chest again and kissed my temple. Then, in one swift, expert move, he popped open the champagne. A few lanky teenage girls in line for cupcakes jumped at the sudden noise and stared at Wes, twittering. He shot them a sparkly, gallant grin and then pulled two plastic cups from his coat pocket. "Cheers," he whispered, bending his head toward me. "To my bride-to-be, the smartest, most beautiful, sexiest woman I've ever met."

I took a sip of champagne and dropped my head to Wes's broad shoulder, gazing out at the street. "Annie's coming shopping," I told him. "I somehow roped her in."

"Is she?" Wes asked. I heard the surprise in his voice and wondered how much he'd figured out about my checkered history with Annie. "I'm glad. She'll make it fun. Hot damn, Jules! Does this mean I should be looking for a best man? Have you changed your mind about the whole no-wedding-party thing?"

"What? No," I said quickly. Then I thought for a moment. "Well, maybe. I don't know. Let me think about it."

"No rush." Wes glanced at his watch. "I should get out of here so you ladies can get on your way. Wouldn't want you to keep Lolly waiting." He tapped the half-full bottle of champagne. "This will make for an excellent cab refreshment, if you're in the sharing mood. You gals shouldn't let it go to waste."

I rested my chin on my hand and watched him stand. It felt like ages since I'd seen him last, though we'd spent the night together during one of his San Francisco stopovers just a week earlier. The secret between us made me feel like even when we were together, we weren't; the memory of that day in the hospital was still lodged like a stone in my chest, making it hard to take deep breaths. *Maybe this is the afternoon I should tell him everything*, I thought for probably the hundredth time. "I don't have to go dress shopping today, you know," I heard myself saying before I could stop myself. "I could reschedule. We could spend the afternoon together."

Wes's face fell. "Well, shoot. I've got to catch a flight to Palm Springs to meet with some investors. I'll be back tomorrow though. Dinner then?"

"Okay," I said, that stone in my chest settling deeper between my ribs. I hugged Wes and inhaled the scent of his neck—a reas-

suringly familiar combination of coffee and leather and something sweet I always had trouble putting my finger on. What
was it? Butter from his morning toast? A package of chocolates
left over from some hotel stay? Maybe a hint of the honey he
liked to drizzle on apples. I smiled, allowing myself a moment
to believe in the possibility of a shared life full of sweet things.

At the bridal gallery, a saleswoman led Annie and me to a
little waiting room where my mother sat perched on the
edge of a white damask settee in front of a huge, three-panel
mirror. She rose when she saw us, smoothing her powder-blue
tweed suit.

"Oh good, you've actually materialized," she said, kissing
my cheeks. She nodded to the saleswoman. "You can bring
those dresses we discussed now." She turned back toward us and
seemed to notice Annie for the first time. "Hello, Annie! What
a delightful surprise. I'm sure you'll have a very interesting take
on all of the dresses."

Inwardly, I grimaced, but Annie seemed to take the comment
in stride. I breathed out, realizing that Annie knew my mother
well enough to know that below her cool exterior beat a very
warm heart. Or maybe Annie's tolerance had something to do
with the fact that we were both a little loopy from finishing that
bottle of champagne on the cab ride over.

"You know me, Lolly," Annie said, pulling the skirt of her
red paisley shirtdress out to perform a little curtsy. "I'm not one
to avoid making a fashion statement."

"Good. If there's one thing this wedding better not be, it's
dull," my mother said. She pulled Annie close for a hug. "I'm so
glad you've joined us."

When the saleswoman returned with several gowns, I followed
her into the dressing room, leaving Annie and my mother in the

waiting room outside. I looked at the dresses my mother had picked for me and was not at all surprised to find that they were beautiful, and exactly what I would have selected for myself. Classic, strapless, luxurious. My mother knew my taste well. I undressed and pulled the prettiest gown on, listening to it rustle around my legs as the saleswoman zipped up the side. I swayed a moment, feeling the effects of all the champagne I'd drunk.

"Oh," the saleswoman breathed. "How will we do better than Vera Wang? You make such a beautiful bride. As perfect as a cake topper."

Suddenly, I felt my throat tighten. My voice sounded clipped when I asked for a moment alone. Once the door had clicked shut behind the saleswoman, I turned back to face the mirror. A bride stood before me—tall and beautiful and blinking back tears.

In that dress, there was nowhere to hide. As much as I'd been trying not to face the reality—the uncertainties, really—of the future, the future was fast approaching. I tried to picture myself walking down the aisle toward Wes, but could summon only a black, gaping hole. I closed my eyes and tried to see Wes's face. Why was he so hard to conjure? I'd just seen him! If I could visualize his eyes—clear and loving and valiant—I would feel better. Or would I? I'd been keeping this terrible secret for so long that it was starting to feel more like a lie than anything else—a lie of omission, perhaps, but a lie nonetheless. How would Wes ever trust me again?

At twenty-eight, I felt damaged beyond love. *Am I going to feel this way, raw and exposed, for the rest of my life?* I desperately missed the old me. I sank down on the bench in the dressing room, wishing I could tear the dress off, wishing I hadn't drunk so much champagne.

The door clicked open and shut before I could say anything, and then Annie was looking down at me with her hands on her hips.

"Oh, Julia!" she said, her eyes widening. "What's wrong?"

I stood quickly and brushed my hands briskly down the gown, a move that made me feel exactly like my mother. "Nothing's wrong," I said. "I'm just so happy."

Annie cocked her head, a droll half smile playing on her face. "Tears of joy don't usually come with so much snot."

I laughed despite myself. It was better, I realized, not to be alone. Snatching a tissue from a dupioni-covered box on the table, I looked in the mirror and dabbed expertly at the mascara that had trailed below my eyes. Watching my appearance improve made my spirits improve, too. "Well," I said, glancing at Annie in the mirror. "Are you going to stand there all day gaping or are you going to tell me I look gorgeous?"

"You look gorgeous," Annie said without any hesitation. I heard the warmth in her voice, the utter absence of envy or bitterness or anger. It was the voice of my old friend Annie, the voice of the best friend I'd had before I managed to ruin everything so many years ago. I breathed out, smiling at her through the mirror, and sniffling just a little, tried to be happy.

Annie plucked the price tag from where it dangled along the side of my dress and raised her eyebrows, laughing a little. "Remember that game we used to play with your mom's magazines?"

I shook my head and did a half spin before the mirror, letting the gown's lush silk skirt swish and fall back into place.

"We'd pretend that we could have one thing from every page," Annie said. "But we couldn't look at the price or the brand or anything, we just had to do a quick pick of what caught our eye first. I was like a bird. I always picked the sparkliest, most colorful thing on the page."

"Just what you needed." I laughed. "Another lime-green vest with bedazzled pockets."

"Hey! I loved that vest."

I shrugged, smiling wryly.

"Anyway," she continued, "the point is you always managed to pick out the most expensive thing on the page, even though you swore you weren't cheating. I never knew how you did it! Even then, you had expensive taste."

The game rang a distant bell, but I couldn't in all honesty say I actually remembered playing it. It was strange to consider the things that Annie remembered from our shared childhood that I didn't. *This is what it would be like to have a sister.* It felt good. I was glad I'd invited her on this outing. Even though I knew champagne was making my thoughts sepia-toned, I vowed then and there to never do anything to risk losing Annie's friendship again.

I turned back to look at myself in the mirror again, a feeling of confidence blooming in my chest. "This is the one," I said, cupping my hands around my cinched waist.

"That's the dress?" Annie asked, surprised. "I mean, it's amazing, but isn't it the first one you've tried on?"

"Sometimes you just know," I said.

"Wow, okay. I guess all that practice making quick decisions with those magazine pages is coming in handy. Should we bring in The Lolly?"

"Yes." I laughed, turning in front of the mirror. "Bring in The Lolly!"

Later, with Curtis silently guiding the Bentley through the Mission's chaotic streets, and my mother, Annie, and I all sharing the ample backseat despite Annie's attempt to sit up front, the car buzzed with the excitement of a successful shopping trip. My mother peppered us with questions about the bakery, though rarely allowed either of us a chance to answer.

"Your mother's passion fruit meringue is on the menu, I

hope," she said to Annie. "Isn't it? It would really be a shame if it weren't. I don't think I've ever tasted anything so sinfully perfect in my life. I know you probably enjoy creating your own recipes—and I've certainly tasted for myself that you're very talented at it—but sometimes there is nothing quite like a recipe from an older generation. Every bite is a taste of history! You don't get a lot of history in experimental pastry, do you?"

"Mother," I broke in, "we'd love to include some of Lucia's recipes, but as I've told you a million times, we haven't been able to find her recipe book."

"Oh." She turned from me to Annie as if to confirm this bit of news. Annie nodded glumly. "Well, that won't do! I'll get Jacqueline and the girls on it immediately," she said, referring to her housekeeping staff. "Operation Lucia's Recipe Book. Those ladies could find a hay-shaped pin in a haystack, though I must say they don't seem to have much luck locating my husband's jewelry." She sighed. "Then again, I'm not sure I would turn in a very expensive missing watch if I were in their position. Would you?" she asked Annie pointedly.

I felt my mouth drop. Annie and I locked eyes and pulled nearly identical faces.

"Here's my apartment," Annie called out without answering, tapping on the window as we stopped in front of her building. "You'd love it," she said teasingly to my mother. "It's very quaint. Very charming. Surprisingly few rodents. Can I give you a tour?"

My mother sat up, buttoning her blazer, and cleared her throat. "That would be lovely, darling. Another time."

Annie shrugged, grinned at me, waved good-bye to Curtis, and hopped out onto the sidewalk, where several passersby made subtle efforts to peer in at whoever was driving through the Mission behind the tinted windows of a Bentley.

A few blocks later, Curtis dropped me off at my car. Alone

once more, doors locked, with the key in the ignition but the engine off, the dense fog of a champagne-fueled headache set in and clouded my good spirits. I leaned my head back against the car seat. These relentless mood swings were exhausting. *Enough is enough. Tomorrow at dinner, I'll tell Wes everything.* The thought produced a taut feeling in the pit of my stomach, like a rope that was being pulled to the point of vibration, the point of fraying. If tomorrow was the day I would tell Wes everything, tonight I needed a drink. I removed the key from the car's ignition, stepped back out into the crisp evening air, and headed toward the closest bar I knew.

From my seat at the back of the 500 Club, I watched Jake step through the front door and felt a wave of gratitude. I hated being there by myself. No one should suffer the indignity of drinking alone—and certainly not in a place like that. Although the seedy bar did offer a shield of anonymity that was appreciated. *Anyway,* I reminded myself, *if I'm just meeting an old friend for a cocktail, nothing sordid is going on.*

Jake slid in beside me in the booth and took a long slug of the scotch I'd ordered for him. His biggest strength, I thought, was the apparent flexibility of his schedule. If he had a schedule at all. I knew Jake talked up this surf foundation he was supposedly starting for city youth, but I'd heard from mutual friends that he spent more time surfing than actually building anything of lasting value. Unlike Wes, who was actually doing something with his life, Jake had always had big ideas and little follow-through. But that was Jake, and you could either appreciate him for who he was or not. Anyway, I realized with a pang, who was I to judge anyone for anything? Jake and I had been getting together in dive bars across the city every few weeks, and even though my subsequent hangovers were increasingly tinged with guilt,

I still enjoyed the comfortable, no-strings-attached banter that these meetings offered. *I've gone through so much this year,* I told myself. *I'm allowed to indulge in a little fun. Who's it hurting?*

"So I realize I never apologized to you about tattling to Annie about your marriage," I said once we were comfortably a few drinks into the evening. "I've been meaning to. I'm sorry it came out the way it did. I just didn't want to see her get hurt."

Jake shrugged, grinning. His dimples were truly unfair. How did any unsuspecting girl stand a chance?

"It's okay," he said. "We've moved past it."

I set my drink down on the sticky table and stared at him. "Wait, what? She didn't break up with you?" Strong, spitfire Annie hadn't kicked him to the curb the moment she learned he'd been lying to her? I hadn't wanted to risk another fight by asking Annie what had happened when she confronted Jake, but I'd always assumed they'd broken up. She hadn't mentioned one word about him since that morning in October when I had told her he was married.

"Nope," Jake said. "She was very forgiving."

His nonchalant attitude made me want to slap him. I sat back against the hard booth, furious, wishing I weren't trapped in the seat beside him. "But what are you doing here with me if you're still seeing Annie?" I asked. "If I'd known, I wouldn't have called—"

"Julia, I think the better question is what are *you* doing here with *me*?" he interrupted. He sounded more amused than defensive. "Annie and I have never talked about being exclusive, but aren't you engaged to be married? I'm just a single guy hanging out with an ex-girlfriend, but what are you?"

I stared down at my drink. He was right. I was every bit as guilty as he was. Or more. Suddenly, I couldn't wait to get out of there. I was supposed to be safe in my bed in my childhood home, calling my fiancé to see how his meeting in Palm Springs had gone, not sitting in some dive bar with my ex-boyfriend. What was I trying to prove by being there with Jake Logan? What had I hoped to gain? Being with him no longer felt like an uncomplicated sojourn to happier times—instead, I realized, it was making me more anxious. The rose-colored glasses were officially off.

Jake threw his arm around me and gave me a chummy little rattle. But when I looked up, his face was close and the look in his eyes wasn't chummy at all. In an instant, he was kissing me. Stunned, I pressed my hands hard into his chest and pushed him away. And that was the moment I saw Annie, standing in the open doorway of the bar, staring at us, the color drained from her face.

21

{

Annie

Do you know how every once in a while you have one of those almost out-of-body experiences where you're both living through some experience and simultaneously watching the whole thing unfold from a distance? Seeing Jake and Julia together was one of those moments. I stepped into the bar, did a quick scan for Becca, and found myself instead staring at Jake and Julia kissing. Physically, the pain was as shocking and visceral as grabbing a hot pan from the oven with my bare hands—though more accurately akin to laying that three-hundred-degree pan straight across my bare chest. At the same time, I felt like I'd been sucked out of my body and was hovering somewhere above the whole scene, watching everything unfold with the interest of a primatologist studying the mating rituals of monkeys. *This moment is now a critical part of my life history*, I remember thinking. *The image of the two of them kissing will never go away.*

I stood in the doorway of the 500 Club, unable to move. Part of me wanted to stride across the room, picking up drinks from the bar and tables along the way to hurl at them, screaming like a banshee at the top of my lungs. Another part of me felt immediately deflated and humiliated and wanted to hightail it home for a good cry and a couple dozen cookies. As I stood frozen in the doorway, trying to decide between the two options, Julia shoved Jake out of the booth and came running toward me.

"Annie!" she cried, her blue eyes huge. "I . . . I don't know why he just kissed me. We're not . . . we're not doing anything." Her shoulders began to shake. "This must look awful, but I swear, we're not—"

"Just shut up," I said.

When I saw Jake striding up behind her, I finally worked up the wherewithal to turn on my heel and walk outside. Out on the sidewalk, I heard him calling after me.

I spun around. "What were you thinking?" I hissed, ignoring the fact that Julia was just a step behind him. "Is this fun for you? Are you having a great time with the two of us?"

He reached out and held my arms, his brow furrowed. Sniveling drunkenly behind him, Julia had a kicked-in, crumpled look. I fought the urge to take a picture with my phone and e-mail it to her mother.

"I'm sorry," Jake said. "This shouldn't have happened, even if it was . . . nothing. And it wasn't calculated—I hope you don't think that. We're just"—he glanced back at Julia and sighed—"drunk."

Looking up at him out there on the street, I suddenly found myself staring at the man behind the contrite, concerned look. It was like seeing a face behind a veil. *This is all an act*, I realized. Practically *everything* about him was an act. He didn't care. About me, about Julia, about those kids he professed to want to help, about anyone but himself and his easy, no-consequences life. How had it taken me this long to discover the real Jake Logan? Seeing the man behind the veil—the man who, I saw now, looked at me distantly, as though I were a mildly amusing stranger—somehow came as a relief. The spark in his eyes that I'd always interpreted as mischievous but inherently kind I now saw signified insouciance, plain and simple. He wasn't at all the man who I'd thought he was—or had wanted him to be. It crushed me to think that I'd opened up to him, that I'd shared parts of myself I could never take back. I probably should have been used to the humiliation of breaking up, of losing pieces of myself to the wrong guy, but the act never lost its sting.

I shook my head, at a loss for words.

"Why don't I call you in the morning," Jake said softly. I realized he was still holding my arms. "We can talk about this with clear heads."

Without hesitation I stepped back, out of his grasp. "I think it's better to just end things now. There's really nothing to say, is there? Where could we possibly go from here? Whatever it was that was happening between us is over now."

Jake blinked. "Why don't I just call you—"

"Please don't," I said, and turned around before the tears could start. I heard Julia calling after me, but I ignored her, as I should have done months earlier.

It was impossible to completely avoid Julia at Treat, but each time she approached me, I shot her a warning look that must have been pretty fierce because she managed to basically keep her distance. I could tell she was dying to speak to me, but what could she say that I would want to hear? What could possibly make up for what she had done? I still couldn't understand why, out of all the bars in the city, Julia and Jake had picked the 500 Club for their little rendezvous. The bar was in *my* neighborhood. Had they wanted me to find them there?

Sadly, like some masochistic idiot, the person I really blamed was myself. After all, I *knew* Julia St. Clair. I knew exactly what she was capable of, and still I had found a way to trust her again. Her betrayal really shouldn't have come as such a big surprise. You know how the saying goes: *Fool me once, shame on you. Fool me twice. . .*

So I found myself in the exact position I'd feared from the start—professionally bound to a person I loathed. The words *It's just until May, It's just until May,* echoed through my head like a mantra keeping me sane. Come May, Julia would be married and, as contractually bound, would leave Treat and my life for good.

Meanwhile, the customers continued to line up at Treat's counter on a daily basis, so I poured myself into work and simply turned up the radio when Julia's bright, phony voice oozed into the kitchen from the shop. It was times like these that I felt my mother's absence acutely, like the unrelenting throb of burned skin long after the initial injury. I wished I could feel her arms around me one more time, or see her warm brown eyes searching my face with maternal concern. A distant second would have been to gorge myself on the ginger cookies she used to make when I'd had a bad day, but even those were out of reach. I'd tried for years to figure out the recipe to those cookies but never came close to getting it right. I seemed to be missing something completely obvious, and it drove me nuts.

I started waking up earlier and earlier, eager for those hours of time in Treat's kitchen before the day officially began, when it was just me and my old friends, the appliances. One morning in mid December I stood hunched over the counter, practically basking in the silence of the kitchen and scribbling out some ideas for new cupcake flavors that had come to me in the fog of half sleep the night before, when I was startled by a loud knock at the front door of the shop. I glanced at the clock. Five. Who the hell was knocking at five a.m.? I heard my heart pounding in my ears as an image of the man in the hooded sweatshirt flashed across my mind.

The moment I stepped through the door of the kitchen into the shop, I breathed a sigh of relief. It was only that blowhard Ogden Gertzwell; I could see through the door's window that he was holding a large crate of fruit.

I unlocked the door and resolved to not be immediately exas-

perated with the guy. It was going to be tough, though; he seemed
to have a tendency to show up and subject me to a lengthy description of his latest crop during those moments when my enjoyment
of the shop's morning silence was at its peak.

"Hi, Ogden," I said, working to keep my tone polite but
brisk. "This is an early stop on your route, isn't it? I didn't expect
you for a couple more hours."

"I was driving by on my way to another delivery and saw
the light was on. Figured I might as well drop off the fruit now,
while I'm in the neighborhood. Do you mind?"

"It's fine," I said. "Need help?"

"No, I've got it," he said. "Just hold the door for me."

I stood at the front door as he made several trips from his
truck to the kitchen. When he'd brought the last crate in I
clicked the deadbolt in place and followed him back into the
kitchen. Already, he was at the sink, washing a large persimmon that glowed as orange as the Technicolor sunset on one of
the vaguely penitent postcards Jake had been mailing me from
Costa Rica. Jake hadn't made it easy for me to stop thinking
about him, sending one gorgeously lush bouquet after another
to the shop. I sensed he had them delivered to Treat instead of
my apartment to show that he was not trying to keep anything
from Julia. The action seemed insincere to me, reeking of obsti-
nance and strategy. I didn't respond.

Ogden pulled a pocketknife from his jeans and sliced the persimmon expertly in his hand. "Raw persimmon is an acquired
taste," he said, handing me a slice, "but I have a feeling you'll
like this one."

I resisted the urge to roll my eyes. *I'm a baker, Ogden*, I wanted
to say. *Of course I know what persimmon tastes like.* I bit into the
fruit. It had the texture of a firm heirloom tomato and a heady,
semisweet taste as though infused with a tiny drop of honey. I
nodded and made a sound of approval.

"You didn't order any, but I brought you a few to try anyway. I wondered if maybe they might inspire a new cupcake flavor for the holidays," Ogden said. He kept his serious brown eyes trained on the persimmon in his hand while he spoke, a gesture that seemed oddly bashful and entirely unlike him. "You'll have to excuse me if that sounds presumptuous. I'll be the first to admit I know nothing about the recipe creation process."

I took another bite of persimmon, considering. Ogden held himself very still as he watched me chew, and I appreciated the restraint he showed in not jumping in to fill the silence. I knew it couldn't have been easy for him.

"You have good instincts," I said finally. "A persimmon cupcake could be a great addition to the menu. Add some chocolate, a little cinnamon and cardamom, some sweet vanilla icing, and I think we'd have a new Christmas favorite."

"You don't think persimmon is too adventurous for your patrons?"

"Nah," I said. It was actually nice to talk to someone who took food as seriously as I did—I only wished he could do so without sounding so pompous. "But we might have to lead with the chocolate. Chocolate Persimmon Spice. That wouldn't offend you, would it? If I promised to use organic chocolate?"

"I think my ego can handle a little organic chocolate," Ogden said. His long eyelashes had a softening effect on his otherwise rugged face. "I came to terms years ago with the fact that my control over the fate of my produce ends the minute it gets carried off my truck."

"It must be like sending the kids off to college," I said. "If you love them, set them free."

"Right." He had a nice smile. Not too broad, but just big enough to show off a handsome row of white teeth. Apparently, life on the farm had been cushy enough to allow for braces. I realized I was smiling back at him, and that the two of us had been comfortably silent for yet another long beat of time. Suddenly, his eyes clicked away from mine. I looked over my shoulder and there was Julia, all freshly scrubbed and peaches-and-cream in an ivory angora sweater and perfectly blown-out hair. She must have been up for hours.

"I didn't hear you come in," I said coolly.

She flushed. "Sorry. Just wanted to get a jump on some accounting. Good morning, Ogden."

"Hi, Julia," Ogden said politely. I could see him looking discreetly back and forth between the two of us, clearly sensing the friction in the air. "Well, I should hit the road and finish up my deliveries. Annie, you'll call me?"

I hesitated, confused. Had I said I'd call him? I felt thrown off balance by Julia's sudden appearance.

"If you decide to make a persimmon order," Ogden clarified quickly.

"Oh, right. Yes. I'll call."

"Great." Ogden nodded at each of us and exited through the kitchen door. His boots left a little pile of mud on the linoleum floor, and I saw Julia's nose scrunch up in displeasure at the sight of it. I smiled to myself, secretly happy with Ogden's unintentional act of transgression, and Julia, catching this smile, seemed to misinterpret it as an opening to chat.

"He's totally into you, you know," she said.

I looked at her evenly and shook my head. "We're not doing this."

Her face fell. "Please, Annie, at least let me apologize."

"Why? Do you think I owe you that?" As much as I wanted to remain cool and distant, I felt my blood starting to boil just thinking about her and Jake kissing in that booth. All it took was to let my guard down for an instant, and the image of the two of them seared its way through all of my other thoughts. "I just can't believe I was so shocked. It's not as though this is the first time you've done something like this."

"What do you mean?" she asked quietly.

I looked at Julia. She was practically begging me to yell at her, to rehash everything we'd been through a decade earlier. And I took the bait. Before I knew what I was doing, I'd slammed my palms down onto the counter. "I've been wanting to put this in the past, but you're still the exact same person you were when you were a conniving, backstabbing teenager, aren't you? You started those awful rumors about me in high school! I never had a chance to repair my relationship with my mother," I said, choking on the word. "She died before my name was cleared!"

"But, Annie, that doesn't matter," Julia whimpered, taking a step toward me. "She always believed you."

I ignored her. "You tried to ruin my life—for what? The fun of it? Because you were jealous that someone like Jake Logan might actually like me? Just admit it already! What's the point of pretending? You were a bitch then and you're a bitch now."

Julia was shaking her head, tears running fast down her cheeks, but the set of her face was indignant even beneath the tears. She opened her mouth and I steeled myself, prepared for a slew of defensive lies. But she just looked at me. After a moment, her mouth closed. She seemed to crumple before me, slumping against the counter. I stared at her, refusing to speak another word. If she thought tears were going to work this time, she was even more delusional than I'd given her credit for.

"You're right," she said then. "It was me."

I sucked in my breath and felt my whole body go still.

"But I never meant for it to get as far as it did," she said. "I never wanted you to get suspended from Devon. I never wanted Cal to get involved. I never wanted your mom to find out. I made one stupid offhand comment to someone, and it got completely out of control. But it doesn't matter to you if I made one comment or twenty, does it? Because either way, I caused something terrible to happen. You're right, I was a complete bitch. And I guess . . . I guess my behavior with Jake proves that I still am. I don't feel like I'm the same person I was back then, but I guess I am. I don't deserve your trust. I certainly don't deserve your friendship. I don't deserve Wes. I don't deserve . . . a lot of things. Maybe anything."

I stood completely still as I listened to her. I guess I thought that if I moved, this mirage of honesty might waver and fade, and I might ruin my chance of finally getting some answers. So it really had been Julia all along! I'd known it, I'd been sure of it, but I suppose some small part of me had held out hope that she would prove me wrong. Now that that hope was gone, I hardly knew how to feel about her.

"I know my apology is much too late and totally worthless. I don't expect forgiveness," Julia said quietly. "But I am so very, very sorry. More sorry than I've ever been for anything in my entire life." She wiped at her eyes, but they were already pretty dry. I marveled at her newfound ability to turn her tears on and off; she seemed to have taken to crying in the same way she took to everything else—effortlessly, like a fish to water. When I cried, my eyes were red and puffy for days.

I don't know what either of us would have said after that, because a turning key in the front door signaled the arrival of Tanya and the start of the baking hours at Treat. Julia nodded at me, gave a pitiful little half shrug, and disappeared into the front of the shop for the remainder of the day.

On my walk back to my apartment that night—I was no longer sharing rides with Julia, having decided getting mugged by Our Guy was the better of two evils—I slowed as I passed the open door of the bodega on my corner. On the news rack the latest issue of *San Francisco* magazine displayed a photo of a giant cupcake on its cover. I stepped inside and read the headline. "The Cupcake Craze: How Two of San Francisco's Native Daughters Are Leading the Charge."

Does Julia know about this? I wondered. The magazine had run a brief, but positive mention of Treat when we first opened, and I'd thought that was all the coverage they were planning on giving us. But this was clearly a much larger story. I paid for a copy and one of the inexpensive bottles of Pinot Noir by the counter—after the day I'd had, I figured I was showing some restraint by not moving straight to vodka.

Twenty minutes later, nestled in my couch with a large glass of wine on the coffee table in front of me, I opened the magazine. An image of Julia at Treat's opening party—her head thrown back mid-laugh, cupcake and enormous engagement ring on equal display in her hand, one black heel lifted daintily behind her—filled an entire glossy page. On the other side, mid-text, there was a small image of me that I remembered the magazine's photographer taking the week after Treat opened. Leaning against the shop's counter in my burgundy apron, I looked tired and chunky, like the eccentric sidekick of the leading lady on the opposite page.

When the daughter of one of San Francisco's most well-known families decided to open a cupcake shop earlier this year, it was not the culmination of a lifelong dream. In fact, Julia St. Clair readily admits the whole endeavor began on a whim. At a time when most small businesses close within a year of opening, starting a cupcake shop is the kind of whim that those of us who don't have a trust fund estimated in the millions can only dream of chasing.

"I just love cupcakes," St. Clair admitted at Treat's opening party this fall. Her sleek blond hair was shiny even under the shop's seductively dim lights. "After a month of taste testing, it's a wonder I still fit into this!" she said, gesturing at the black Prada cocktail dress that hugged her trim figure.

I closed my eyes and sank back into the couch, rubbing at my temples. The article was nothing more than a puff piece about a bored, capricious socialite with money to burn. With all of Julia's resources, with all of the weird public interest in her and her family, she had had the opportunity to shine a light on how Treat was different from other bakeries, how we were special. But no, she'd simply taken the moment to show off her legs. I could have killed her.

After a long spell during which I muttered colorful death threats in between long sips of wine, I finally pulled out my cell phone and called Becca. I filled her in on the confession Julia had made that morning and then told her about the article.

"I'm seriously thinking this whole thing isn't worth it," I told her, nearly out of breath from rambling for so long. "Why am I putting myself through this? Believe me, I love Treat. The thought of leaving destroys me. But I can open up another shop someday, can't I? Why am I doing this to myself?"

"Annie," Becca broke in when I finally paused. "Did you read the whole article?"

"What? Well, no. Once I started imagining impaling Julia with a spatula, the page went a little out of focus. But I got the gist."

"I read it when I got home from work," she said. Her voice had a funny tone. "I think you should read the whole thing."

"Now?"

"Now."

"You're not just trying to get me off the phone so you and Mike can have happy couple sex, are you?"

Becca laughed. "Hey," she said. "There's nothing wrong with killing two birds with one stone."

"You suck." I sighed. "Have fun."

I picked the magazine back up and flipped to the article, rolling my eyes anew at the horrendous juxtaposition of photos. I skimmed down to where I'd stopped reading the first time and resolved to finish the article. It wasn't easy. There were more references to Julia's family, her wardrobe, her perfect highlights and impressive résumé, blah blah blah. And then.

"Annie Quintana is quite simply the most talented, most inventive person I've ever known," St. Clair says. There is a new note of earnestness in her voice. She seems to focus when she talks about her business partner, becoming more present in the conversation than when the talk is of her family or upcoming nuptials. "I can't begin to fathom how her brain works. Her mother was a fabulous baker as well and shared a lot of her secrets with Annie. But it's more than just inherited knowledge—Annie can taste one ingredient and immediately develop an entire recipe around it. And I guarantee that that cupcake, whatever ingenious combination of flavors it is, is going to be the most delicious and surprising cupcake you've ever eaten."

The rest of the article was about me—my training and career to date—and included a few quotes from me that I now remembered the journalist jotting down at the party. There were glowing descriptions of some of our menu's most popular cupcakes, as well as a couple of the more experimental ones. The journalist, perhaps entranced by Julia's enthusiasm, seemed to think Treat was the best thing to happen to the Bay Area's baking scene in years. I shut the magazine and sighed, feeling utterly confused.

Which Julia is this? She had as many faces as a set of Russian nesting dolls. Still, I had to admit, she'd done exactly what moments earlier I'd been wishing she had done. She'd used her resources—in this case an obsequious journalist who was clearly enthralled by Julia's societal standing—to successfully promote our little cupcakery.

When my phone rang, I picked it up immediately, expecting it to be Becca. But it was Julia.

"It's Treat," she said, her voice tight with what sounded like a mix of rage and fear. "I'm already in the car. Can you meet me there?"

Someone had spray painted the words "GET OUT" in thick black letters across the front window. From the *inside*. Whoever had done it had managed to get through the front door but hadn't been able to disarm the alarm and it must have finally driven him away. Inspector Ramirez and several other officers were already inside the shop with Julia when I arrived.

"This feels like déjà vu," I muttered, crossing over the threshold. Everything in the shop looked normal except for those thick black letters on the window. I checked the kitchen, but nothing appeared out of place. I walked back into the shop, arms crossed tight across my chest. Just the idea of some ill-intentioned stranger in my shop made me sick to my stomach.

Ramirez was crouched by the front door shining a flashlight at the locks. "There isn't sign of a forced break-in," he announced, a little out of breath as he hoisted himself out of the squat. "Who else has keys other than the two of you?"

Julia and I looked at each other. "Two of our assistant bakers," I said. "But this wasn't either of them. I'm sure of it." The idea of Tanya or Elisa yielding a can of spray paint was laughable.

"I don't think you should feel sure of anything right now," Ramirez said. "I'll need contact information for all of your employees."

"Fine," Julia said. "Whatever you need."

"Can you think of anyone who might not want this shop to stay open for any reason?" Ramirez asked.

I shrugged. "The Council on Obesity? Militant Mothers Against Refined Sugar? The list of enemies of the cupcake is long."

"Annie." Julia sighed.

"What?" I said, turning toward her. "You think someone we know did this? Come on! That's ridiculous."

"What else can I think?" Julia asked, her voice shaken. "You have to admit this is beginning to seem calculated."

"You'd be surprised what a disgruntled employee—" Ramirez began to add.

"No one is disgruntled," I interrupted. "But we'll give you the contact list and you can question everyone yourself."

Ramirez's eyes skimmed the ceiling, slowing as they reached the corner of the shop near the front door. "If you're going to stay open, I recommend a security camera. I'm sure your alarm company can install one."

"*If* we're going to stay open?" I asked, surprised.

Ramirez puffed out his pudgy cheeks and shrugged. "It's obviously up to you. But it's clear that someone is targeting your shop. No other businesses in the vicinity have reported such a pattern of incidents. A camera could confirm if it's the guy you've seen hanging around the shop before, or if it's someone else . . . someone you know."

"I'll call the alarm company first thing in the morning," Julia said. She pulled out her phone and typed a note into it.

Ramirez drummed his pen against his notebook and the noise seemed to echo ominously through the shop. I shifted uncomfortably, wishing I were back on my couch with that glass of wine. "So there's nothing else I should know?" he asked. Again, he was looking at me. "Nothing else out of the ordinary that's happened lately that needs to go in the report?"

I thought about this for a moment. "There was an article that came out today in *San Francisco* magazine about Treat," I said slowly. I felt Julia's eyes on my face but didn't look over at her.

"I can't imagine there's any connection, but if someone really doesn't want the shop to be open, I guess they might be pissed about the good press?"

Ramirez jotted this down in his book. "Okay," he said. I wished he would give more insight, but he just looked around the shop one more time, stifled a yawn, and snapped his notebook shut.

After we'd reactivated the alarm and locked the shop back up, Ramirez walked us to Julia's car. Once we were inside, the car's heavy silence took over.

"My next investment will be in a graffiti-removal company," she said after a moment.

Humor. An unusual choice for Julia. I looked over at her, thinking of what she'd said in that magazine article. Finally, I sighed.

"Why don't you come over," I said. "We could probably both use something sweet. I made some cookies."

Her eyes widened. "Okay," she said quickly, and started the car. A few minutes later, as we were driving, she asked, "Are they your mom's ginger ones?"

"Their bastard cousin."

Julia smiled, twisting to look over her shoulder as she expertly parallel parked near my building. "Sounds delicious."

We sat on the couch in my apartment, a plate stacked high with soft ginger cookies on the cushion between us. I saw Julia eyeing the *San Francisco* magazine on the coffee table.

"Why didn't you tell me about that?" I asked, nodding toward the magazine.

"I didn't know about it. I thought the little write-up they ran right after the shop opened was all they decided to do." She hesitated, nibbling delicately at a cookie. "What did you think of it?"

"It was pretty perfect," I said matter-of-factly. "I'm sure it will be great for business."

Julia seemed confused by this. "Yes, but—I meant everything I said about you. About how much I admire you. I wasn't saying that stuff for the publicity."

The weird thing was that even after everything we'd been through, even though I was still incredibly angry with her, I believed her.

"I know," I said. I pulled my knees up to my chest and peered over them at her. "I believe you think I'm a good baker, and I believe you when you say you want Treat to do well." I paused and took a deep breath. "What I have trouble believing is when you say you're sorry for what happened with Jake. How could you have done what you did to me and still claim you want us to be friends? Friends don't go on secret dates with their friends' boyfriends. Friends don't kiss their friends' boyfriends. Those are probably rule number one and two in the friend handbook."

"You're right," Julia said simply. "I'm a horrible person. I'm the world's worst friend."

"They should make a coffee mug."

"I would use it every day as penance," she said. I got the sense she actually meant it.

I sighed. "Seriously, Julia, what were you thinking? Something must have been going through your head."

Julia's lip trembled for a moment, sadness looming in her eyes. She shook her head slightly—I'm not sure she even knew she was doing it—and looked away.

"I'm listening," I said. Despite my anger, something instinctively made me ease some gentleness into my tone. "Just talk to me."

And then, to my surprise, she did.

22

Julia

"I was pregnant," I said. Annie's eyebrows shot up and I could practically hear her thoughts begin to race a mile a minute down a not so flattering, though not, I knew, terribly unwarranted path. "No, no," I said quickly, feeling my face grow warm. "Not with Jake. I was pregnant back in the spring. With Wes's baby."

I waited for Annie to say something, but she just looked at me, her heart-shaped face cocked to the side with all of her long, dark hair spilling around her shoulders. Something about her hair—its messiness, maybe—comforted and emboldened me. She seemed to display her flaws proudly, like well-earned war wounds. If I wanted any hope of repairing our friendship, I realized, I had to tell her everything. There was no other way.

"I was working like crazy then," I said quietly, "and I didn't even realize I'd missed my period until I was nearly two months along. Wes was in China, so I took the test alone one morning. When I saw it was positive I was shocked. But happy." I swallowed and breathed deeply through my nose. Strangely, I had no urge to stop talking. After all those months of keeping this inside of me, barely allowing myself to even think in any concrete way about any of it, I suddenly needed to articulate out loud exactly what had happened. This wasn't just about repairing my friendship with Annie, I realized. This was about repairing *me*.

"Wes and I had talked about how we wanted to start a family," I told Annie. "Not right then, of course—not before we were married. But eventually. Kids were part of our plan. I remember looking at the pregnancy test that morning and thinking, *Well, this is ahead of schedule.* And then, I don't know, I felt this flood of happiness wash through my whole body. I was standing there grinning ear to ear, all by myself in my bathroom.

"I had an ultrasound to confirm the pregnancy and was amazed when this tiny little bean with a flickering heart popped up on the screen. I hadn't wanted to tell Wes the news over the phone, but in that moment when I saw the baby for the first time, I wished he were with me. The ultrasound technician gave me a few photos and I decided I would surprise Wes with them when he got back from China the following month. It was a long time to keep the news to myself, but I had so much going on at work that I figured the time would fly by. I didn't realize that being pregnant seemed to put everything else in slow motion." I closed my eyes, thinking back to that time. "I'd sit in my office knowing I was supposed to be working on a presentation, and then I'd realize I had my hand on my stomach, and my eyes were half closed, and I was thinking about the bakery down the street from my apartment and whether it would still be open by the time I got out of work. I was beginning to have this strange stretching sensation in my lower abdomen, and I'd find myself envisioning my uterus growing to contain this life that was now, according to my online research, the size of a lime. I wasn't sick, but I felt exhausted a lot of the time. I did everything you're supposed to do—I stopped drinking, I stopped eating sushi, I choked down enormous prenatal vitamins every single day. It was hard to concentrate on anything but the thought of that little heartbeat inside of me. I'd get these crazy joyful tears in my eyes when I saw babies in strollers out on the street—me, teary-eyed! I've never even had PMS, and there I was, crying at soup commercials and *American Idol*.

"And then, a few weeks after that ultrasound, I noticed a little spot of blood in my underwear. Of course I went right to my computer and learned that a lot of women have some bleeding during their first trimester and it was likely nothing to worry about. A part of me was concerned, but a larger part of me felt confident everything was fine. It had to be. The bleeding was scary, of course, but how could anything be wrong? I'm young and healthy."

I swallowed. How could I describe to Annie just how sure I'd been that everything was okay, how impossible it had been to even fathom that anything had happened to the little baby growing inside of me? How I had never expected to feel the way I felt when I was pregnant—that something I'd never known was missing had clicked into place inside of me, that I felt a new sense of purpose, a sudden and deep understanding of some critical part of life that I'd never before even realized existed?

Annie looked at me, her brow furrowed with concern and encouragement, her front teeth pressing anxiously into her bottom lip. Still, she didn't speak. I took another deep breath through my nose and continued, telling her how my OB had asked me to come in for an ultrasound just to be sure everything was fine. The nurse had me get into a gown in the ultrasound room and wait for the technician, who of course took forever. I must have looked at my watch a dozen times over the next twenty minutes, getting more and more uneasy as each minute ticked by. Finally, the technician came in. Right away when she touched my stomach with the ultrasound wand, an image of the baby came up on the screen. Even in the few weeks since the first ultrasound, the baby had grown so much. There was the little head, the round little body. Our perfect peanut-shaped baby. I remember just staring at the screen—at my baby—in awe, for several long seconds. And then I realized the room was silent. The tech hadn't said a word.

"She pushed at my stomach with the wand a little to get the baby to move, but nothing happened. The baby just lay there, black and solid in profile, with its back curled against my uterus. There was no flicker of life. No heartbeat. I looked at the technician, and the look on her face said everything. I started sobbing—" My voice caught on the word and I cleared my throat before continuing. "The tech wiped the goo off my stomach and slipped out of the room. She never said anything.

"My OB explained that it appeared the baby's heart had stopped beating at some point in the previous week. So all that time that I'd been sitting at my desk with my hand on my stomach, my baby was dying. My doctor said there was nothing anyone could have done—miscarriages happened all the time. I wanted to scream. I'd never felt so betrayed in my entire life— and it was my own body. I just couldn't believe this was happening—had happened—to me." I took a breath and then plowed ahead with the truth. "It was the sort of bad luck, the sort of failure," I said, "that happened to other people, not me."

I looked at Annie, almost willing her to roll her eyes at this comment—anything that I could use as an excuse to stop speaking. But she just sat there with her gaze locked on mine, her brown eyes deep and sad.

I told her that my OB recommended a procedure called dilation and curettage. "It's when they dilate your cervix and surgically remove the fetus. It was scheduled for the next morning, so I went all the way home and spent the night lying in bed cradling the little swell in my abdomen that held the baby whose heart had stopped beating. Even though I knew the baby had died, the thought of someone removing him or her from me was . . ." I swallowed, unable to finish this thought. "It was a very difficult night. The next morning, I cried the entire way to the hospital, the entire time while I waited to be put under, and woke up sometime later to the sound of myself still sobbing. The whole thing seemed surreal—the procedure is matter-of-fact to the hospital staff; they do that kind of thing every day. But it was the worst day of my life."

The sum of these words felt horribly, almost viciously inadequate. How to explain to Annie that losing a baby had felt like having my heart permanently branded with a feeling of loss? That it had produced a cloud of toxic smoke in my chest that hung dark and suffocating to that day, crowding my ability to think, to breathe even, the way I once had?

"I was still crying when I went back to my OB a few days later. She told me that the hormones my body had been producing at that point in the pregnancy were at the same level they would have been had I carried the baby to term. I guess she was trying to make me feel better—I was dealing with the crazy hormones of a woman who had recently delivered a baby, but I had no baby to show for it. She told me she hoped that if I felt I needed to speak with someone, I would. She meant a therapist, of course. But I didn't want to talk about it. I didn't want to tell a single person. I didn't want to do anything. I quit my job. I moved home.

"And then I saw you at my mother's party and I ate one of your cupcakes, and I felt, I don't know, one tiny bit better. A tiny bit normal. It was something. It was a start. At least I thought it was."

I shrugged, my eyes finally welling with tears. My throat felt raw, like I'd been talking for hours. At some point, I realized, Annie had taken my hand in hers. Her eyes, too, were wet with tears.

"Oh, Julia," she said, her voice wavering.

I wished I were done, but there was still more I needed to tell her. "And then," I said shakily, "I started getting drinks every once in a while with Jake Logan. Being with him made me feel like the person I used to be—confident and strong and . . . unbreakable. It was selfish. But I swear I didn't know you were dating him at that point, and I never meant for anything to happen between the two of us. I love Wesley. I would never want to hurt him. But being with Wes makes me think of losing the baby, and there's this huge secret between us now, and it taints everything. When I saw Jake again, that last time, I thought you had broken up with him. I never expected him to kiss me. I didn't want that—I wanted the opposite. I just wanted to spend a few uncomplicated moments with someone and not think about anything that had happened or that might happen in the future."

I looked down at my hand in hers. "I know I've been incredibly selfish. I understand if you can't forgive me. I don't know if *I* can forgive me."

Annie sighed. "You should never have gone through all of that alone," she said softly. "I can't begin to imagine how hard it's been for you. I wish I'd known. I wish you'd told Wes, or me—or anyone. You have people who really care about you who might have been able to help."

"I know," I said. "I don't even recognize myself anymore. I've behaved so badly."

"It's not that," Annie said quickly. "I'm not trying to make you feel any worse. I'm just so sorry that this happened to you. Losing a baby . . ." Annie paused and gave my hand a squeeze. She looked me right in the eye and said slowly, "I am so sorry." She waited, letting her words catch hold, before continuing. "I guess I don't understand why you still haven't told Wes. He seems so supportive and clearly loves you so much. He could have helped you through all of this."

It was hard to explain my actions to Annie when they hardly

made sense to me. "My whole life has been smooth. Things come very easily to me," I said. "And that's the sort of person Wes expects to marry—someone perfect. I know that sounds crazy. But the woman he fell in love with had everything together, and now . . . I'm completely different. I'm not the same person. My body is . . . flawed. Maybe seriously flawed. I don't know. I know miscarriages are relatively common, but mine was—later than most. I just have this terrible feeling this is just the beginning of a long, hard road. Wes didn't sign up for this. His whole life is about helping children—that's the mission of his company! He loves kids. I can't take that dream of a family from him."

"Wes loves you for *you*. That was evident the moment I saw you guys together. He will love you no matter what."

I smiled wearily and pulled my hand away to take a sip of wine. "That's nice to think. But I'm guessing the reality is a little more complicated." ·

"Julia, you have to give Wes a chance. You can't make up his mind for him."

I stopped myself from responding right away and allowed her comment a moment to sink in. She had a point. Already, now that I'd told her about the miscarriage, my heart felt a little less leaden. Maybe she was right. Maybe Wes would love me no matter what.

"In fact," Annie said slowly, "I really think it's time you tell Wes *everything*."

I looked at her. "You mean about Jake?"

She shrugged. "I'm no relationship guru. I've never been engaged. Hell"—she smiled ruefully—"my last boyfriend turned out to be married *and* he hooked up with my friend."

Given the context, I tried not to smile too broadly at her use of the word "friend." *Still*, I thought, *if Annie forgives me, maybe Wes will, too.*

"I'm sure you're right." I sighed. "Wes should know every-thing." I thought about the upcoming weeks—Christmas and then the New Year's Eve engagement party that my mother had planned for us. "Maybe after the holidays?"

Annie smiled. "You'll probably know when the time is right."

I smiled back at her. A feeling of relief swelled inside of me. I felt lighter and more hopeful than I had in ages. Having Annie by my side didn't make the pain of losing the baby any less acute—that was something I would live with forever—but I did feel stronger. I had been right to tell her everything. *No more secrets*, I thought. It was as good a New Year's resolution as any.

23

Annie

IF LOLLY ST. Clair was meant to do one thing with her life, it was throw parties. To see her in action as she directed her staff before Julia's New Year's Eve engagement party was to watch a veteran captain lead the crew of a large sailing vessel to port through a particularly treacherous stretch of coastline. I'd arrived at the mansion early to put the finishing touches on the cupcakes I'd made for the party and had watched as Lolly clicked her way from one room to another, directing small teams of black-uniformed employees, turning enormous flower arrangements a half inch counterclockwise, sending monogrammed linen cocktail napkins back for a third round of ironing, and shaking her head tersely enough that even her lacquered bob shook at the caterer's suggestion that the filet mignon station be placed near the entry to the living room rather than by the farthest set of French doors.

By the time the grandfather clock in the foyer struck eight, the house was filled to the brim with extravagant holiday cheer—flickering candles in oversized crystal globes, giant red poinsettias, lush arrangements of white hydrangea and roses, strands of twinkling holiday lights, and a monumental, red-ribbon-swagged

Christmas tree that would have given the tree at Rockefeller Center a run for its money. My cupcakes, on which I'd placed meticulously molded fondant stars and trees and doves, lined tray after tray along the kitchen counter, waiting to be passed to the more than one hundred guests expected that evening.

The seven-piece swing band was three songs into the evening by the time Julia finally appeared downstairs, looking exceptionally thin and glamorous in a pale gold, one-shouldered dress. She hugged me so tightly that my shimmering red trapeze top crinkled like wrapping paper in her embrace. Before we had a chance to speak, Wes strode up and took Julia's hand.

"Hello, gorgeous bride of mine," he drawled, spinning her skillfully into his chest and dipping her backward for a kiss. When he righted her, I saw her eyes were glittery with emotion. "Hey there, Annie," Wes said, kissing my cheek warmly.

"Happy engagement!" I said, hoping my voice sounded cheery. I'd never been particularly good at keeping secrets, and I had a terrible feeling that if I were left too long in Wes's presence, I would let slip some hint about Julia's miscarriage and emotional state. Perhaps Julia had anticipated this, because she suddenly looked beyond my shoulder and smiled, waving her wrist so rapidly that the tinkling of her diamond bangles could be heard even over the band.

"I have a little surprise for you," she said to me.

Behind me stood Ogden Gertzwell. "Hi, Annie," he said, kissing my cheek before turning toward Julia and Wes and congratulating them on their engagement. "Thanks for inviting me," he said as Wes clapped him heartily on the back.

Julia hugged him. "We're so glad you made it!"

I glanced at her, puzzled by her enthusiasm. When I looked back at Ogden, he seemed amused.

"She didn't tell you she invited me, did she?" he asked.

"No," I admitted.

He laughed. "Do you mind?"

"Of course not."

Sure, I could have been annoyed with Julia for inviting Ogden. After all, wasn't it bad enough that I had to attend a party with a crowd of people I didn't know, people with whom I had nothing in common? Why add insult to injury by inviting a windbag like Ogden and then springing him on me like I should be grateful for the super fun surprise? So I could have been irritated. But I wasn't. Or at least I was trying not to be. I was newly resolved to give Julia the benefit of the doubt, and step one in that process seemed to be allowing for the possibility that inviting Ogden Gertzwell to her party wasn't just her way of torturing me.

"How's the produce business, Ogden?" Wes asked. "Keeping you busy even through the holidays, I imagine?"

"Oh, always," Ogden said. He seemed like he was about to go on, but he looked at me and appeared to change his mind. "But I'm off duty tonight. When someone manages to get me in a tux, I figure I owe it to them to take the night off from farm talk."

"Fair enough," Wes said, grinning.

As Ogden and Wes tended to what was clearly a blossoming bromance, Julia suddenly grew pale. I followed her gaze to where Lolly and Tad stood nearby. They seemed to be engaged in some sort of spat, their faces drawn and tense. It wasn't at all like them to be so public with their emotions, and I felt that old anxious, tingling sensation in my legs as I watched them abruptly leave the room.

"I'm sorry, but will you excuse me?" Julia said, interrupting Wes's enthusiastic description of the exotic Chinese vegetables he'd discovered on his latest business trip. "Oh, and Wes, I see Joan and Devon over there. Would you mind introducing them around? I don't think they know anyone."

"Of course," Wes said. Within moments, Julia had delivered

Wes to the lost-looking couple in the corner and then exited through the same door her parents had just used.

Left alone, Ogden and I were saved from awkward small talk by a pallid, mousy member of the waitstaff who approached with a tray of golden crostini slivers topped with soft cheese and some sort of dark fruit jam. I loaded several onto a napkin while Ogden took a step closer to the tray.

"Is that fig jam?" he asked the girl, peering at the hors d'oeuvres skeptically.

"Yes," the girl said, smiling. A smattering of pimples was inexpertly coated with cover-up on her chin. "It's delicious."

"Hmm," Ogden breathed. He lowered his large nose to the tray, his tan forehead creasing as he inhaled deeply. "Black mission or brown turkey?"

The girl glanced back and forth between Ogden and me, but by then my mouth was too full to intervene on her behalf. "Excuse me?" she asked.

"Well, they're obviously not white kadota"—he sniffed—"so I'm guessing either black mission or brown turkey."

"I think it's Brie?" the girl murmured.

"No, no. I'm asking about the figs. Are they black mission? Most likely."

I sighed. He'd obviously already forgotten his resolution to not discuss the farm.

"I'm really not sure. I'm sorry," the girl said. She legitimately looked apologetic, and I felt a strong urge to pull her aside for a pep talk on how to deal with smug men. Unfortunately, I had a feeling Ogden wasn't the only one of his ilk she was likely to encounter that night, odd duck that he was.

"That doesn't look like Brie to me," Ogden responded, clearly oblivious to the anxiety he was inducing in the girl. "It's most likely goat's cheese. Is it organic?"

I stared at Ogden. Was he serious? *Organic?* "Oh for chrissakes, Ogden," I said, never mind my half-full mouth. "The figs are black mission and hail from a biodynamic farm in Central California where they were harvested on a partly cloudy morning by women wearing red merino wool gloves. The cheese comes from a three-year-old goat named Ethel who lives in Marin and subsists on a strictly organic diet. The wheat for the bread was harvested by friggin' environmental PhD students interning at a cooperative farm in Kansas. And the sum of these fabulous crostini is even greater than the parts. It's time to shit or get off the pot."

The waitress coughed to cover a laugh. Ogden's thick blond brows furrowed together. *He has absolutely no idea how ridiculous he sounds when he talks like that*, I thought, surprised. The realization chastened me a little. Ogden took a crostini from the tray and bit into it slowly, looking around the room as he chewed. The waitress nodded at me gratefully and made a quick escape.

"I'm sorry," I said. I tried to mean it, but the apology just wouldn't stick. "Okay, no I'm not. You were harassing that poor girl who is probably just trying to make a few bucks before going back to college! Not everyone knows the origin of every ingredient they're serving."

"Well, maybe they should! People who serve food have a responsibility to know what it is they're pushing on people. I'm sure the St. Clairs would be mortified to know that their staff is so poorly educated."

This comment, tossed off so flippantly, enraged me. "My mother was an integral part of the St. Clair staff for a very long time," I snapped. Luckily, the music was loud enough that my raised voice didn't turn any heads. "She never graduated high school, but she would have been smart enough to know that telling you that you're a pretentious ass is just a waste of breath."

Ogden's mouth fell open. "Oh, Annie. I didn't mean—"

"And," I continued, cutting him off, "she knew more about the importance of good food than you ever will. She presented it with *heart*."

Ogden shook his head. He reached out his big hands toward me for a moment before letting them fall awkwardly to his side. "I'm sorry. You're right. I don't know why I gave that girl such a hard time." He sighed and looked down, his face softening. "I was probably trying to impress you."

"What?"

"You're a hard nut to crack, Annie. I talk too much when I'm with you. I swear, I'm not usually so loquacious." He pulled at his sandy hair so that it stood askew off the top of his head and smiled at me ruefully. "I seem to leave every encounter I have with you with my own words ringing unattractively in my ears and the distinct taste of my own foot in my mouth."

I studied him. This Ogden Gertzwell was full of surprises. "Well," I said. "I'm sure of all feet, it's safe to guess that yours were raised biodynamically. If that's any consolation."

He laughed, and the act seemed to relax him. His whole body was suddenly looser, his muscular shoulders less tense. "So that's how you know Julia?" he asked. "Through your mother?"

"I guess you could say that. She was Julia's nanny and also cooked a lot for the whole family. Her role sort of shifted over time as we grew up. We lived in the carriage house you walk through to enter the courtyard."

"You grew up here? That sounds—complicated," Ogden said. "No wonder it always felt like there was tension between you and Julia. If you don't mind me saying it, you always seemed like an ill-matched pair. I could never figure out how you wound up in business together."

"No, you're right. Pairs don't come much more ill-matched. We've hit our rough patches over the years. But things are better now, I think."

"I'm glad to hear it. Sometimes," he said slowly, "the things that happen when we're young are the hardest to let go of."

"Exactly," I said, eyeing him with new appreciation. "Frankly, I find that whole idea mortifying. Will we ever grow up and stop being stuck in childhood?"

"Probably not." Ogden cocked his head, and I saw a little glint of mischief in his eyes. "But perhaps as a seller of cupcakes, that works to your advantage."

"Oh God, you're right!" I said, laughing. "I'm like a Freudian capitalist!"

He grinned. "Hey," he said. "If I promise not to say another word about the food or the waitstaff, do you think we could pretend to start the evening over?"

"Deal."

He looked surprised.

"What?" I laughed. "I'm trying to not be so hard on everyone. It's just one of many New Year's resolutions."

"Ah," he said, and snagged us a couple of champagne flutes from a passing tray. "It seems like I'd better start making a few myself."

24

Julia

AFTER A QUICK search for my parents in the kitchen, I hurried up the stairs to the second floor. The sound of my mother's agitated voice floated toward me from the direction of my father's study.

"I just don't understand, Tad!" she was saying when I entered the room. "I asked you to do one thing, just *one* thing in preparation for this event, and you didn't do it?"

My father was sitting dejectedly in his office chair as my mother darted around him, opening and banging shut his desk drawers.

"What happened?" I asked.

My mother straightened, startled. She blinked a few times and made a quick, irritated adjustment of the dramatic cowl-neck collar on her black gown. "It's nothing, darling. Everything's fine. Go back downstairs and enjoy the party."

I looked at my father. He seemed smaller than usual, sitting like that in his chair with my mother straight-backed and bristling with annoyance at his side. "Dad? Are you okay?"

He smiled, shrugging sheepishly. "Oh yes. Just dealing with a minor setback. I was tasked with supplying the cash for the staff tips tonight and I seem to have fallen short in my duties."

My mother pursed her lips. One of her prime rules for party throwing was to have all staff tips divvied out in individual envelopes at the start of the night so as to avoid any last-minute snafus or drink-induced overpayments at the end of the evening. It was Lolly St. Clair Party Planning 101. My father knew these rules as well as anyone—as far as I could tell, his role as the pre-party bank runner had been established decades ago.

"You forgot?" I asked.

"Absolutely not," he said, a little louder than necessary. My mother and I exchanged a quick glance. "I went yesterday."

"So the money is missing?"

"Misplaced," he clarified. "I thought I put it in the top right drawer of my desk the way I always do. But it's not there, or anywhere else in the office."

I thought for a moment, watching my mother become more agitated by the second. "Did you check the jacket you wore to the bank? Maybe you left it in a pocket. Or the car?"

My father's face brightened. With surprising grace for such a large man, he leaped out of his chair. "The car! Of course. I probably just forgot to bring it in. Hang on, girls, I'll be back in a wink."

Alone with my mother, I gave her a pointed stare. She straightened a bit taller. "It's nothing, darling," she said. "I know what you're worrying about and I think it's just ridiculous. On a special night like this!"

"Ridiculous to worry about Dad? Or ridiculous to worry about anything on the night of my engagement party?"

"Either one. Take your pick."

"Mother," I said, speaking quickly before my father returned. "Something isn't right. You see it, too, don't you? This isn't like him. He isn't himself."

For just one moment, my mother's steely gaze flickered. I saw then that, in her own way, she was worried, too. I heard my father's heavy footsteps in the hall.

"Just promise me we'll make him see a doctor next week," I whispered. "Promise me now so I can enjoy the evening."

My mother's shoulders fell an inch before she gave a brisk nod. I felt my father standing beside me then.

"So much for the hope of having fathered the next Sherlock Holmes. The money isn't in the car," he announced. He had a hangdog look on his face, and I could tell the whole situation perplexed him. "Curtis is going to drive me down to the bank. We'll be back before most of the fashionably late crowd arrives."

"Drive like the wind," my mother said, her tone nearly imperceptibly softer than it had been ten minutes earlier.

The party was in full swing by the time I made it back downstairs. When I entered the living room Wes immediately appeared beside me and pulled me out onto the dance floor. We spun over the gleaming marble floor, inhaling evergreen-scented air and the slight smokiness of the enormous wood-burning fire; it seemed both an ideal beginning and picture-perfect ending to an evening. I think, in the pit of my stomach, I knew then that I really would tell him everything that night, let the chips fall where they may. Ever since I'd told Annie about the miscarriage and my meetings with Jake, I'd felt the weight of keeping those secrets from Wes more strongly than ever. *This year might end with my engagement party*, I realized with a pang, *but the next one has a reasonable chance of kicking off with me as a newly single woman.*

When the band took a break, Wes and I slowed to a stop in the middle of the room and I looked up into his eyes, feeling my love for him beating its wide wings, frantic in my chest. *That*

250 • Meg Donohue

might have been our last dance. The thought terrified me. I held his hand in mine and resolved not to release it all evening.

"Took me a second to figure out what was going on there with Ogden and Annie," Wes said as we walked toward the bar. "You didn't tell me you were throwing your hat in the match-making ring."

"I'm trying out something different. Thought it might be time to learn some new tricks."

"Well, you seem to be taking to it like a bear to honey."

"He's perfect for her. They're two odd peas in a pod. She just doesn't realize it yet." It was more than that, really. Ogden and Annie seemed to share a solid self-confidence; both seemed immune to any outside pressure to disguise their quirks.

"You're a good friend to her," Wes said.

"Oh, I don't know. Maybe." I looked down at our entwined hands and took a deep breath. "You know, Wes," I said, "we haven't had a moment alone together in ages. Maybe we could sneak upstairs before the countdown begins and no one will even know we're gone."

A mischievous grin spread across his face, and I saw a glimpse of the devious, too-clever-for-his-own-good child he must have been. "Lead the way, my lady."

If only either of us knew the path I was leading him down, I thought as we climbed the stairs. But if we did, he might not follow so willingly.

Upstairs, leaning against the pillows on my bed with the sounds of the party drifting up from below, Wes and I kissed for a long time. As his hands began to push down the gold strap atop my right shoulder, I stopped him. He looked at me, flushed.

"It's good to be alone with you," he said. "I missed you."

"I missed you, too," I said. I took his hands in mine and stared at them, blinking back tears. "I have so much to tell you."

Wes shifted. "What do you mean?" When I was quiet, he lifted my chin gently until our eyes met. "What is it, Julia?"

And so I told him everything—the miscarriage, that long awful night knowing the baby had died but was still inside of me, the terrible procedure the next day. Instead of delivering our baby, whose due date I was all too well aware would have been that very week, I was delivering the truth. And then I told him about Jake—the drinks, the kiss, the misunderstanding with Annie. Haltingly, through tears, every tiny detail spilled out of me. While I was speaking, Wes held me, then stood angrily, sat back down abruptly, held me again, squeezed the blanket fiercely with his free hand, shook his head, and cleared his throat, his eyes red behind his glasses.

"I don't give a rat's ass about this Jake character," he said when I was finished. It was the first thing he said, so I knew his words weren't entirely true, but I appreciated hearing them nonetheless. "It sounds to me like he took advantage of you. Maybe you let him. That shouldn't have happened. But I believe you when you say you don't feel anything for him and that that kiss was his doing, not yours. I believe you one hundred percent. And I don't want to talk about him anymore." This last bit came out as low and angry as a growl, and I swallowed, nodding.

"But the baby—" The word caught in his throat. He looked away. "Why wouldn't you tell me, Julia? All this time. That was my baby, too. That was our baby."

"I know," I said. Tears were streaming down my face. "At first, I just wanted to tell you the good news in person. And then it became bad news so quickly, and I . . . shut down. I didn't tell anyone. But I should have told you. Of course I should have. And then at some point I think my anxiety shifted away from what had happened and focused more on what could still happen."

"What do you mean?"

"I just have this feeling," I said, barely getting the words out, "that something is wrong with me. That I'm saddling you with marriage to a woman who can't have children. And I know how much you want a family."

"Oh, but Julia, that's why I'm marrying you—to be a family. You and me. *We're* the family."

I pulled back and looked at him. "You're being kind," I said carefully. "It's easy for you to say those words now, when we both feel young and optimistic. But please think about all of this more before you say anything you might regret later. You want children. I know you do."

Wes took off his glasses and wiped his eyes. In his long silence, my chest seized painfully. "Julia," he said at last, clasping my hands. "I'm sure the miscarriage was a one-time thing. And even if it turns out to be more than that, we *will* be parents. That's not just some hunch—as far as I'm concerned, it's a fact. There are lots of ways to be a family. Look at Karen and Fo . . . or Rick and Monica. Those are picture-perfect families—I can't think of them in any other way. They're families I would be thrilled to be a part of."

Karen, the chief technology officer at Wes's company, and her husband, Fo, had used a surrogate and were now the parents of beautiful, ringleted boys. Rick, Wes's best friend from college, and his wife, Monica, had adopted a plump, perpetually happy baby girl from South Korea. I had always thought of them as bittersweet families, cobbled together through disappointment and tears and modern science and airplane tickets, but now, looking at them through Wes's clear eyes, I could begin to understand that they were just families like any other—complicated, messy, and forever bound. I thought of Annie and Lucia and how when I was growing up, the two of them had always seemed as much a part of my family as my own parents, how the lack of blood connection didn't mean anything when you were a child who needed love, or an adult with an open, generous heart.

"You're going to be an amazing father," I said softly.

"Only if you're by my side," Wes answered. I saw in his eyes that he meant it, and the frantic flapping in my chest finally slowed. I took a deep breath. Through the open door we heard the sound of our engagement party guests beginning the countdown to midnight.

"TEN! NINE! EIGHT!"

Wes and I smiled at each other. He stood and pulled me to my feet and together we hurried down the hall.

"FOUR! THREE! TWO!"

At the top of the stairs, with the sounds of the party loud in our ears, Wes wrapped his arms around me and kissed my collarbone, and then my neck, and then my cheek, and then finally my lips, until we had kissed away the old year and kept kissing right into the new.

January

25

Annie

AS THE FIRST month of the new year neared its close, Julia and I sat at Treat's counter and peeled the liners off our cupcakes while we ran through our weekly business agenda. It had been impossible not to notice the change in Julia since New Year's Eve. Her smile seemed broader, her eyes brighter, her step quicker. Things had clearly taken a turn for the better with Wes, and I felt happy for her and proud that she'd finally been able to unload the secret that had been weighing her down for so long. Now, as though awakening from an extended sleep, she talked nonstop about her wedding and everything there was to do. It was enough to make a single girl like myself want to scream, but I managed to hold it together. She deserved to feel happy—even if happiness for Julia meant endless discussions of calligraphy and orchids and *custom-dyed parasols*. To each their own, I suppose.

"My mother has been driving everyone in the house absolutely nuts looking for your mom's recipe book," Julia told me after she'd taken her first careful bite of cupcake that night. I looked up sharply, my heart skipping a beat. She pressed her lips into an apologetic smile. "It hasn't turned up, but she asked me to give you this. I guess it's a consolation gift."

She pulled from her bag a chocolate-brown box tied with a sumptuous white silk ribbon. Inside, I found a thick blank book, its cover a swirling Venetian pattern of blues and greens. On the first page, in her confident, graceful cursive, Lolly had inscribed:

Dear Annie,
    A recipe book for the next generation—perhaps now is the time for new traditions after all.

Love always,
Lolly St. Clair

P.S. I have all the faith in the world that it will not be long before your mother's book joins this one on your bookshelf.

"It's beautiful," I said.

"It is," Julia agreed, sighing. "But, still, I'm sorry."

For the first time all month, Julia's mood seemed damp. She plodded through the week's agenda in a weary monotone. Even our discussion of the projected sales boost from the upcoming Valentine's Day didn't seem to lift her spirits. Most telling of all, her cupcake, since that initial bite, had sat untouched in front of her. And even though the sight of her perpetually perfect manicure no longer annoyed me the way it once had— *because, really, what productive member of society has time for weekly nail appointments?*—listening to said perfect nails drum anxiously against the counter for five minutes straight was enough to test the patience even of those freshly committed to kindness via the power of the new year.

"Okay, out with it already!" I demanded at last, pressing her laptop closed before she could argue. "I refuse to listen to one more ingenious marketing strategy without first learning what has brought on the sour face. You've been rainbows and kittens all month and now suddenly you look like someone slid right down that rainbow and landed squat on your kitten. So spill."

Julia sighed. "Is it that obvious?" she said. "I swear, I used to have a killer poker face, but I can't keep anything from you, can I?"

"Not when your mood swings threaten to give me whiplash. I have a kitchen to run."

Julia bit her lip and glanced outside. For a moment, I wondered if something had happened at Treat that she hadn't told me. As far as I knew, there hadn't been any more break-ins or sightings of Our Guy around the shop. At Inspector Ramirez's advice, we'd installed a camera, but so far it had only recorded customers during the day and an empty shop at night. I think Julia and I were both beginning to relax a little, though if I were honest with myself, I'd admit that there were still times when I stood at the front window of the shop, or when I walked around the neighborhood alone, that I felt a prickly, on-edge sensation in the pit of my stomach. But I chalked the feeling up to residual unease and tried not to think about the other possibility—that I was being watched.

So I was a little surprised when it turned out Julia's mood that day had nothing at all to do with Treat or the break-ins.

"It's my dad," she admitted quietly. She told me that Tad had been misplacing things, and his out-of-character behavior had been weighing on her. I remembered that day in her kitchen months earlier when she had asked whether I noticed a change in him. He'd seemed a little different, I remembered thinking, a little more talkative than he'd been when we were kids, but fine. I hadn't realized just how worried Julia had been. She told me he had been evaluated for Alzheimer's earlier that week.

"But he's okay." Strangely, she delivered this news with a tight, unhappy smile. "All the preliminary tests have come back totally normal. The doctor thinks it's just age-related forgetfulness."

"Well, that's a relief. Isn't it?" I asked, confused.

"Of course. It's funny, though," she said, and then hesitated. "All this time I've been worried about my dad. But if it turns out I shouldn't be worried about him, who am I supposed to be worried about?"

"I'm not sure I follow."

"It's just that all those things that are missing—they're really valuable. He's not misplacing his pen or his glasses—he's losing jewelry and cash."

I looked at her carefully. "So you think someone might be stealing from him?"

Julia sighed. "I don't know. I'd really hate to think that."

"Well, it sounds like it's too late. You're already thinking it. Have you talked to your mom?"

"Do you think I should?"

"If I know her at all, I bet she has similar concerns."

"But the people who have access to our house are people who've been part of our family for years. Which of them would do such a thing to us?"

Julia and I were both silent. I guessed we were both doing the same thing: running through the list of St. Clair employees. Stoic, steadfast Curtis? Of course not. Round-faced, blue-eyed Sonja who had been cooking their meals for a decade? Un-thinkable. Quiet-as-a-mouse Jacqueline or chatterbox Angela who, as a team, had managed to keep the house sparkling and dust-free for years? Highly unlikely. Adolfo, the gardener who dutifully clipped flowers from the garden before the sun had even risen so that Lolly would have a fresh arrangement on the hall table each morning? Ridiculous. The whole train of thought was disturbing.

"You should talk to your mom," I said. I hated feeling at a loss as to how to help Julia, but that's where I found myself.

And then, just as Julia picked up her cupcake and took one

slow, almost mournful bite, it happened again. I was swept by that prickly, stomach-churning sense that someone was watching me, or her, or both of us. I gave the street a surreptitious scan, not wanting to alarm Julia, but it was empty. I decided I was simply hopped up on one too many cupcakes, dieting being the one resolution that I'd forsaken within an hour of the new year.

26

Julia

OUR HOUSE COULD seem warm and reassuring one day—every piece of furniture, every rug, each piece of art as familiar to me as my own face—and creaking, huge, and foreboding the next. It had always been that way. I remember afternoons when I came home from a long day of social strategy at Devon Prep and, throwing myself into the maroon couch in the dark upstairs den, felt there was no place where I could more easily be my true self, no place where I felt safer and more secure. Other days—when my parents were off at some event or another, and Lucia and Annie were happily tucked away in the cozy carriage house for the night, and I lay below an airy summit of duvet in my bed waiting to hear my parents' key in the door downstairs and feel my mother's light kiss on my forehead upon her return—I was certain that no lonelier, colder, or more cavernous place existed on earth.

My father's diagnosis was good news, of course. Great news. The very best news. I didn't even like to think about what the alternative would have been—the idea of losing him slowly—or, worse, quickly—to Alzheimer's was . . . unthinkable. And yet, since his return from the doctor, the house had begun to feel more and more like that creaking, cold place of my youth and less like the safe haven I had run to that spring when my world had crumbled around me. I tried to pinpoint exactly what I felt as I walked down the gleaming mahogany stairs, or opened the door to my carpeted walk-in closet, or stashed another wedding present in one of the sun-filled spare bedrooms. It wasn't that I felt antsy, exactly—though it would certainly be nice when Wes and I moved into our own place after the wedding. There was only so much parental contact that any decently well-adjusted twenty-eight-year-old could stand. So, yes, I was feeling eager to move on, and yes, I did have the sense that my time at home had reached its natural conclusion. But it was more than that. I stopped, midway down the stairs at nine in the morning, about to head to Treat for the day, my hand on the cool banister, and probed my emotions. What did I feel? Unease, I supposed. Apprehension. I could hear Sonja in the kitchen, her familiar voice quick and warbled like water running over rocks, and Curtis's occasional low response. They were far enough away that I couldn't make out their words; their conversation was punctuated by the bang of a pan being placed on the range, the click of the gas flame igniting.

Unsafe, I thought with a start. The word chilled me. *I feel unsafe.*

My mother's sudden voice from her bedroom upstairs was as distinct as if she were speaking directly in my ear and I flinched, watching my hand jump on the banister. I hurried back up the stairs.

She was perched on the edge of her bed, one hand tangled in the curlicue cord of the old-fashioned black rotary phone she insisted on keeping on her bedside table. It was a position I'd seen her in a thousand times: one earring off, bolt upright, brow smooth but still somehow emitting an aura of perturbitude. She eyed me in the doorway and motioned for me to come in. I shut the door behind me.

"Faye? Faye? *Faye!* I'm going to have to call you back." She paused. "Yes, we absolutely are going to need the south field behind the machinery barn cleared and mowed for the wedding—that's where the staff vehicles will go." Pause. "The *staff* vehicles." Pause. "No, the *south* field. Yes, that's right, but—" She looked at me and pulled her mouth down at the corners. "Faye? Faye, we're going to have to go over the entire list another time. Just please don't do anything until we talk. There's no point in rushing and getting things wrong. *Don't do anything.*" Pause. Large sigh. "Yes, that's right. *Yes, Faye.* Sit tight. Good-bye for now."

Whenever my mother set that phone down on its cradle, I understood her attachment to it. Ending a cell phone call could never hold the same delicious finality.

"How is she?" I asked. Faye was the house manager for Wood-stone, our family's home and vineyard in Napa where Wes and I would be married. We'd inherited her from the home's previous owners. Faye was now partially deaf, though my mother insisted the deafness was simply a strategy she employed to do exactly what she wanted with the home that she'd lived in most of her life and—probably rightfully—thought of as her own.

"Oh, Faye is Faye," my mother said, clipping her earring back into place. "Faye is fine. You might need to be married in a field steaming with horse manure, but Faye is just dandy."

I laughed. "We'll tell the guests to bring their mucking boots."

"We will *not*," my mother said.

I dropped my smile. "No," I said. "Of course not." *Without Lucia and Annie around when I was young*, I wondered, *would anyone in this family ever have cracked a smile?*

"What is it?" my mother asked. "You look worried."

"I've been thinking about Dad and all of those missing things."

My mother waved her hand, and her diamond ring caught the light for one blinding moment. "Oh, that? But he's fine. You know what the doctor said. He needs to do more brain teasers. Crosswords, that sort of thing." She sighed. "Aging is a beast,

Julia darling, but you've got to take the bull by the horns. I've been telling your father that for *years*."

"So you think it's as straightforward as that?" I asked.

"Well, yes." Something in the tense set of her jaw when she said this made me feel apprehensive. I thought back to when we'd talked about my father before, how I'd had the sense that she was not telling me everything. I bit the inside of my lip, trying to think of how to get her to be open with me. Now she tucked her chin down toward her chest and studied me, her gaze darting back and forth between my two eyes. "Julia, you're being uncharacteristically quiet. What is it?"

"The things going missing," I began slowly, swallowing. "That started happening right around when I came home, right?"

"Yes," my mother said. I tried to keep my expression nonchalant, but encouraging. "Well, no. Not exactly. I suppose it had been going on for some time before that. Years, maybe. But sporadically. Nothing that alarmed me. I really didn't think anything of it. I still don't."

"You don't?"

"No."

"I don't think I believe you."

My mother sighed. "Julia, will you please tell me what on earth we are talking about? I don't particularly enjoy feeling like a character in an Agatha Christie novel."

"Do you ever wonder if maybe one of the people who work for us has had something to do with the lost items?" I took a deep breath, then said quietly, "Like maybe Curtis?" With his access to my father, he was the only one who truly made sense, but he was also the one whose betrayal would hurt the most.

My mother pressed her lips together, a habit I'd long ago realized I'd acquired from her but nonetheless could not shake. "Curtis has been with our family for ages. Forever."

"Yes," I said. "I know."

"He is one of your father's closest friends."

I didn't say anything.

"I'm not sure you realize how incredibly difficult it is to find trustworthy people to work in your home. These people that we surround ourselves with—they're privy to everything. We *must* believe they are good, loyal people or the equation simply does not add up." My mother seemed to be steering herself toward something, so I didn't interrupt her. She gazed at me calmly the whole time, but I could sense her mind working furiously behind her cool blue eyes.

"Lucia Quintana," she said. "Now *there* was a loyal person." She held a thin finger aloft. "A loyal *friend*. Lucia was a completely open book—such a refreshing characteristic in a person. Just like Annie, wouldn't you say? I would have trusted her with my most valuable possessions. And I did, of course. I trusted her with you. I trusted her judgment unconditionally."

"What do you mean?" I asked. This mention of Lucia threw me—of all the possible scenarios I had steadied myself for leading up to this conversation, none had involved Lucia.

"Curtis has struck me as . . . less than ideal over the years. He's *not* an open book. I consider myself an excellent judge of character, but Curtis is remarkably tough to read. There's something unnerving about having someone know the intimate details of your life while you know next to nothing about his. Not that that ever seemed to bother your father."

"So that's why you never let him go? Because of Dad?"

"Well, yes, of course. Your father was a big part of it. But it was Lucia, really, who convinced me all those years ago. I trusted Lucia and she trusted Curtis, so, transitively, I believed I could trust Curtis. *Believe*," my mother said, correcting herself. "I still believe I can trust Curtis."

I thought about this. "How did you know Lucia trusted Curtis?" Even as I asked, I realized I knew the answer.

My mother looked at me and blinked. "Well, they were to-gether, of course. Lucia and Curtis. They were—let's see—I suppose you would say they were dating."

As my mother spoke, a long-forgotten memory flashed through my mind. I must have been ten or eleven years old at the time. I was walking down the hall to the kitchen when I spotted Lucia and Curtis standing close together in the little room off the hall where the staff ate their meals and stashed their coats and bags for the day. I remember feeling there was something vaguely off-kilter about what I was seeing, the slant of their bodies toward each other was both unfamiliar and un-settling. Curtis looked over then, suddenly, and without chang-ing the look on his face at all, without saying anything, abruptly closed the door. I remember thinking that he must not have seen me there—the hall was dark—and that, anyway, there was probably nothing strange at all about what I had seen. This was simply the other side of the lives of the people that worked for us. Even my beloved Lucia had a whole other life that didn't involve me. That sounds like it was a weighty moment for me—some pivotal awakening. The end of ignorance. It was not. I simply kept walking down the hall and forgot the whole thing had ever happened. Until now.

"I can't say I ever understood exactly what Lucia saw in him," my mother continued. "But she saw *something* and I decided that was enough for me. I certainly didn't want to let Curtis go and risk losing Lucia—and little Annie!—to boot. That was out of the question."

"But Mom," I said, "we lost Lucia and Annie years ago. Why have you kept Curtis around all this time if you don't really trust him?"

My mother's eyes softened. When she spoke, her voice, too, had softened. "Well, because Lucia loved him. And I missed her. She was a dear, dear friend. She took care of all of us really, not just you and Annie. With Curtis still around, I could imagine Lucia was still here, too. I suppose it made me feel that I remained close to her, even in her death. I couldn't lose all of you in one fell swoop."

I thought of my mother clicking briskly around our huge house in the year after Annie and I had left for college and Lucia had died. It had never occurred to me that she might feel unsettled by the house's yawning quiet in the same way I sometimes did. I always pictured my mother hurrying toward something, always busy, always efficient, never allowing herself to linger too long over unproductive feelings like loneliness or sadness.

As though reading my thoughts, my mother sat up a little straighter on the bed and toyed with the thin gold band of her watch. "The whole thing is really very silly. In fact, I remember having the distinct sense that things between Lucia and Curtis had cooled a bit that fall before she died. So, there you have it. The truth revealed: I'm a sentimental fool and I can't bear to let him go." She waved her hand in front of her face. "No, no. Really, the fool is your father. He is very attached to Curtis, you know. I'm sure if he caught Curtis trying to steal the shirt off his back he would just throw open his closet to give Curtis a few more options."

My mouth fell. "So you really do think it's been Curtis all this time! Why haven't you said anything? Why hasn't anyone confronted him?"

"Oh really, Julia darling, what's the point?" my mother asked airily. She stood from the bed and busied herself with an examination of her forehead in the mirror over her nightstand, her long, arched brows raised high, undoubtedly checking to see if this unpleasant conversation had noticeably aged her in any way. "We have the money to spare. If he needs it that badly, let him have it. He's practically a member of the family at this point."

Our eyes met in the mirror. "If he's stealing from us," I said, "I don't think he feels the same."

The corners of her mouth quivered. She looked at me for a long beat of time in the mirror before turning around to face me. "Julia darling," she said, not bothering to mask the sorrow in her voice, "I'm afraid you're probably right."

That night, after we'd locked up the shop and I'd dropped Annie off at her apartment, I pulled a sheet of paper from my bag and studied it below the light of my car. It was a list of the contact information for each of our family employees; I'd printed it out in my father's office that morning after the conversation with my mother. My finger moved slowly down the page until I reached Curtis's name. I knew he lived down in Daly City, but I'd never been to his house before. I don't think any of us had.

It was ten p.m.—late to show up unannounced. But I knew my parents were staying in that night and didn't need Curtis to drive them anywhere, so he'd likely be at home by then. I don't know what I wanted from him exactly. But I knew I didn't want to embarrass him or make the situation any more awkward by confronting him in our house. I wanted him to be honest with me. I guess, really, I just wanted some control. I wanted things back to normal, back to the way they were supposed to be. My body had betrayed me, but there was nothing I could do about that. This, though, I could do something about. I wanted to feel safe again. If I'd learned anything from my newly strengthened relationships with Wes and Annie, it was that I needed to be brave, to take risks, and to be honest. I plugged Curtis's address into my car's GPS and pulled out onto the street.

27

Annie

I CAN'T SAY exactly why I returned to Treat that night after Julia dropped me off at home. I wish I could hang the impulse on the hook of intuition, but I think it was something more along the lines of run-of-the-mill insomnia that drove me down to the bakery at eleven o'clock at night. Julia had tasked me with developing a new cupcake for her wedding and I'd found myself stumped by the challenge. I wanted to create a cupcake that reflected Julia herself in some way—beautiful and immaculate on the outside, with a flavor profile that was elegant and brave and laced with surprising, but delicate sweetness. I'd been playing with the idea of a classic lemon cake with a hidden heart of wild berry custard, topped with sweet vanilla buttercream, but so far I hadn't been able to get all of the flavors quite right. I could have continued working on the recipe at home, but something—I really can't say what—prompted me to pull on my jacket and walk the long blocks back to Treat.

When I stepped through the cupcakery's door, I sensed immediately that something was wrong. The air, usually warm and sweet, smelled acrid and thin. Distracted, I must have forgotten to turn the deadbolt on the door. I flicked on the light and scanned the shop. Nothing seemed astray: the register gleamed beneath the chandelier and the glass display counter bore a few streaks from the wipe-down Devi had given it earlier that evening.

Then I saw it: a thin, steady plume of dark smoke rising up from the crack below the kitchen door.

Now, I know what I *should* have done at that point. I should have turned right around, walked out onto the sidewalk, and called 911. But the smoke was coming from *my* kitchen. The kitchen that had become my second home. The kitchen that was the very heart of the little shop Julia and I had turned into a successful business. Without giving myself a second to think too deeply about what I was doing, I grabbed a burgundy dish towel from a shelf behind the counter, held it to my mouth, and nudged open the swinging door to the kitchen with my foot.

The smoke in the kitchen was still diaphanous at that point, a dark haze moving through the air in a manner that in any other circumstances I might have described as beautiful. I stepped inside and felt a suffocating blanket of heat drape over me. Across the room, a wide crest of fire lapped at the back wall, eating its way up toward the ceiling faster than I could ever have imagined, coughing out black clouds with each leap upward.

Peering through the thickening smoke, I made out what appeared to be a pile of recipe folders engulfed in flame on top of one of the ranges. *How the hell did they get there?* I reached for the fire extinguisher that usually hung beside the refrigerator and saw that it was gone. My heart began to beat even more furiously in my chest, my mind racing indignantly. I remembered seeing the fire extinguisher there earlier that day—someone must have purposely removed it. *Who would do this?*

Enraged, I lowered the dish towel from my face and began to whack it against the flames. I'm not sure how long I stood there, smacking that towel against the wall, determined to stop that fire from devouring my kitchen. Time seemed to slow and then quicken at the same pace as my ever-shifting thoughts. A searing heat pulsed against my face as the fire grew until, exhausted and defeated, I turned back toward the door to the shop and saw that the path had been swallowed up by smoke. My eyes were stinging by then, leaking hot tears that further blinded me. I stumbled toward where I thought the door should be and slammed my foot into the stand mixer. Foot throbbing, I fell to the floor. A strange, itching, tightening sensation clamped down on my throat. Suddenly, I couldn't stop coughing.

And then I felt the hot floor beneath my cheek, and then nothing at all.

I awoke to find myself lying on a stretcher in an ambulance, a darkly bearded EMT hovering above me.

"You're going to be okay," the EMT said loudly. He smiled a rueful smile at me—*was he disappointed I wasn't in worse shape?*—revealing a row of small, coffee-stained teeth.

"Okay," I croaked. My voice was foreign-sounding and muffled by what I discovered was an oxygen mask over my mouth. My head throbbed and my throat and eyes burned, but a quick test of my limbs reassured me that he was right. I was okay.

A dry crescendo of a cough rose from a corner of the car. I lifted my head to peer around the EMT—the movement required a surprising amount of effort—and there, hunched on a seat near the foot of my stretcher, wearing his usual hooded sweatshirt but now an oxygen mask over his face, too, was Our Guy. The Mystery Man. The Stalker. I pressed my head back down against the stretcher, panic and confusion colliding painfully in my already pounding head. My mind raced. I motioned for the EMT to bend down closer to me and pulled the mask from my face.

"That man," I whispered hoarsely. "What is he doing here?"

The EMT glanced over his shoulder and then looked back at me, his dark eyebrows knotted close together. "He pulled you out," he said slowly, enunciating each word as though clear diction might help me understand. "He got you out of the fire."

I closed my aching eyes, but, annoyingly, this motion sent hot tears down my cheeks. The man released another torrential cough behind the EMT. I pulled the mask aside to speak again, but the EMT moved it back over my face. His face was blurred now by my involuntary tears.

"Keep the mask on," he ordered. "Don't try to talk."

I shook my head, the motion sending another crackling peal of pain through me, and yanked the mask aside. "No," I choked. "No! You don't understand. That's him! That's the guy who set the fire!"

The EMT looked back at the man and then at me again, concern spreading over his face. "She's confused," he murmured, and hearing myself spoken about in the third person only served to confuse me more. His eyes did a quick scan of a machine that I realized was connected to me via a cord clipped to the end my finger. Apparently satisfied by whatever he saw on the screen, the EMT turned his attention back to me, lowering his face close to mine. For a moment, it almost seemed like he was planning to whisper something in my ear, but then he stopped inches from my face. His eyes were strange—slightly yellow and catlike—and he looked tired.

"That man saved you," he said again, settling the oxygen mask back on my face. "That man," he said, "is your father."

28

Julia

CURTIS'S HOUSE WAS dark when I pulled up. It was a small, detached bungalow with some straggly bushes dotting a mostly paved front yard, stucco walls, and a stark white door that seemed to glow in the inky night. *So this is where Curtis lives,* I thought, a little ashamed to realize I'd never wondered what his home looked like in all the years I'd known him. I parked in the street, crossed the yard, and rang the doorbell. When no one answered, I returned to my car and sat in the front seat, my hands on the wheel. I decided to wait there, figuring he'd most likely be home soon. Somewhere nearby a dog barked sharply, and my hand immediately shot out to lock the car doors. I sank down into the seat and took a few deep breaths.

At some point, despite my unease in the unfamiliar neighborhood, I must have fallen asleep. When I opened my eyes, I was blinded by Curtis's car lights swinging across my face as he pulled into the driveway. I sat up, a sharp crick in my neck adding to my flustered, disoriented haze, and glanced at the clock. *Midnight?* Was it really possible that I'd been asleep for more than an hour? The sound of Curtis's car door shutting was jarring in the still night air. He ambled up to his front door, hands pressed deep in his pockets. Oddly, despite the late hour and my reasons for being there, I felt relieved to see him.

"Curtis!" I called, stepping out of my car. I rubbed at my sore neck with one hand and walked toward him.

He turned, his sunken eyes squinting in my direction. His face fell into a frown as I approached.

"Julia," he said slowly. "What are you doing here?"

"I need to speak with you about something," I said.

Curtis glanced beyond my shoulder into the street, and then back at me. "Little late for a chat, isn't it?" he asked. He seemed different here, out of the context of my house and the city I knew. His broad face was shadowed, deep wrinkles cutting into his forehead. It occurred to me that he might have been drinking, and the relief I'd felt at seeing him moments earlier evaporated. *What* am *I doing here?* I wondered. Then I straightened my shoulders, determined to chase the worry from my thoughts. *I'm taking charge*, I told myself. *I'm getting my life back.*

"Please," I said. "Can I come in?" Despite the little pep talk I'd given myself, my voice sounded small.

For a moment, I wasn't sure Curtis was going to answer. Finally, he nodded and turned back toward the front door. I followed him inside the house, down a short, dark hallway, and into the living room. Curtis flicked on the light. The room was cold and sparsely furnished with little more than a small brown sofa and a television on a stand in the corner. It felt like the home of someone who lived a very solitary life. How strange it must have been for him to have spent nearly every day in our spacious, professionally decorated Pacific Heights house, only to come back each night to those tight, sterile quarters. *We live in two very different worlds.*

"Have a seat," he said. "I'm getting a beer. Do you want anything?"

"No, thanks," I stammered. I perched on the edge of the

couch, rubbing my hands on my legs to warm them. "I'm fine." I'd known Curtis my entire life—why did I suddenly feel like I was talking to a stranger? I swallowed, realizing my mouth was dry. "Maybe some water," I called after him as he crossed through an arched doorway into the kitchen.

Alone in the room, I looked around. It was only then that I noticed several cardboard boxes beside the couch, including an open one filled nearly to the brim with miscellaneous household things. Was Curtis one of those people that lived out of boxes, never bothering to unpack? He didn't strike me as the type. In our house, he always dressed neatly, if humbly, in tan slacks and neutral-colored sweaters. He filled every request the household threw at him quickly and with an air of silent efficiency. Did you need someone to pick up a visiting friend from the airport in two weeks? You only had to ask Curtis once. Did you request a ride to the gala and then realize you forgot the address? Curtis seemed to always know exactly where you were going and when you wanted to be there, turning through the city streets with quiet confidence, never relying on GPS.

And yet, looking around, it did appear that most of his possessions were crammed into boxes. Glancing behind the sofa, I saw another open container packed full of things wrapped in newspaper. A small black box near the top of the heap drew my eye. My stomach flipped. Before I could stop myself, I was turning and kneeling on the couch. I grabbed the small box, opened it, and found myself staring at my father's Cartier watch.

The sound of Curtis setting a glass of water down on the coffee table made me jump. Spinning around, I looked up at him, my heart racing, the watch still in my hand. Curtis was very close. I'd never realized how big he was, never before thought of him in a remotely menacing light. The air reeked of an acrid smell I could not place.

"This is my father's watch," I said quietly.

To my relief, he turned and walked back across the room. Folding his large frame into a metal chair by the entry to the kitchen, he took a long swig of his beer, then said, "Yes." He voice was flat and I had trouble reading it. Was he apologetic? Did he feel ashamed? Embarrassed? Defiant? I couldn't tell. "He gave it to me."

I looked at him. *What would Annie do in this situation?* I wondered. *What would Lucia have done?* "No, Curtis," I said, drawing myself taller. "He thought he lost it."

He shrugged. "Does it matter?"

"Of course it does!"

Curtis took another long slug of his beer.

"It's been you this whole time, hasn't it?" I asked. "You've been taking my father's things."

He shrugged again. "Did he miss them? Did not having those fancy things change his life in any way?" I realized I'd been holding out hope that he'd deny everything, or that he'd at least have some plausible explanation for his actions, and my heart now dropped. "Who cares, really?" His lips curled around these words, his face setting into a sneer I'd never seen from him before. I felt as though I'd been slapped.

"I care, Curtis! We all care. We all trusted you. My father has known you for nearly half his life! He considers you one of his best friends."

"No!" Curtis slammed the side of his fist into his muscular thigh. My cheeks burned and I found myself wishing the unaffected Curtis of a moment earlier would return. "Was he my friend when he told me he wouldn't loan me money fifteen years ago? When I'd gotten myself into a tiny bit of trouble and was about to lose my house? No!" A burst of spittle flew from his mouth. "You know what he gave me? More *hours*. He wanted me to *earn* that money. And he's the boss, isn't he?"

I thought about this, my mind working quickly. My father,

for all his conservative fiscal practices, was at heart a very generous person. If he hadn't loaned Curtis money, there must have been good reason.

"I'm sure my dad had your best interests in mind," I said evenly. It was important not to provoke him, and realizing this only served to make me more anxious. What had I expected to happen when I confronted Curtis? A tearful confession? A promise to be a better person? A renewed allegiance to our family? I was embarrassed by how juvenile my little fantasy seemed now as I sat across from a man who was beginning to show a side I'd never seen in all the years I'd known him.

He snorted. "My best interests? Julia, he's *your* father, not mine. I didn't need his *best interests*, I needed his money. He refused. So I got creative." In one long gulp, Curtis drained his beer and set it down hard on the floor.

Something about the sight of his large, now empty hands made a lump form in my throat. "Well," I said. "Everyone will understand." I stood slowly from the couch, itching to be out of that house and back in my car, speeding home. "We'll figure this out. We all care so much about you."

"Sit down," Curtis said quietly.

I froze. "What?"

He didn't repeat himself, just glared at me until I sank back down to the couch. I stared at my lap blindly and worked to think straight. Beside me, my purse held my cell phone. Even as I realized this, Curtis was crossing the room toward me. He grabbed my bag, then turned and settled back in his chair.

"Curtis," I whispered. "What are you doing?"

He set my bag at his feet and didn't answer.

29

Annie

WHEN WE ARRIVED at the hospital, I gathered I was to be admitted and that Our Guy was deemed well enough to accompany me. No one seemed to question his presence at my side, and, out of curiosity, I suppose—*This guy pulled me from the fire? And he's claiming to be my father?!?*—I didn't draw attention to fact that he was, in fact, a stranger. I eyed him as he walked beside my stretcher down one long hall after another. With the hood of his sweatshirt hanging limply down his back, the man looked older and shorter than he ever had before, as though the bright, unforgiving hospital lights deflated him. Finally, I was deposited in a room, checked over briefly by a doctor, and told that I needed to be monitored while I rested for a bit. As long as I felt okay, I would be released in an hour. Then I was left alone with the man.

I pulled the mask off my face.

"I think it's better," the man said in a thick Spanish accent, gesturing toward the mask, "to keep this on."

For some reason, I obeyed. The mask made me feel slightly cross-eyed, but the oxygen was silky and cool in my nostrils. I pressed my head into the bed and tried to breathe deeply. My body craved rest, but my mind charged forward, relentlessly compiling and sorting and interpreting information.

"I did not want to scare you," the man said sadly. His light brown eyes searched the ceiling as though the words he needed might be there. "I'm sorry. I wanted to find you finally. I wanted to see that you are okay. But you were not. I see there is a bad man, so I stay to help you. I want you to be safe."

"I don't understand," I said. Something in the set of the man's face as he leaned toward me seemed oddly familiar. The EMT's words echoed through me. My heart began to race.

"Do you speak Spanish?" he asked.

I lifted my hand and made a so-so motion. It didn't seem wise to trust something as potentially life-altering as a conversation with a man who claimed to be my father to my dodgy college-level Spanish.

And then, in halting Spanglish and elaborate hand gestures, the man told me his name was Miguel Patilla. He said he was my father. After that, he seemed stumped. He stared at his hands. "I was married many years," he said finally. "My wife died last year. I have thought of you many times. I have so many . . ." He struggled, paused, and began again. "I feel very bad. I was so young when I was with Lucia. I should have done something when her mother made her leave the house, but I was . . . a stupid boy. She left Ecuador and I never met you. I try to forget about you. I was not good."

I stared at him as he spoke, spiky ropes of anger and disbelief and confusion and, what? hope? knotting together in my chest. I was listening to him intently but somehow, at the same time, I realized I was counting my own breaths. *In, out. One. In, out. Two. . .*

"I am a father. I have a son and a daughter." His eyes shone. "And you, of course," he said, hurrying. "Two daughters. I am a good father to them, my children in Ecuador. And I am a bad father to you. I did not know that Lucia died and you were alone. You have been alone so long and I am so sad for that."

I suddenly realized why he looked familiar: he looked like me. As he spoke, I could sort of see my own face floating up behind his. In the arch of his eyebrows, I saw the arch of mine. In the little point of his chin, I saw my own. While my mother had been darker than me with coffee-hued eyes and milk-chocolate skin, this man had my coloring: eyes the hue of caramel, skin the color of honey. I stared at him in shock, grateful that the mask on my face gave me an excuse to not speak.

"I come to see you, but I don't know if you want to meet me. You seem good. You are very successful. I am very proud, and I think maybe I should leave. Maybe I should not bother you. Maybe," he said sadly, "maybe you hate me. I can understand. I am no father to you. I am a stranger.

"But I watch you and I see this man who is doing bad things to your store. I decide I cannot leave you. So I stay and get work in a restaurant. I live near you. I call my children and they un-derstand—they want you to be safe, too. So I watch, and some nights I scare away this man who is trying to hurt your store. Other nights, I want to warn you, but I end up scaring you and your friend. So I keep my distance again. And tonight, there is a fire. When you need me most, I am not there. I walk by on my way home from work and I see the smoke and I hear the alarm and the door is open and I find you." He slumped in his chair. "I should be there before. I was so late. All this time, I want you to be safe, and then . . ." His voice choked.

I stared at him. I had spent so much of my life not think-ing about my father, and now, apparently, here he was. *I have a father.* My thoughts darted and buzzed and stung as quickly as bees swarming out of a hive that has been hit by a stone. If I had spent some amount of time imagining, fantasizing, about our meeting, I might have been better prepared. As it was, I felt baffled. I had never really thought about my father, long ago dismissing the idea of him just as it seemed my mother had. I had no script to follow. I didn't know what to say. My mother had never given me any clues to help me determine how I should feel about him. Had she loved him? Had he treated her poorly? What would she have thought about him showing up in my life like this? Without her guidance, I was left to make up my mind entirely on my own.

I looked at this man. I didn't feel coldly toward him. To the contrary, I realized I was glad he was there, even if attempting to wrap my mind around the fact that Our Guy was in fact my father was as dizzying as trying to see every image in an Escher drawing at once. I took a deep breath. My lungs felt clearer. I pulled the mask from my face.

"You saved me," I said. "Thank you."

He blushed and looked at his hands. "I wish I had done more. Your store—it's not good."

My kitchen! I bit my lip. "Is it gone?"

Miguel—it would take some time for me to call him my father—shook his head. "No, it's there. But the kitchen is very bad. There will be a lot of problem from so much smoke and the water from the firemen." He reached out toward me, but then seemed to reconsider and dropped his hand. "But I think it will be okay."

My thoughts raced back to what he had said earlier. It was easier to think about Treat than to think too deeply about the fact that I was speaking to my father for the first time in my life. "So you saw who set the fire?" I asked. "You know who did it?"

Miguel frowned. "No," he said. "I did not see. But I think it is the same man who did all of the other things I seen him do. He wrote those words in the shop. He broke the glass. I see this. He is big. Tall. White. Ah!" He released a frustrated bark—half snort, half cough. "I point him out in a picture. I know him if I see him again." He slumped in his chair. "I don't know. I don't think this helps."

I pushed myself up in bed, thinking. "It's okay. The shop has a security camera now so we should have a video."

Miguel brightened. "Yes? Oh good."

We smiled at each other. *This man is my father.* How bizarre. Our little moment was cut short by a knock on the open door.

"Ogden!" I said, startled. "What are you doing here?"

Ogden quickly crossed the room to my bedside and surprised me by taking my hand. "Thank God you're okay! I was on my way home from the opening party for a friend's restaurant and I saw the fire trucks outside of Treat. I headed right to the hospital when they said you were here." He glanced at Miguel and then back at me. "I'm sorry—am I interrupting?"

"No, it's fine. Thanks for coming." I looked over at Miguel. "Miguel," I said, "this is my friend Ogden Gertzwell. Ogden, this is Miguel Patilla." I hesitated a moment and then just went for it. "Miguel is my father."

Ogden's thick blond brows rose in his forehead. He turned and took a long step toward Miguel, who had risen from his chair, and shook his hand heartily. "Mr. Patilla! What a pleasure. I'm sorry to meet like this, though, when our girl is in the hospital."

"Our girl?" I said. Ogden glanced toward me, embarrassed.

Miguel smiled at him. "I'm happy you are here," he said. "It's good for Annie to have someone with her."

I shook my head, not knowing what to make of this alternative universe I suddenly found myself in.

"I should go now," Miguel said. He handed me a slip of paper on which he'd written his phone number. "Will you call me?" his eyes flicked between mine nervously. "I'd like to speak with you more, if it's okay."

"I'd like that," I said. I looked at him, memorizing his face. "Thank you."

After Miguel left, I sank my head back into the pillow. Before I knew what I was doing, I was laughing in disbelief at the turns the night had taken. My laughter quickly dissipated into a chain of dry coughs.

Ogden looked at me with worry in his eyes. "Are you sure you're okay? Do you want me to get a doctor?"

"No, I'm fine." As soon as I said it, I realized it was true. My headache seemed to have lifted and my throat no longer ached. "They're going to discharge me soon. It's nice of you to come by, but you don't have to stay."

Ogden pulled the chair Miguel had sat in up close to my bed. "But I want to."

For a moment, a wave of prickliness ticked over my skin. I'd been on my own for years, and suddenly men were coming out of the woodwork to protect and care for me. *They can disappear just as easily as they arrive*, I warned myself. "I don't need you to," I told Ogden, straightening. "I can get home on my own."

"Oh, I know," he said hurriedly. "But I'd like to stay anyway, if you don't mind."

Even as he said the words, I understood just how much I wanted to hear them.

"Besides," he continued, a serious set to his eyes. "I think I just promised your father I'd keep you company."

I laughed. If only he knew how odd that sentence was. Julia would have appreciated the strangeness of this whole situation. Where was she anyway? I was surprised she hadn't shown up at the hospital yet. "Did you see Julia at Treat?" I asked.

Ogden paled. "No—she wasn't in there with you, was she?"

"Oh no. But I'm sure the security company called her when the smoke alarm went off." I reached into my pocket, relieved to find my phone still there. I had several messages from the security company and one from Inspector Ramirez, but none from Julia. That was odd. I called her cell phone but it went to voice mail. Maybe Wes had whisked her off somewhere romantic for the evening and she wasn't answering her phone. I remembered suddenly that she had mentioned—somewhat cryptically, now that I thought about it—that she had plans for the night when she dropped me off at my apartment after we'd closed the shop. *Oh well. Good for her.* There wasn't anything to be done now anyway but worry about the damage to Treat.

"So how bad is it?" I asked. "Did you get a good look at the shop?"

Ogden grimaced. He laid his hand on mine again. What was with him tonight? I looked down and realized I didn't actually mind the feeling of his big old paw covering mine. "It seemed pretty bad," he said. "I was really worried about you."

"You were?"

He nodded, then hesitated. "I've been thinking about you a lot," he said.

"Really?" I asked slowly. I was enjoying watching him struggle.

"Yes, really," he said. "I've been thinking that maybe we have more in common than you think."

"Is that so?"

"We both like feeding people. Good food is our best gift."

"You might be wrong there," I said, shifting in the bed. "I also have sparkling wit to offer."

Ogden smiled. "Well, that's true." He paused for a beat, then cleared his throat. "But I think the place you feel most at home is in your kitchen, when you're not trying particularly hard to be . . . sparkly. I'm the same way. With my farm."

I was on the verge of responding with some light retort but the earnest set of Ogden's face stopped me. Looking at him then, really looking at him, I saw that what I'd once attributed to a lack of passion in his eyes was in fact exactly the opposite; he had the intense, intelligent gaze of a man who knew exactly what he loved in life, and why. I couldn't believe what I'd missed seeing all that time I'd been so busy looking for something else.

And he was right, of course. I thought of Treat's little kitchen charred by fire and swallowed deeply. When I stood in that kitchen, I felt my mother by my side. Her favorite place in the world had been standing in front of the stove not in the St. Clairs' fancy kitchen, but in our little carriage house—our *casita*, as she called it. That was where she seemed to feel the most at peace with herself and the choices she had made in her life. Over the years, I'd learned that standing by her side at the carriage house stove was where I had the best chance of hearing some story about her childhood and family. As I thought of this, an idea occurred to me—both troubling and startling in its simplicity.

"Hey, do you have your truck here?" I asked Ogden, propping myself up on my elbows.

He nodded.

"There's something I'd like to do, but I need your help. Can you help me?" I wondered if he had any idea what it took for me to say those words.

"Of course," he answered immediately. I wasn't sure I'd ever seen him look so pleased.

When we pulled up in front of the St. Clair mansion, all of the windows were dark. I punched the old code into the gate and held my breath until, after a pause, the gate unlocked and swung open.

"Annie," Ogden whispered, keeping pace with me as I walked hurriedly through the arched porte cochere. "What are we doing here?"

It was the first time he'd questioned me since we'd left the hospital. He'd been remarkably quiet on the drive to the St. Clairs', only nodding as I'd directed him through the series of turns that led us to Pacific Heights. I'd been grateful for his silence—I felt shaken by the events of the night and I was filled with conflicting feelings of hope and dread as we drove through the city. What was I suddenly afraid I might find at the St. Clairs'? The very thing I'd hoped to find for all those years?

"Don't worry," I whispered over my shoulder as we climbed the steps to the carriage house door. "They won't mind that I'm here." I bent down, lifted the small stone duck beside the door-mat, and breathed out in relief when I saw the key glimmering there in the darkness. "See?" I said. Ogden's expression told me that my knowledge of the key's location did not do much to al-leviate his concerns. Still, he followed me over the threshold and closed the door behind him.

I flicked on the light. The smell of the carriage house was exactly the same as it had always been, even after all those years: a woolly carpet smell, an undertone of muskiness that must have risen from the garage below, and, inexplicably, pine.

"In here," I said, motioning for Ogden to follow me into the kitchen. The stove was a small white relic from the eighties, but it gleamed spotlessly below the kitchen's track lighting. I looked at Ogden. I had the sense that he would do exactly what I asked, whatever it was, and I felt a rush of gratitude toward him. De-spite his willingness, or perhaps because of it, I wanted him to understand.

"I've been looking for something of my mother's for a long time," I told him. My voice sounded croaky and small in the kitchen. "I've been looking since she died, actually. It's a book with no value to anyone but me, and I know she would have wanted me to have it." I lifted my chin then, daring Ogden to think I sounded silly as I said, "There's a very small chance it's behind that stove."

Ogden looked at me and without hesitation said, "Well, let's take a look." He shook off his jacket and draped it across the kitchen counter. Then he stretched his arms out, took hold of the back of the stove, and began to pull it toward him. The stove was wedged snugly into place, but he rocked it back and forth so that it hobbled forward inch by inch. As he did, I grabbed an old flashlight from the cabinet below the sink. Once the stove was six inches or so from the wall I hoisted myself up on the counter, flicked on the flashlight, and peered down into the dark space that was now exposed. There, amid tumbleweeds of dust, various wires, a set of kitchen tongs, a wooden spoon, and a salt shaker, was my mother's journal. I looked back at Ogden, my mouth open in surprise.

"It's there!"

I hopped off the counter to let Ogden take my place. He reached his long arm down into the space behind the stove, pulled the book out, blew the dust off its cover, and handed it to me, beaming.

"I can't believe it," I murmured. It must have fallen behind the stove in the days before my mother's death. The book was smaller than I remembered, its black leather cover butter-soft in my hands. I flipped through the pages and the sight of my mother's sloped handwriting drew a knot in my chest.

"Why don't you sit?" Ogden suggested softly. When I didn't move, he took my elbow and guided me over to the couch. I sat down heavily. Passion fruit meringue. Ginger cookies. Apple-cinnamon empanadas. Coconut flan. The recipes were all in English—my mother had wanted me to read them someday. But jotted down here and there in between the recipes were my mother's diary entries, and those were in Spanish. I let the pages fall slowly through my fingers until, about halfway through, the writing stopped. *So many blank pages left!* My throat tightened with sorrow. She'd only just begun.

The final pages she'd written were in Spanish—not reci-pes then, but diary entries. I let my eyes work their way slowly down the pages, translating the words as best I could. I felt an icy chill run through my body as I realized what I was reading. I was so immersed, forgetting even that Ogden was still there, that I jumped when the door to the carriage house swung open.

"Annie?" Tad said, his brow furrowing as he crossed into the room. Lolly stepped out from behind him looking strangely pale in her cornflower blue silk robe. They glanced at Ogden and then back at me. "Are you all right? What are you doing here?"

"I—I found my mother's book," I gasped. I held the book in front of me, as though it might explain everything, and then, thinking better of it, clasped it tight to my chest again.

"We heard about the fire, dear," Tad said gently. "Inspector Ramirez—"

Lolly interrupted, "We wanted to come to the hospital, but we've been waiting for word from Julia."

"What do you mean?" I asked. "Where's Julia?"

"We don't know. She's not here. She's not answering her phone." Lolly's voice was as close to panicked as I'd ever heard it. "Wesley is out looking for her now." She seemed to be thinking something, on the verge of saying more, but before I could question her, my phone rang. I fumbled in my pocket and pulled it out. *Ramirez.*

"Annie, hi," he said quickly. "We were able to pull an image of the arsonist from the security camera. We haven't been able to ID him, but maybe you can. Can I e-mail the image to you?"

"Yes, go ahead. I can look at it on my phone."

"Good. Is Ms. St. Clair with you?"

"No," I said, nearly swallowing the word. "We don't know where she is."

There was a beat of silence. "When was the last time someone saw her?"

"I'm not sure," I said. "A few hours ago?"

I heard Ramirez breathing into the phone as he considered

this. "Let's start by seeing if you can ID this guy," he said finally. "I'll send the photo now."

I ended the call and looked around the room at the solemn faces gazing at me. "Inspector Ramirez is sending me a photo of the guy who set the fire." Ogden took a step closer to me and squeezed my arm. We all stood in silence, listening to the refrigerator click and hum in the kitchen. When my phone chimed, Lolly sucked in her breath and seemed to grow even paler.

As I pulled up the image, I felt a mounting sense of dread in my heart. I'd already guessed whose face I would see on the screen—my mother's diary had told me all I needed to know. I realized then that everything I'd believed about my mother's death was wrong, that a person I had thought of almost as a father figure for much of my life was not who he pretended to be. And I suspected that Julia, wherever she was, was in much more danger than she realized.

30

Julia

CURTIS HADN'T SAID anything in what felt like a very long time. Whenever I began to speak he glared at me until I fell quiet. He was on his fourth beer by then, and each time he'd left me alone to retrieve a cold bottle from the kitchen, I'd half risen from the couch and then sat back down heavily when I'd heard the fridge shut. *It's just Curtis!* I told myself, trying to slow my nervous, shallow breaths. I'd known him my entire life. He was my father's friend. This was simply a huge misunderstanding.

"Curtis, it's really late," I said, trying again when he returned to the room and sat back down. "Why don't I head home now and we can talk more in the morning?" I started to stand from the couch. As I did, Curtis rose abruptly and his chair made a heart-rattling clatter as it toppled over backward behind him.

"Sit," he said.

I sat back down heavily, and he righted his chair and did the same. I felt my teeth begin to chatter. Was I really being held captive at Curtis's house? Despite everything, the idea was ludicrous. When another long stretch of stony silence had passed between us, I decided to try again.

"I don't understand. You're going to keep me here all night but not say anything?"

He shrugged and took a long slug of beer.

"It's just me, Curtis," I said quietly. I had to find a way to get him to remember that I wasn't the enemy. "You *know* me. We can figure this out. I don't blame you." When he didn't say anything, I continued. "Don't you remember when I was little and you'd drive Annie and Lucia and me to get ice cream after school? And we'd always bring you a chocolate-fudge scoop on a pretzel cone? You told me once it was your favorite. I never forgot."

The overhead light cast long shadows below Curtis's hooded eyes. He seemed to sway a moment before speaking. "I never wanted to hurt her," he mumbled. His voice was so quiet that I almost wondered if he realized he was speaking out loud. "That wasn't supposed to happen."

"Hurt who?" I asked. I regretted the question even as I asked it.

"Lucia," he choked, his voice suddenly thick with anguish. "Stop lying! That's the real reason you're here. You don't give a damn about your father's watch or any of that crap. Everything I did tonight was for nothing, wasn't it? I was too late. You found the book."

I stared at him. "Curtis, what are you talking about?" My mind bounced over his words like a needle hitting a snag on a record. What did Lucia have to do with anything? What had Curtis done tonight?

"I loved her," he said. "I never meant to hurt her, but she found out about the stealing." His eyes roamed the room and for a moment he looked so agonized that I had an urge to comfort him. Then, slowly, what he was saying began to sink in. "She didn't like it. The second she found out about the whole thing she decided she was too good for me. She didn't like that I gambled. She didn't like that I owed people money. What she *did* like was pretending she was all prim and proper, but wasn't she the one who got pregnant at sixteen?" He barked out a laugh and then glared at me, daring me to argue. I wanted to scream for him to stop speaking. I wanted to press my hands to my ears and not hear another word. But all I could do was look at the floor.

"She said she was going to tell Tad everything," he continued. "Interesting where her loyalties lay, isn't it? Who knows—maybe she was sleeping with him, too. That might explain something. Maybe I'm on to something there." Curtis suddenly bent forward and cradled his head in his hands. "No," he muttered. "No. She wasn't like that." Now, again, he seemed to be speaking to himself. I stole a glance at the door to the living room, wondering if I could outrun him if I needed to. As if reading my thoughts, he lifted his head and stared at me, his eyes narrow and gleaming.

"She just made me so mad," he hissed. "Why would she tell on me? I needed that money. She knew that. So we argued and I shoved her, but I never meant to hurt her. I just forgot she was so little. I get so angry sometimes. Her head hit the wall and she shut her eyes and she just looked like she was smiling a little or sleeping. But her eyes were just shut a minute! Not even—a few seconds! Then they were open again and she was fine. She said she was fine and I trusted her because I loved her. And then a few days later, in the kitchen . . ."

My mouth fell open. "She died," I said before I could stop myself. *Curtis killed Lucia.* I felt my entire body begin to tremble and struggled to hold myself still.

Curtis's face seemed to crumple. "But that wasn't because of me," he said. "That wasn't me. The doctors said it was an aneurysm. That's what everyone said."

I nodded and tried to blink back the tears that had sprung to my eyes. As Curtis watched me, his face hardened again. "See—you're blaming me." He shook his head angrily. "Everything would have been fine if Annie hadn't come back," he said. "You two couldn't stand each other. Why couldn't you have just kept hating each other?"

He seemed to really want an answer to this, but I could think of nothing to say. I looked at the floor and swallowed.

"Instead you had to team up and hunt for Lucia's journal," he muttered. "I know she wrote some really big lies about me in there, didn't she? She was always writing something and she'd never let me read any of it. But that was all in the past and everything was fine and then you girls had to come back and stir things up. I'd forgotten all about the whole mess, really. That book, and whatever lies it had in it, was gone—I'd looked everywhere! But you wouldn't let it drop. And then you made me start doing those things to the bakery. I didn't want to do that! But I knew if Annie were gone you would all forget about looking for that book, and that stupid cupcake shop was the only thing keeping her around. She certainly wasn't hanging around because she actually liked you. And then last week your mother starts following me around the house looking for the damn thing. That woman always gets what she wants. All of you do. One of you was going to find that book sooner or later. I had to do something."

Curtis was the one who broke into Treat and spray painted the window and bar! Of course. He was the only one who could have known how hurtful those particular words would have been to Annie. He'd been trying to tear us apart for months. Stealing my father's watch was one thing, but trespassing? Destroying property? Threatening us? And most terrifying and heartbreaking—Curtis was responsible for Lucia's death. *I don't know this man at all.* A chill ran down my spine. *What exactly had he done to Treat tonight?*

"You're wrong, Curtis," I told him quietly. "I don't have Lucia's journal. That's not why I'm here. Besides," I said, thinking quickly, "it really doesn't matter. What happened with Lucia was obviously an accident. And my father's things—I think that was all a big misunderstanding. I think my father knew the whole time. He *wanted* you to have those things. They were gifts."

Curtis shot me a plaintive look. "Do you think so?" he asked. An instant later, his face darkened. "You're lying."

He stood, swayed a moment, and then took a step toward me. I felt myself sink back into the couch, my body coiling into a position of defense or offense, I had no idea which. Suddenly, there was a rapid burst of knocking at the front door and Curtis immediately stretched out his arm and flipped off the living room light. I gasped as the room fell into darkness.

"Get down," he hissed, and before I realized he'd crossed the room, I felt his hands on my shoulder shoving me down into the couch cushions. I lay there with my face pressed into the couch, Curtis's grip painful on my shoulder, listening as the knocks grew more urgent at the door. Moments later, Curtis seemed to change his mind. He sat up.

"Don't move," he whispered. His sour breath was warm on my face. He crossed the room and turned the light back on. Before me stood the old, familiar Curtis, his face a stoic mask, his dark, sunken eyes distant, but almost kind. "It was an accident, like you said," he whispered. "So don't move, okay?"

I nodded silently from my half-curled position on the couch. He nodded back at me, a grateful smile playing at the corner of his lips. And then he was gone. I listened to his footsteps in the short hall and heard him open the door. From the front steps, a man's voice, familiar but unplaceable, drifted toward me. I strained to make out their words. The man outside sounded brusque; Curtis answered him in a slow, detached voice. I straightened to a seated position on the couch and rubbed my throbbing shoulder.

What the hell am I waiting for?

I stood and as quietly as I could darted across the room and into the kitchen at the back of the house. My heart leaped when I caught sight of the door in the corner of the kitchen and I ran to it, no longer caring how loud I might be, just wanting to be out of that house. I pulled the door open, felt the crisp night air fill my lungs, and hurled myself down the steps and then down the long, narrow walkway next to the house. If I hadn't seen the police cars, I might have run all the way home. I could have done it if I'd needed to—I'd been training for a run like that all my life. But there they were: three cop cars lined up on the street in front of Curtis's house. I slowed and looked back at the house. Inspector Ramirez was in the process of putting handcuffs on Curtis, who looked out onto the street, his face a blank, shadowed mask.

I jumped when a cop cleared his throat near me. "Miss?" he asked. "You all right?"

I looked beyond the cop's shoulder and saw Wes sprinting down the sidewalk toward me, trailed closely by my parents and Annie. "Yes," I said breathlessly, and began running toward my family. *I am now.*

May

31

Annie

JULIA ST. CLAIR and Wesley Trehorn were set to be married on the sort of mild-weathered, raspberry-sunset-sky, bug-free spring evening on which you might expect a couple like Julia St. Clair and Wesley Trehorn to be married. I had spent the entire afternoon scurrying around the sprawling Woodstone property, trying to help Lolly and the wedding coordinator and her team of vendors as much as possible without imparting sweat stains on my pale pink maid of honor dress. That's right: Julia had asked me to be her maid of honor. And, yes, I was wearing pink.

Over the previous few weeks, I'd finally perfected the Julia St. Clair wedding cupcake: classic lemon cake with a hidden heart of my mom's boldly flavored passion fruit filling, slathered high with Julia's favorite vanilla buttercream icing and glammed up a bit with sparkling curls of candied lemon rind. The entire Treat baking team had worked through a late night of frenzied mixing and pouring and icing to create the three hundred and fifty cupcakes that would be wheeled into the dining tent on an enormous tiered stand after dinner. Despite my desire to keep a close watch on that precariously cantilevered display of cupcakes, Julia, who had made a complete about-face on the whole wedding involvement thing following her New Year's Eve heart-to-heart with Wes, had decided that it was perfectly within her right as bride to micromanage my every move that day. In between trips to ensure the menus lay straight on each plate ("Yes, Julia, they're perfect. Yes, I *promise*."), the peony to ranunculus to garden rose ratio in the centerpieces was just right ("Three to two to one, Julia. Yes, I *counted*."), and the espresso-stained Chiavari chairs were in perfectly straight rows ("Straight as an arrow, Julia. Yes, I used the *yardstick*."), I kept ducking my head into the kitchen to ensure the swarm of caterers and waitstaff hadn't smudged any cupcake icing or knocked loose any candied lemon rinds.

As I was about to pop into the kitchen yet again, Julia, still in her white terry-cloth sweat suit ("Mrs. Trehorn" bedazzled in Swarovski crystals across the sweatshirt's back), strode down the long stone hallway toward me. With her blond hair styled in glamorous, Old Hollywood waves behind her ears, and her makeup a slightly more dramatic version of her usual refined peaches-and-cream look, even the ridiculous sweat suit couldn't keep her from resembling Grace Kelly—a semblance that I was fairly certain she'd cultivated as precisely as a gardener prunes and shapes a rosebush.

"Julia!" I cried. "Why aren't you dressed?" I checked my watch. "The ceremony starts in less than an hour!"

Julia pursed her glossy lips and glared pointedly at my oversized man's watch. I'd chosen to forget that she'd instructed me not to wear any jewelry save the glittery diamond stud earrings—*blood-sweat-and-tears diamonds*, as I'd joked to Becca— she'd gifted to me in thanks for finally accepting my role as her humble servant. Er, maid of honor. Whatever. I put my hand over the watch, and she raised her eyes to my face.

"I need to talk to you," she said solemnly.

"Okay, sure," I said. I glanced toward the kitchen door. "Let me just check on one—"

"Annie! I'm about to get married!"

"Right. Excellent point. I can check on the cupcakes later. Let's chat." Julia had been expertly playing the I'm-getting-married! trump card for weeks, and today, I realized, was not the day to rebel.

I followed her down the hall into the bedroom she was using as a base camp for all things bride. Her sumptuous silk gown hung on the door of an antique armoire, and her whisper-thin, elbow-length veil was draped carefully over a gray velvet slipper chair in the corner.

"Sit down," she ordered. I flopped onto the bed, my dress rustling loudly beneath me. Julia cringed. "Maybe you should stand. You still haven't mastered the whole sitting-without-wrinkling thing we talked about, have you?"

"No," I said, gravely. "I'm afraid I haven't. And, geez, time is really running out!" I stood up and leaned awkwardly against the nightstand.

"Ha-ha. Okay, listen." Julia suddenly began wringing her hands—an uncharacteristic gesture that made me straighten up a bit. "As you know, lately I've been doing a lot of *soul-searching* . . ." She paused, wincing at the expression. " . . . and I just can't seem to shake some of the second thoughts I'm having."

I'd been dreading this moment. I looked around the room, wishing that by sheer desire alone I could summon another, better, more practiced bridesmaid for Julia. But alas, I consti-tuted her entire wedding party. "Oh, Julia," I sighed. "You know I don't know the first thing about marriage, or relation-ships, or, you know, normal, earnest human interaction, but I feel like I've heard that it's totally common to have cold feet right before the wedding. The important thing is to remember that you really do love Wes. Focus on that."

Abruptly, Julia laughed, her expertly made-up face breaking into an affectionate, cockeyed grin. "You are absolutely bizarre," she said, shaking her head. "*Of course* I love Wes. We're about to get married, you moron. I'm talking about Treat."

I breathed. "Oh! You are? Thank God." I blinked. "Wait, what? Why? You're about to get married!"

In the months after the fire, we'd rebuilt the cupcakery as quickly as we could—Julia's old affirmation that lots and lots of money really could make people, even *contractors*, move more quickly, proved irritatingly accurate yet again—and reopened within two months. In the meantime, we'd filled catering orders out of the St. Clairs' kitchen and managed to maintain, maybe even grow, the positive buzz for the cupcakery right up through our grand reopening party. It had felt indescribably *right* to step back into Treat's kitchen again in April, to hear Julia out front in the shop, charming customers with her old flair, and to listen as the register rang up order after order, the air filling all the while with the sweet smell of cupcakes, the dank, bitter smell of smoke and water damage a quickly fading memory. That first day back at the shop was when I decided that all of the drama of that year had been worth it; stepping through Treat's door with Julia by my side felt like coming home, and there was no better feeling in the world.

Now, Julia rolled her eyes. "Getting married doesn't mean the rest of the world stops, does it?" I eyed her, not sure if this was a trick question. "Treat's business has been booming since we reopened," she continued. "We've been written up in a slew of papers and there's that article about innovative cupcakes coming out in *Food & Wine* next week—plus the mention that's going to appear in our wedding announcement in the *Times* 'Vows' section tomorrow. I'd say things are right on track, wouldn't you?"

I nodded. I had no idea where she was going with all of this, or what "track" she had in mind for Treat, but I knew Julia well enough to know she was working herself up to something big.

She put her hands on her hips and grinned. "In other words, I think the timing is perfect to consider expanding Treat to other cities! Los Angeles, New York—can't you just see a Treat shop nestled into one of those darling little streets in Nolita? The neighborhood is practically *begging* for a cupcakery!"

I didn't have the slightest clue as to where Nolita was, but I decided to brush over that and get right to the point. "But Julia," I said quietly, "you're leaving. You've always said you just wanted to help get Treat off the ground, get married, and then go on your merry way. Which is totally fine—I get it. Running a cupcake shop wasn't how you envisioned your career when you were networking your way through business school. But I can't handle expanding the shop by myself. It's hard enough to run one kitchen, let alone multiple ones spread across the country. And besides, I'm happy being a one-shop gal. I don't need to run a cupcake empire."

Julia fiddled with the zipper on her white sweatshirt, pulling it up and down. She cleared her throat. "Well," she said. "What if I do?"

"What do you mean?"

"If I wanted to stay on," she said. "If I wanted to stay your partner—would you have me?"

I breathed out, a swell of relief rising steadily inside of me as I understood what she asking. "Of course!" I said quickly. I hadn't even realized until that exact moment just how much I'd been dreading the idea of running Treat on my own, how much I'd sensed I would miss Julia when she left. "It's *our* business. We built it together. We're *building* it together."

Julia shook her head. "No, it's your business," she said adamantly. "That's the agreement we made at the beginning. As of today, Treat is yours." Julia played with her zipper again, seemingly searching for words. "Listen, I know how you felt when you agreed to this whole thing. You wanted to own your own business and my involvement was a means to an end." I tried to interrupt, but she held her hand out and smiled. "It's okay! It's okay. I know you don't feel the same way about me now as you did a year ago. But I would understand if you wanted to uphold that contract. Really, I would. I know how it is to have a dream. And you're right—the cupcakery was never mine. I was just borrowing it when I really needed something positive to dream about. At least, that's what I was doing at the beginning. Everything is different now, but I would never want you to feel like I was forcing something on you. I want you to know this is entirely—legally, even—your decision to make."

I laughed. "Oh, Julia, come on. Legally? I think we've been through enough in the last year to not resort to invoking the law here. Treat is *ours*. Even if I wanted to, I would never be able to think of it in any other way. And honestly, it would be a huge relief to me if you remained my partner. You know I'd take balancing flavor profiles over balancing checkbooks any day. Besides," I said, shrugging, "it turns out we make a good team."

Tears sprang to Julia's eyes. "We do, don't we?"

"Oh no. None of that!" I ordered. "The makeup artist already left and if I'm required to do touch-ups you're going to walk down the aisle looking like a cross between Tammy Faye Bakker and Lady Gaga."

Julia grimaced and waved her hands at the corners of her eyes, drying her tears. "I just wish," she sighed, "that your mom was here today."

I reached out and squeezed her hand. "Me, too."

The knowledge that my mom's death had been caused—accidentally or not—by Curtis still pierced me as sharply as it had the day I'd read her final journal entry. She'd written, her cursive growing long and shaky, that she'd confronted Curtis about his stealing and he'd shoved her against a wall. *My head*, she wrote, *still throbs*. Those words were written three days before she collapsed in the St. Clairs' kitchen. I wasn't sure if the acute pain of that knowledge would ever lessen for me, nor was I sure if I would ever want it to. The fact that Curtis was now in jail—and would be for a long time—didn't help me feel any more at peace with what had happened. It confused me that a part of me still mourned the loss of the Curtis I had known and loved for my entire life. On the other hand, I burned with rage over what he had done to my mother and felt immeasurably relieved that he was out of all of our lives for good. As much as I wanted to come to terms with everything that had happened, I understood that for the pain to truly lessen I would have to let go of my mom in some way, and I wasn't sure I'd ever be ready for that. I wanted to feel her with me every time I baked. I wanted to think about how proud she would have been of Julia and me and our bustling little business. I wanted to read the recipes in her book and hear her voice reciting them to me, as clear as if she were standing beside me. Still, I knew my mom would not have wanted Julia to dwell on the past on her wedding day.

"But at least we're not alone," I said brightly. "*Your* mom is here. And your dad."

"And *your* dad," Julia said, smiling.

"Yes," I said. "How crazy is that?"

After the fire, Miguel had returned to Ecuador to see his children, but had flown back to San Francisco a couple of weeks before Julia's wedding so we could spend some time getting to know each other. He was helping me with my Spanish, and as I improved in the language, I realized that underneath his shy exterior and halting voice, he had a wicked sense of humor and a loud, crackling laugh. Julia had pressed him to extend his visit long enough to be a guest at her wedding, and to my surprise he'd accepted. I'd caught a glimpse of him through the window earlier as he'd stepped off the bus the St. Clairs had chartered from San Francisco. It was hard to believe that this man who looked so dapper in a gray suit, his hair slicked back against his head, had once terrified Julia and me on dark nights in the Mission. *There's my father*, I thought when I saw him. Even thinking the word still felt like a trial run—the title didn't yet quite hold. But I was getting there. He was trying to convince me to visit him in Ecuador later in the summer to meet the rest of my family. *Strange how things turn out.* I wasn't ready to meet everyone, and of course Treat was just getting back off the ground, but maybe, I'd said. *Maybe in the fall.*

"And Ogden," Julia said. "He'll be here, too. Have you seen him yet?"

"No, but I'm sure he's out there. He's always early." I rolled my eyes. "Farmers."

Julia eyed me appraisingly, looking disconcertingly like her mother for a moment. "He's going to say you look beautiful."

I shrugged. "I think he likes me best in an apron."

Now it was Julia's turn to roll her eyes. "Farmers."

There was a light rap on the door and then Lolly herself was peeking her head into the room. "Julia St. Clair!" she rasped. "Why on earth aren't you dressed? The guests are already seated!"

"Well, they're not going to start without her, are they?" I said, striding over to take Julia's gown off its hanger.

"They might," Lolly warned. She clicked the door shut behind her. "This will *not* be one of those weddings that starts twenty minutes late. I've already informed the wedding coordinator in no uncertain terms that we will be sticking to a strict schedule. 'St. Clairs are schedulers!' I told her just this morning. We are! Aren't we?" She was, I realized, looking at both of us when she asked this.

Julia and I glanced at each other, communicating a thousand things in one arched brow, one hint of a smile, and then burst into a fit of laughter.

32

Julia

I TOOK A deep breath as Annie and my mother helped me into my wedding gown and shoes. This was the very moment I'd been so anxious about all year, but now that it was here I felt exactly how I'd always wanted to feel on my wedding day: calm and confident. I watched in the armoire's mirror as my mother slid the veil's diamond-studded comb into the crown of my blond hair.

"Oh, Julia," she said, stepping back for a moment. "You are absolutely stunning." She looked back and forth between Annie and me, her cool blue eyes glistening. "*Both* of you girls look beautiful."

"I'm a bride," I said. I heard the dreamy softness in my voice and didn't cringe. I was beginning to see the benefit of allowing a little candor, a little vulnerability into my life.

My mother walked up beside me, looked for a long moment into my eyes through the mirror, and took my hand in hers. Ever since the Curtis incident, things between us had been warmer. We seemed to be on the same learning curve of figuring out how to express our emotions more freely. When I'd finally told her about the miscarriage, she'd begun to cry immediately.

"I don't ever want you to go through anything like that again!" she'd said, nearly growling with rage. Her eyes had glimmered angrily through her tears—anger directed not at me, but at a world that dared to do something like this to her daughter. "But if you do, I want to be by your side. Promise me you'll let me." I'd never seen her look so ferocious, and I'd nodded, struck mute by her reaction.

Someday, I'd told myself with a searing burst of faith, *I will love my own child this much, too.*

It was moments like those that made me realize just how much Wes's unflagging optimism had worn off on me. My old confidence was blooming again under the warmth of his support; even in the weeks following the terrifying hours when Curtis had held me captive in his house, I'd felt buffered from the possibility of sleepless nights by Wes's attentiveness and concern. Of course, I still couldn't see exactly what the future held for us, but I now felt certain we were each better off facing that uncertain future together.

Interestingly, in the weeks after the fire, my mother had seemed to take cues from Wes's relationship playbook. Before I even had a chance to worry too deeply about how Curtis's betrayal and subsequent absence would affect my father, my mother had started eschewing her morning power walk in favor of joining us at the breakfast table. There, she'd pestered my dad for sections of the paper, loaded up his plate with three slices of melon for each slice of coffee cake, and one day had even shocked us all by expressing interest in finally learning how to play golf. The grin on my father's face when she'd continued to appear at the table morning after morning was priceless. I'd watched my mother's efforts with admiration and relief and as I'd packed my things and prepared to leave the family home for good, I'd taken comfort in knowing that I left each of my parents in good company.

Now, the grandfather clock in Woodstone's hall began to chime loudly. "Showtime!" my mother rasped. "I'm going to duck outside and check that your father is ready for the big walk. Annie, you'll make sure the two of you are on the other side of that door in thirty seconds?"

"Aye, aye!" Annie said, snapping her silver heels together.

As soon as my mother shut the door, I threw my arms around Annie, nearly smothering her with my veil.

"Death by bride!" she mumbled through a mouthful of tulle. "After this year, I probably should have seen this coming."

"Thank you for being here," I said, still hugging her.

She pulled back and looked at me, jutting her chin into the air. "Where else do you think I would be?" She gripped my arms gently before releasing me. "Now let's get out of here. There's a scary mother to obey."

"And a handsome man to marry," I said. My gown rustled elegantly as I made my way across the room.

"And cupcakes to eat!" Annie added, pulling open the door.

"Yes." My mouth watered a bit at the thought. "Always."

Acknowledgments

I am eternally grateful to my wise editor and dear friend, Jeanette Perez, who has made a dream come true. It is both a comfort and a luxury to have such an insightful editor ready and willing to flip on her flashlight when darkness falls on the writing path. My heartfelt thanks to all at Harper who have helped along the way, including, but not limited to, Carrie Kania, Brittany Hamblin, Jennifer Hart, Mary Sasso, Eleanor Mikucki, Dalma De Leon, and Elizabeth Thompson. Thank you also to my wonderful agent, Elisabeth Weed, for taking me under her wing, and to the talented Alyce Shields, for giving me insight into life as a pastry chef.

Thank you to my parents, whose generosity, voracious love of learning, and enthusiasm for life will always inspire me.

Above all, thank you to my husband Phil—my happily ever after, my voice of reason, and my first reader—and to our children, for giving me the gift of knowing infinite love.